The Cruel Ever After

ALSO BY ELLEN HART

The Cruel Ever After

ELLEN HART

MINOTAUR BOOKS ≋ NEW YORK

This is a work of fiction. All of the characters, organizations, and events portrayed in this novel are either products of the author's imagination or are used fictitiously.

www.minotaurbooks.com

Library of Congress Cataloging-in-Publication Data

Hart, Ellen.
    The cruel ever after/Ellen Hart.—1st ed.
        p. cm.
    ISBN 978-0-312-61476-8
        1. Lawless, Jane (Fictitious character)—Fiction.   2. Art—Collectors and collecting—Fiction.   3. Theft of relics—Fiction.   4. Lesbians—Fiction.   5. Minneapolis (Minn.)—Fiction.   I. Title.
    PS3558.A6775C78 2010
    813'.54—dc22

                                                              2010035813

First Edition: December 2010

10   9   8   7   6   5   4   3   2   1

For Lev Raphael

Half of the harm that is done in this world
Is due to people who want to feel important.
They don't mean to do harm—
But the harm does not interest them.
Or they do not see it, or they justify it,
Because they are absorbed in the endless struggle
To think well of themselves.

—*T. S. Eliot*

Cast of Characters

Jane Lawless:	Owner of the Lyme House Restaurant and the Xanadu Club in Minneapolis.
Cordelia Thorn:	Creative Director of the Allen Grimby Repertory Theater in St. Paul; Jane's oldest friend.
Chester (Chess) Garrity:	Antiquities Dealer.
Melvin Dial:	Retired businessman.
Irina Nelson:	Curator at the Morgana Beck Gallery of Antiquities in St. Paul. Steve's wife, Dustin's mother.
Steve Nelson:	Iraqi war veteran. Irina's husband.
Majid Farrow:	Curator at the Morgana Beck Gallery of Antiquities in St. Paul.

Morgana Beck:	Owner of the Morgana Beck Gallery of Antiquities in St. Paul. Irina and Misty's mother.
Julia Martinsen:	Doctor of oncology. Jane's ex-girlfriend.
Peter Lawless:	Documentary film maker. Jane's brother. Sigrid's husband. Mia's dad.
Sigrid Lawless:	Peter's wife. Mia's mom. Grad student.
Mia Lawless:	Peter and Mia's eleven-year-old daughter.
Misty Beck:	Unemployed. Irina's sister. Morgana's daughter.
Lee Northcutt:	Itinerant preacher.
A. J. Nolan:	Private investigator. Jane's good friend.
Raymond Lawless:	Criminal defense attorney. Jane and Peter's father.

The Cruel Ever After

1

Even before Chester Garrity opened his eyes, he knew this wasn't going to be one of his better days. Birds trilled, a lawn mower hummed in the distance—signs pointing to a beautiful spring morning, and yet the pounding inside his head was so intense that every bird chirp sounded like a horn blast.

Rolling onto his back, he stretched his aching limbs. When he worked up the courage to pry his eyes apart, he saw that he was lying outside under a pergola, his right leg hard up against the side of a hot tub. He couldn't imagine why he hadn't tried for something more comfortable, but then he couldn't remember much of anything about last night, except an excess of liquid celebration.

The next thought to pierce his throbbing consciousness was that he was back in Minneapolis. Once upon a time, he'd promised himself that he would never return to the Midwest unless it was in a body bag or at the point of a gun. Cows and milk-fed morons weren't his idea of culture. He'd lived all over the world, most recently in Istanbul, but money, as it always did, had grown tight. The need to replenish his dwindling bank account was the only force on earth that could have pulled him back to the middle of nowhere.

Propping his back against the plastic faux wood, Chess counted to three and then heaved his girth to a standing position. He wobbled a little, steadied himself, and finally dragged himself into the back entry of Melvin Dial's house, glad to see that Dial hadn't locked him out. He made a mental note to cut back on the booze. At fifty-one, he wasn't old exactly, but his out-of-shape body couldn't tolerate the level of abuse he'd once considered the price of a good time.

He entered the kitchen, rubbing his eyes, not really watching where he was going. He nearly stumbled when his foot hit something hard. Struggling to focus, he saw that all the drawers and cupboards had been opened, the contents dumped out. It looked like a high-priced kitchen equipment store had belched all over the travertine tile.

Shuffling through the mess into the living room, he pressed a palm to his eye. "Oh, right," he whispered. The card game. He wondered how much money he'd lost. Dial had deep pockets. More to the point, he wasn't the least bit frightened of illegalities. He was just the man they'd been looking for.

The living room was every bit as torn apart as the kitchen. Sitting down on the edge of a chair to get his bearings, he saw that the card table was still upright, covered with not only cards but empty glasses and filled ashtrays. A champagne bottle rested on its side—and, Jesus, a bottle of absinthe. Not a drop was left in any of them. No wonder he had a hangover the size of the Great Pyramid of Giza. But where was Dial?

A crumpled potato chip bag lay on the floor next to one of the wing-back chairs; chips were scattered across the tabletop and onto the bijar rug, as if someone had tossed it in a fit of temper. With a hand resting on the back of a chair to steady himself, he bent down to pick up one of the larger chips. He wasn't the least bit hungry, but the taste in his mouth was so foul that anything to make it go away seemed welcome. As he scooped the chip up and into his mouth, he spied a dark red stain near the footstool. The sight of it kick-started the part of his brain that was still asleep.

His gaze zipped from the stain to a pair of brown Cole Haan tassel loafers. The rest of the body was hidden behind the couch.

As Chess edged forward, his breath caught in his throat. "I am so screwed," he whispered, fighting back a burst of panic.

Dial lay on his back, the front of his white dress shirt soaked in blood, the beautiful Kurdish rug beneath him stained a dark red. The old man's eyes were open and staring blankly at eternity, leaving no doubt in Chess's mind that he was dead. He bent down to examine the deep gash in Dial's chest. Someone had knifed him and left him to die.

What, exactly, had happened last night? Chess recalled the bar where they'd cemented the deal. Irina, knowing the area much better than he did, had picked the place for its old-world charm, its pricey wine list, and the absence of blaring music. With adrenaline flowing as freely as the wine, none of them had wanted the evening to end, but end it had when Irina announced that she needed to get home to her baby and her husband. Chess and Melvin Dial had been left to their own devices for the shank of the evening.

Shivering as he lowered his aching body down onto one of the wing-back chairs, Chess closed his eyes and tried to picture what had happened after they arrived back at the house. He thought he remembered Dial popping a champagne cork and pouring them each a glass of bubbly. He made the same ironic toast he'd made at the restaurant: "To Don Rumsfeld's magnificent myopia." They took chairs on either side of the antique card table. Chess had shuffled the deck, recalling that they felt sticky. He thought he'd won the first few hands, although he couldn't be certain. With all he'd had to drink he couldn't even remember leaving the table and going outside. He'd

3

been dead to the world, with no memory of anyone coming to the house, the sound of a doorbell or a fight. The fact that he'd slept right through a murder propelled him out of the chair.

Think, he ordered himself. It seemed more than probable that Chess himself would be sprawled next to Dial if he hadn't wandered outside and passed out. Whoever had come to the house had been looking for something. He couldn't be sure exactly why Dial had been murdered, but there was always the possibility that it had to do with the deal they'd just struck. That's why he couldn't call the police. He needed time to think everything through, to work out the best way to handle it, and for that he needed a cigarette. It could be hours, even days, before the old guy's body was discovered. He was retired, reclusive, lived alone. Chess had time. It might be the only thing he had going for him.

Before he left, Chess bent over the body and dug into Dial's pockets for his keys—just in case he wanted to come back. He hesitated, wondering if he should take the old guy's wallet. Hell, why not?

Stepping over to the front door, he stuck his head outside and looked around. Dial's house was located on a tree-lined street in Linden Hills, a quiet part of the city where leaves flickered in the late morning sunlight, dogs barked in the distance, and nobody, much to Chess's silent relief, seemed to be out and about. He removed a pack of cigarettes from his shirt pocket, tapped one out, and slipped it between his lips, cupping his hand around the tip and lighting it with a silver lighter. Then, closing his eyes, relishing the moment, he took a sweet, deep drag and held it, feeling a sense of calm spread slowly into his muscles.

Shutting the door behind him, he proceeded swiftly down the cobbled front walk. The plan forming in his mind was to simply walk away and, when he felt safe, call for a cab to take him back to his hotel. He could phone Irina from there, explain what had happened. Dial's death was a setback, for sure. They would need to look else-

4

where to make the sale. Still, it was doable. This wasn't the end of the road.

"Afternoon," called a cheerful voice.

Chess coughed smoke out of his lungs.

A bald guy in a bathrobe and slippers had just come out on the front steps of the house next door. He leaned down and picked up a folded newspaper.

Cursing his wretched luck, Chess forced a smile. "Afternoon."

"Looks like we've got ourselves another gorgeous day."

Gorgeous, right. The scent of lilacs was so strong it was almost gagged him. "Sure does." Before the man could continue with his Midwestern pleasantries, Chess gave a friendly wave, then turned and headed up the street as fast as he could go without looking like he was about to break into a dead run.

"Shit, shit, shit," he exploded as he rounded the end of the block. The neighbor could put him at the scene of the crime, which would limit his ability to frame a plausible lie. He stuck the cigarette back between his lips and dug his cell out of the pocket of his jacket. As he did so, a white pickup whizzed past, driving way too fast for a residential street.

Asshole.

He forgot about waiting until he returned to the hotel. He punched in Irina's number at the gallery. When nothing connected, he checked to see what was wrong.

"Unbelievable."

The goddamn cell was out of juice.

He turned and began walking toward the lake. He had to find a phone, which wasn't as easy as it used to be, when Ma Bell had been on every other corner.

Walking south, he felt the tension in his stomach continue to build. It surprised him that he remembered the lay of the land as well as he did. As a young man, South Minneapolis had been his playground.

5

He'd lived in an apartment on Bryant Avenue, gone to the U of M, fallen in and out of love at least half a dozen times. Callow youth, he thought to himself, a time when everything seemed possible. Life, he'd learned, was often far more like drawing dead in a poker game. Even if you got everything you wanted, you still couldn't win.

The more distance he put between himself and Dial's house, the better he felt. His head was finally starting to clear. He flipped the cigarette away, supposing that he felt bad about the old guy's death, although he hardly knew him. Irina would take it harder, as would her mother. A guy like Dial had to have his share of enemies. Chess hoped like hell that his murder had nothing to do with the statue.

As he reached the south end of the lake, he noticed a building rising above the trees that hadn't been there twenty-some years ago. It looked like a giant log temple. Could it be? Was that the restaurant? He made a quick left into the parking lot, crossed a grassy patch that led to the front sidewalk, and climbed the log steps up to the front door. Before he went inside, he shrugged into his safari jacket and finger-combed his unruly hair back into place. He was older, for sure, but still looked pretty much the same. His body—that was a different story. Would she recognize him? Would he recognize her? He stepped up to a petite young woman behind the reception desk. "Can you tell me who owns the restaurant?"

"Sure," said the woman, pulling a menu out from underneath the reception stand. "Jane Lawless."

He digested the information, giving nothing away. Holding up his cell, he said, "Do you have a house phone? This thing's out of juice."

"Is it a local call?"

"St. Paul."

She handed him a cordless. "Dial nine to get an outside line."

Walking over to a quiet corner, he tapped in the gallery number. It rang five times before a woman's voice answered, "Morgana Beck Gallery."

6

"Morgana? It's Chester Garrity."

Morgana Beck was Irina's mother, the owner of the gallery and a visiting professor of the science and ethics of antiquities at Basir University in Ankara, Turkey. Irina had been working for her mother for nearly ten years.

"I need to speak to Irina," said Chess.

"Not here."

He shoved a hand into his pocket. "Do you know when she'll be—"

"I'm with a client right now. Call back later."

"Could you at least give me some idea of when she'll be in?"

Morgana and Chess had met on several occasions over the years, but for some reason, the great Morgana Beck didn't seem to like him.

"She and Steve drove down to Rochester this morning."

Steve was Irina's husband. "So, later in the day? Three? Four?"

"Is something wrong? You sound upset."

"Will she be in at all today?"

"I don't know. I'm hanging up now."

Chess turned his back to the receptionist as he cut the line. Morgana understood just how to yank his chain, and seemed to take great pleasure in it. Morgana Beck, a fifty-eight-year-old St. Paul matron, believed down to the soles of her Jimmy Choos that she was better than everyone else. People were always disappointing her, or trying her patience, or boring her into a state of stupefaction. People like Chess. *This* from a woman who'd undergone more cosmetic surgery than Michael Jackson and who had all the personal charisma of a boiled egg.

Pulling his shirt cuffs out from under his jacket sleeves, Chess gave himself a brief pep talk and then turned around and walked back to the receptionist, handing her the phone.

"Is Jane here?"

"She is," said the receptionist. "But she's tied up at the moment. If you'd like to make—"

7

"She'll see me."

"If you could give me your name—"

"Garrity." He allowed himself a small smirk. "Just tell her that her husband is here and wants to talk to her."

Where are we on the birthday invitations?" asked Jane, easing back in her chair as a waiter poured more coffee into her cup. Coffee was the last thing she needed. She'd been thoroughly buzzed since seven.

"I sent them all out at the beginning of last week," said Cordelia, gazing through her rhinestone-studded horn-rimmed glasses at her notes. She never went anywhere these days without her Moleskine notebook. In its pages were her overwrought thoughts on life, her to-do lists, and famous quotes—often her own—she wanted marked down for posterity. "What else needs to be done?" She whipped off the glasses, all business today.

"Have you heard from my brother and his wife? They're coming, right?"

"Haven't you talked to them?"

Cordelia knew there was a rift between Jane and her brother, she just didn't know why. "I haven't talked to him in months."

"You two are behaving like children. Just bury the hatchet—not in each other's backs—and get on with it."

"It's not that simple."

"You know, Janey, if you told me what was going on, I might be able to help. I've had vast experience when it comes to empiric family warfare. Besides, Peter adores me."

"Everyone adores you."

"It's my cross."

Jane gazed past Cordelia to a table at the rear of the deck. A waiter appeared to be having an extended conversation with a customer who didn't look happy.

"Excuse me," she said, getting up. She wove her way through the tables. "Is there a problem?" she asked, moving up next to the waiter.

"You seem to be out of everything," said a sandy-haired man in a business suit.

"He wanted the lamb stew," said the waiter, looking apologetic, "but we ran out."

"So I ordered the Galway corned beef and cabbage. Your waiter just informed me that you're out of that, too."

Jane recalled that they'd been shorted on their corned beef order on Monday. "I'm the owner. Let me suggest a couple of specialties you might like. Have you tried our savory beef and mushroom cottage pie? It comes with a cup of potato leek soup and a small salad. Our Cumberland sausage and mash is another favorite. Or you might like today's fish entrée—pan-fried striped bass in a citrus butter. Comes with sweet potato chips. I sampled it this morning, and it's wonderful."

"I suppose the fish," said the man, glancing at the woman across from him. "If you can make it fast."

"We can," said Jane, "and it's on the house."

He looked up at her, no longer quite so disgruntled.

"I'm truly sorry for the inconvenience. I want you to be happy with your food. If there are any more problems, just let me know." She nodded to the waiter, and he took off. On her way back to her table, she spotted a pair of longtime customers—an older couple, with a grandson in Afghanistan.

"Nice to see you," she said, smiling down at them. "Everything okay with your order?"

"Wonderful as always," said the woman.

"How's your grandson doing?"

"He should be home next month," said the man. "We're keeping our fingers crossed."

"When he's back, bring him by for a piece of our turtle cake—on me." The grandson loved sweets.

"We'll do that," said the man with a grin.

Sitting down again, Jane picked up her coffee cup and took a sip. She should probably have been working the lunch crowd, seating customers, expediting orders in the kitchen, but because Cordelia had arrived ready to discuss Jane's father's birthday "extravaganza," she had decided to take a break.

Cordelia Thorn was Jane's oldest and best friend. They'd known each other for so many years that the word "friend" hardly seemed adequate. They were more like family, or perhaps somewhere in between. Jane's life would be far less colorful without Cordelia's angst and opinions.

Jane was a restaurateur, Cordelia the creative director of the most prestigious regional theater in the Midwest. They shared a love of food and a personal history that took them all the way back to high school.

On a day like today, with sunlight glinting off the choppy waves of Lake Harriet, a breeze ruffling the leaves, and sailboats, their white sails billowing in the wind, skimming across the water, it was hard to believe problems existed in the world. Yet Jane and her brother were a case in point. She was holding her breath, praying that Peter would come to the party and not turn it into another battlefield. She was also hoping that if he and Sigrid and their daughter, Mia, did show, they could act the role of a happy family for their father's sake.

"Did you send an invitation to Julia?" asked Jane.

Cordelia glowered. "Yes, with deep reservations."

"I'm a little worried about her."

"You should be. She's a lunatic."

"I've phoned her a couple of times in the past month. She never returned the calls. That's not like her."

"Count your blessings."

"Don't be such a sourpuss. She's Dad's primary care physician now. He considers her a friend of the family. I think he'd be upset if we didn't include her."

"Your paterfamilias is a kind man with a bad case of myopia when it comes to Dr. Julia. *I* consider her a nutcase with an obsessive need to wiggle her way back into your personal life. You may have dumped her, but she's not done with you. Mark my words, Janey, that woman is trouble."

"What's going on down there?" asked Jane, pushing out of her chair. This time she stepped over to the wood railing that surrounded the second-floor deck. Several other customers were already up and watching a man, dressed in a medieval monk's cowl, standing on top of a wooden crate, speaking to a growing crowd of onlookers—or gawkers. Jane strained to hear him, but all she could pick up was the words "spirit" and "deceit."

Cordelia sidled up next to her. "How lovely. An itinerant preacher. One with a highly evolved sense of style. I wonder where he bought that cowl."

"You like the Friar Tuck look?"

"Sexy is as sexy does. Now come on back to the table. We've still got work to do."

Jane wasn't exactly thrilled to have all this commotion going on right underneath her restaurant's deck, but because the man was on public property, she couldn't do much about it.

"Hattie's really looking forward to the party," said Cordelia, pen poised once again over her notebook.

Hattie Thorn-Lester was Cordelia's five-year-old niece. She was back living with Cordelia again, this time as her legal ward.

"She's got her outfit all planned. Black and pink, of course, with her handmade Ziegfeld Follies–ish hat. She wants to make a real visual statement. I can't blame her. She is, after all, a Thorn." She stopped, jerked her reading glasses down to the tip of her nose, and gazed over them. "Lord love a duck, I don't believe my eyes." She stood, drew her arms wide, and cried, "Chester, dear boy! Is that really you?"

"Chester?" repeated Jane, twisting around. She realized it was pure cliché, but her jaw actually dropped when she saw who was striding toward them. She hadn't seen Chess Garrity since . . . since—

Cordelia treated him to her famous bear hug, inching him up off his feet and spinning him around. Chess had put on weight but still wasn't as big as Cordelia. Cordelia's girth was legendary, but her strength, when excited, was the stuff of myth.

"What are you doing here?" demanded Cordelia, setting Chess down, holding on to his hands. "You look marvelous."

"I look older," he said, flashing Jane a help-me-out-here-before-she-breaks-every-bone-in-my-body look.

Jane pulled out a chair. "I'm stunned."

He gave her a peck on the cheek, rubbing his arm as he sat down. "I never thought I'd be back. I guess life has a way of changing our plans."

Cordelia caught the waiter's eye. "A bottle of your finest champagne. Chop chop."

Chess looked around, taking in the broad deck packed with customers. "This truly is amazing. Seeing you two again. This restaurant was your dream, right, Jane? The one you talked about all the time. You actually did it. You didn't squander the money I gave you."

"She's got a second dream made manifest, too," said Cordelia, flapping her napkin before tucking it into her cleavage. "It's more a of nightclub. In Uptown. It's an old restored art deco theater. Very classy. You'll have to come see it. How long will you be in town?"

"A few days."

Chess was older than Jane, but he had a young face. Even now, he didn't look his age, although his hair, an implausible though real shade of red, had thinned. He looked prosperous, his once pale, freckled skin now ruddy and tanned, his teeth so white they could blind. And he was a good fifty pounds heavier. Jane recalled that some of his college buddies used to call him Antinous because he looked like the marble sculpture of the famous Greek, the one found in the temple of Apollo at Delphi. A Greek god like face atop a body that packed on the pounds so easily that Chess often starved himself to stay trim. DNA gave, and DNA took away.

"So," said Chess, pushing his chair back and crossing his legs. "How's Christine?" He seemed uncomfortable, shifting this way and that. Jane had the sense that he was looking past her, that his mind was someplace else.

"She died," said Cordelia, lowering her eyes, then glancing uneasily at Jane.

Making no effort to hide his shock, Chess said, "I'm sorry. I thought you two made a great couple."

"I did, too," said Jane. "We were together for nearly ten years."

The champagne arrived. The timing couldn't have been worse.

Attempting to save the moment, Cordelia said, "So, tell us what you've been up to all these years."

"A little of this, a little of that."

"Still filthy rich?"

He took a sip of the champagne, then set the glass down next to

14

his napkin. "I've made and lost several fortunes since the last time I saw you two. At the moment, I guess you could say I'm between fortunes."

Jane's connection to Chess Garrity was an unusual one, but it wasn't complex. Chess had been a closeted gay man who came from a highly religious—and extremely wealthy—family in Chicago. When the children turned thirty, provided they were married in the Catholic Church and living good lives, they would each inherit nine million dollars. Chess's father was dead, but his mother made sure her children, all four of them, toed the line. The problem was obvious.

Chess had met Cordelia when he tried out for a show she was directing at the Blackburn Playhouse in Shoreview. This was long before her reign began at the Allen Grimby Repertory Theater in St. Paul. They hit it off immediately. Chess got the part, and over the course of the next few months, he and Cordelia began to talk about his predicament.

That was where Jane came in. The scheme that Chess and Cordelia cooked up all depended on her. Chess and Jane would get married in a church in Lake Forest, Illinois, where his mother lived. Jane would act the blushing bride for as long as it took for Chess to pocket his inheritance. For her time and effort, Chess agreed to pay her three hundred thousand dollars. The money would allow her to convince a bank to give her an even bigger loan to build the Lyme House. People always assumed that her father had financed the restaurant, but back then, Jane and her dad hadn't been on the best of terms.

The final part of the plan was, as soon as Chess's nine million was safely tucked away, that he would fly to the Dominican Republic, get a quickie divorce, send Jane the papers, and take off for greener—foreign—pastures. He wanted to travel. See the world. That was his dream.

Jane got cold feet right before the wedding ceremony and had to be dragged by Cordelia and Christine—in her wedding gown and veil—into the limo that took them to the church. Ultimately, though, her marriage to and divorce from Chess Garrity was what had allowed her to make the dream of owning her own restaurant come true. She'd never told another living soul what she'd done to get the financial ball rolling. The only people who knew—and were still alive—were sitting at this table.

Jane and Chess had lived together for three months after the wedding in a small apartment near the university. Chess was a sweet, generous guy, easy to talk to and full of enthusiasm for the recipes she was developing. Many of those recipes would become the Lyme House's first signature dishes. Chess loved to eat, and Jane loved to feed him. She wasn't sorry when he moved out and Christine moved back in, but she missed him—missed his humor, his belief in her abilities, and his encouragement. When he left Minnesota, he said he'd keep in touch, but he never had.

Folding his arms over his chest, Chess turned his attention to Cordelia. "And you. Still working in the theater?"

"You don't know?" She was aghast, quickly filling him in on her illustrious career, underlining her current theatrical glitterati status in the Twin Cities.

"The Allen Grimby," he repeated. "Isn't that the one with the Byzantine interior? The one that looks like it came straight out of a 1920s Hollywood movie set?"

"We call it the AGRT."

"To differentiate yourself from the Tyrone Guthrie Theater?"

"The what? Those are not words I recognize."

Chess laughed. "Same old Cordelia."

The waiter placed Jane's and Cordelia's sandwiches down in front of them.

"Order something," said Cordelia, gazing hungrily at her croquemonsieur. "The food's terrific."

He seemed unsure.

"It's on your ex," said Cordelia. She flashed them both an impish smile. "When you're done eating, I'll drive you over to the theater, show you around. How's that sound?"

He looked up at the waiter, then at his watch. "I'm not sure."

"Of what?" asked Cordelia.

"I might have to be somewhere this afternoon."

"Like where?"

When he didn't answer, Jane said, "Give the guy a break. He doesn't need to tell us his itinerary."

Cordelia grumbled. "Fabulous. Chester Garrity. Man of mystery."

"It's not like that."

"No?"

Glancing at Jane, he added, "Well, maybe a little."

3

That night, Irina waited for her husband to fall asleep. He drank a third beer while he watched the end of a movie, then dithered for a while in the kitchen, standing in front of the open refrigerator. After downing half a roasted chicken and three slices of buttered toast while reading a gun magazine, he drifted off to bed. When he began to snore, Irina took it as her signal to tiptoe down the hall and slip out the back door.

It was going on one in the morning when she pulled up to the curb next to a large elm, where Chess was standing, smoking a cigarette.

"I thought you'd never get here," he said, flipping the cigarette into the street. He pulled her toward him and kissed her fiercely.

"Are you okay?" she asked, breathing in his familiar aftershave.

"Better now that you're here."

Irina had met Chess on a working trip she'd taken to Istanbul last August. She'd flown to Turkey in order to meet with dealers in international antiquities. A mutual friend had introduced them at a cocktail party. Maybe it was being away from home, or drinking one too many martinis, or maybe she just needed the assurance that she was still an attractive, desirable woman. It had been far too long since she'd felt the way Chess made her feel that night. Over the next week, she came to understand how badly her emotions had atrophied while being married to Steve.

"Are you ready?" whispered Chess.

"If you are."

She opened her trunk and removed a sack of cleaning supplies.

"Did you get everything on the list?" he asked.

"Everything."

"I'll pull your car into the back driveway when it's time to carry out the body. I've thought about this and nothing else all day. The only way out of this mess is to make Dial disappear. The blood should be dried by now. We'll wrap garbage sacks around him just in case. Then we'll drive to the river."

The idea of putting Melvin Dial's body into a garbage sack was almost more than she could handle. She felt Chess's strong arms encircle her.

"I'm sorry I had to ask for your help, but the old guy's too heavy for me to handle alone."

"No, I understand."

"Do you?" When he kissed her this time, it made her shiver.

They walked down the street toward the house, hand in hand, Irina steeling herself for what she would need to do. The night had turned chilly, which made her wish she'd worn something more substantial than twill slacks and a light cotton sweater. Chess seemed to sense when she needed his reassurance. Without being asked, he slipped his arm around her waist.

"Look," said Irina, pointing. "There are lights on."

"I'm sure they've been on since last night. Nobody's been around to turn them off."

Irina had been in Dial's home several times, so she knew the layout. The first-floor light came from the living room.

"This way," whispered Chess. He led her through a neighbor's yard, where they paused at the edge of Dial's privacy fence for a quick reconnoiter. Everything appeared to be quiet. The only illumination came from a security light high up on a pole about thirty feet down the alley.

Just as they were about to move through the the gate, a rabbit scurried into the driveway and stopped, raising its head and sniffing the air. At the same moment, the sound of tires grinding on pavement warned them to stay put. An old Chevy van tore down the alley not five feet away from where they hid.

Chess squeezed her hand after it was gone. "Let's go."

He opened the gate, and they crept inside.

"God, but I hate the smell of lilacs," he whispered, digging a key out of his jacket pocket and fitting it into the lock.

Irina wasn't sure how anyone could hate lilacs, although she had to admit that the scent was pretty strong.

Once inside the kitchen, Chess took a flashlight out of his back pocket and switched it on.

"Where's the mess?" asked Irina.

He stood still for a few seconds, looking confused. "Someone must have cleaned it up." He set the sack of cleaning supplies on the kitchen counter and rushed through the pantry into the living room.

Irina followed at a slower pace. She found him standing by the couch with his hand messaging his forehead. "The body's gone. And the bijar rug, the one he bled all over, it's gone, too." His gaze swept the room. "Everything's been put back in its place. What the hell is going on?"

"What's that?" asked Irina, pointing at a small white sack on top of the card table.

He lunged for it, held it upside down. A cell phone, a piece of folded yellow legal paper, and a bunch of snapshots fell out. Backing toward the lamp, he held the piece of legal paper under the light and read the contents out loud.

I took care of the body for you and
all the cleanup. For my effort I expect
to be paid. Keep the prepaid cell
with you. I'll call and give you
instructions. The photos are part of
what will go to the police if you try
to stiff me. I've got more pictures
to show them—and the knife. I want
$50,000. Small bills.

Your Pal, Ed

"Jesus," said Chess. "This guy must have thought that whoever killed Dial would come back to clean up the mess. But how did he get in here?" He walked over and checked the door. "Nobody's forced it. The back door wasn't jimmied either. I suppose he could have broken a window."

They spent the next few minutes looking around, trying to figure out how Ed had entered, but in the end, they came up empty.

"He must have had a key," said Chess.

"Who would have a key to Dial's house?"

"How the hell would I know?"

Irina stepped over to take a look at the snapshots. The first one showed Dial's body behind the couch. The next was a picture of Chess's passport propped up next to one of Dial's tassel loafers.

"Is this really your passport?"

Chess pinched the bridge of his nose. "I'm afraid so. I usually keep it in the inner pocket of my jacket. When I looked for it this afternoon, it was gone. I didn't worry because I figured I'd left it back at the hotel."

"How did it get here?"

He walked a few paces away. "I always keep a couple of extra hundred-dollar bills in it. Maybe, when Dial and I were playing poker last night, I took the money out. I must have dropped the passport or set it somewhere. God knows, I was pretty smashed. I have no memory of any of it, but I'll bet I'm right. This Ed person, he must've found it, jumped to a conclusion, and here we are. I'm on the hook, at least in his mind, for Dial's death."

Irina reread the note as Chess stuffed the contents of the sack into his jacket pockets.

"I don't get it," she said, tucking a lock of hair behind her ear. "The fact that this guy has your passport and that he placed it next to the body doesn't prove anything."

"Let's get out of the light." He motioned for her to follow him back to the kitchen.

Standing in the semidarkness, he whispered, "You're right. It doesn't prove I did it. But if this guy sent the photos to the police, at the very least they'd want to question me. That's the last thing we need. We've got to keep everything under wraps until we can find another buyer. I mean, we can't exactly sell the Winged Bull of Nimrud on eBay."

"You'd be surprised at what you can buy on eBay. Lots of the Baghdad Museum's ancient cylinder seals are there. Coins. Cuneiform tablets."

"Not the Nimrud gold. Nobody's that stupid. We've got to find some way to pay this guy off, make him go away."

Her resolve was beginning to crumble. "This is so much more than I bargained for."

"We talked about the dangers."

"I never expected someone to be murdered."

Hearing a noise, they both ducked down.

"What was that?" whispered Irina.

He put a finger to his lips, waited a few seconds, and then said, "Let's get out of here."

They left the cleaning supplies on the counter, cracked open the door, and ran back through the moonlit streets to her car. Irina unlocked the doors, and they both climbed in. "What do you know about Dial?" asked Chess, breathing hard.

"He's been buying from the gallery for years. I knew he wasn't averse to crossing the legal line if he could get his hands on something really special. That's why I approached him."

"Does he resell what he buys?"

"Sometimes. He keeps a pretty low profile."

"Does he always pay in cash?"

"Always."

"But your mom would never deal in anything illegal."

"Are you kidding? If she knew what we were doing, she'd turn us in."

"The old guy probably had enemies. We can't say for sure why he was murdered."

She sat looking at the deserted street, wondering how everything had gone so wrong. One more day and they would have been home free. "What if his death *was* connected," she said. "You and I both know there are people out there tracking down the looters from the Baghdad Museum."

"Don't go there."

"But you've heard the stories, right? Dealers and buyers murdered in their sleep, drowned in swimming pools, knifed in back alleys. You don't sell antiquities and not hear what's going on."

"I didn't do the looting."

"That's a technicality."

Chess rolled down the window to get some air. "So what do we do? Hide under a rock? We *need* the money from that sale."

"Are you going to pay this guy off?"

"First I have to find the fifty thousand." He looked over at her with a question in his eyes.

"I don't have it."

"Maybe I should start making arrangements to move the bull back to Istanbul."

"You can't leave." She said it too fast, sounded too desperate. She feared that she cared more about him than he did about her. "I've still got a bunch of connections I never approached. I'll start working them tomorrow."

"If you think you can sell it—"

"I know I can."

"But this time, we've got to be even more careful."

She had a sudden thought. "Don't go back to your hotel."

"Where am I supposed to sleep?"

"Don't use your credit cards, either. I'll get you some cash."

He kissed her again, this time more tenderly. "We'll figure out a way to make this work for us."

She couldn't help herself. She twisted the words around inside her mind, made them mean what she wanted them to mean. What they were doing, dangerous as it was, would make their future together possible. That's what he'd said.

For *us*.

4

Jane sat on the wicker couch on her screened back porch, nursing her third brandy and feeling like an insect working its way out of a web. At times, she puzzled so long and hard about life in general, and hers in particular, that her brain hurt. Her dog, a chocolate Lab named Mouse, stretched out next to her, his head in her lap. It was going on two in the morning. If she was smart, which apparently she wasn't, she would already be in bed. She had a full day tomorrow and needed to get some sleep, but she was too restless, too caught in the sticky filaments of thought.

It had been a rough year. She'd broken up with her girlfriend last fall. She'd been estranged from her brother even longer than that. Her emotions had been on overdrive for so long that all she wanted was to kick back and relax. A quiet life was the new goal. A few drinks made the world stop, or at least made it seem manageable, although she'd gone down that road before and knew it led nowhere. She might just take a few weeks off, spend it up at her parents' lodge on Black-berry Lake. She'd barely taken a full day off since March, buried as she was under the daily grind of running two restaurants in an economic recession.

Summer at the lodge was Jane's first memory of Minnesota. She could still call up the image of her mother sitting at the end of the dock, feet dangling in the water, a heavy August sun dipping behind the distant trees. The scene had been repeated often that first summer, the year they all moved back to Minnesota from the southwestern coast of England. Jane's father would walk out to check on her, bending over, touching her back, never staying long because he must have sensed that she needed time to adjust, to grieve the loss of her old home and get used to her new one. Her mother found solace in those sunsets, and perhaps a few answers to the riddle of life. Jane felt the need for a few of those sunsets now, too.

As she stretched her arms over her head, Chess's face bloomed inside her mind. When she thought about him these days, which she rarely did, she still felt, for multiple reasons, that she'd made the right decision in marrying him. Yet a core part of her remained ashamed.

"I was in too much of a hurry back then," she said to Mouse, absently stroking his velvety ears.

She couldn't recall ever being ashamed of being gay. It was just another human variation. She'd been outraged by the inequity in Chess's parents' edict. Still, all the sneaking around, and the fact that she got paid to lie, made her complicity feel sordid.

"We should head up to bed."

Without lifting his head, Mouse raised his eyes.

"But between you and me, sitting in the dark with you, drinking a brandy, it's got to be my favorite part of the day. It's quiet, you know? There's nobody knocking on my door, or phoning me, or asking me to do something, or expecting me to dig my way out of a crisis." In years past, that had been exactly what she loved about her work. It was fast and furious. Something always needed her attention. She would lose herself in the energy of it all, and time would disappear. Where had that gone?

"Maybe I need to learn to meditate. What do you think?"

Mouse's tail thumped.

"Or take up knitting." She swallowed the last of her brandy. "Nah."

As if on cue, the doorbell rang.

Mouse sat up, sniffing the air.

Nobody came to her house at this hour of the morning except for Cordelia. Occasionally, she even brought a pizza, a welcome thought.

"You feel like some pepperoni?" she asked as she headed through the dining room into the front hall, Mouse trotting along next to her. Before she opened the door, she looked through the peephole. "No pepperoni, babe. Sorry."

"I've been mugged," groaned Chess, leaning a hand heavily against the door frame. His jacket was ripped and soiled, and he had some nasty abrasions on his face.

"Come in," she said, holding his arm and helping him inside.

"Cordelia told me where you lived," he said a little breathlessly. "I'm sorry to wake you, but—"

"I wasn't asleep." She helped him to the couch in the living room. Although his legs appeared rock solid—as thick as tree stumps—he was so out of shape that she was afraid he might fall. When his jacket spread open, she could see his belly pushing against his belt. He reminded her of a middle-aged Marlon Brando, before he fell off the weight cliff altogether and ballooned. Chess was still attractive, but he was fast going to seed. "Where are you hurt?"

"I'm just shaken up."

"I'll get my first aid kit."

Mouse, always the gentleman, sat down in front of him and held up his paw.

"Nice dog," said Chess, patting his head with little enthusiasm.

Jane returned with the kit and began to clean the scrapes on his face. Chess winced and pulled away a couple of times but eventually let her finish her ministrations.

"What happened?" she asked, before telling him to close his eyes as she covered the abrasions with antibiotic spray.

"I was coming out of a bar. Two guys jumped me."

"A gay bar?"

"What?" He looked away. "Yeah."

"You're lucky all you have are a few bruises."

He ran a hand through his hair, dislodging several tiny sticks and pieces of gravel. "They took my wallet. All my money, traveler's checks, and credit cards. And my ID. Everything."

"We need to call the police." She started for the kitchen to get the phone, but he gripped her arm.

"No police."

"But you need to file a report."

"What I need is a friend, a place to spend the night."

"Chess—"

"I know what's best."

She stood looking down at him. "Where did you stay last night?"

"With . . . a guy. But I can't go back there."

She wasn't sure she was getting the full story. She sat down across from him, on the rocking chair next to the fireplace.

"Can I stay? Maybe I could sleep on the couch. I promise, I'll leave in the morning. You can trust me. You know that."

"It's hardly a matter of trust. Anyway, you don't have to sleep on the couch. I've got a guest bedroom upstairs."

"No, that's too much trouble. Just let me bed down here. I thought about sleeping outside somewhere, but I'm too rattled."

"I still think you should report what happened to the police."

"I can't."

"Why?"

"Because if it got out that I was at a gay bar—"

"You're still in the closet?"

He wouldn't meet her eyes. "More or less."

"But who even knows you around here anymore?"

"More people than you might expect."

She shook her head. "That's a hard way to live. You still have your suitcases? Your clothes?"

"They're all at Robert's house."

She wanted to ask who Robert was but decided to let it go. As they sat staring at each other, the conversation stalled and then died.

To fill the silence, Jane said, "Want to wash up?"

"Maybe later."

"Want a brandy?"

"Desperately."

She left the room and returned a few seconds later with two glasses and the bottle.

As she poured them each a drink, he said, "Thanks for letting me stay."

"Of course you can stay."

"Still, thanks."

She sat down and studied him for a few seconds. "You never mentioned what you do for a living these days."

Looking relieved that the conversational ball had been picked up, he said, "I deal in antiquities. Mostly jewelry. I work for a broker in Holland."

"And you live in Istanbul?"

"That's where my primary residence is. I live in what's called Cukurcuma. It's the SoHo of Istanbul, although that doesn't do it justice. It's a very West-leaning section, very grand, trendy but ancient. Lots of shops on narrow, winding streets. Lots of new restaurants and nightclubs. It's like nowhere else on earth." He gazed straight ahead into the cold fireplace.

31

"What about when you're in Amsterdam?"

"I have a small flat. Both of my residences are small, bare-bones affairs. You might not believe it, but money has never been important to me. It's simply a means to an end."

"Traveling? Seeing the world?"

"The experience of life in all its varied incarnations. When I was younger, I wanted to visit every corner of the world."

"Have you?"

"I'm still working on it."

"What are you doing here?"

"I'm on a buying trip. Not that I'll be doing much buying without my credit cards. You know—" He glanced down at Mouse, who was lying on the braided rug next to Jane. "I wonder sometimes. Do you ever let your mind wander, think about what our lives might have been like if we'd stayed married? If we'd really been in love."

She found the question strange. "But we weren't."

"No. But what if we had been? You were so beautiful. You're still beautiful. I'd forgotten those amazing icy blue-violet eyes of yours."

Jane wasn't sure what to say.

"You've done well for yourself. Two restaurants. This big old house. I mean, look at you. You're fit and prosperous."

"The recession has hit the restaurant industry pretty hard."

"Didn't seem that way this afternoon." He crossed his legs, leaned back against the cushions. "And Cordelia. She's still as exotic, as curvaceous as ever, although she's put on weight. Then again, so have I."

"She never does anything halfway. If she likes something, she wants to wallow in it. If she doesn't like it, she'd just as soon take a flamethrower to it."

"That sounds about right. Is she seeing anyone?"

"Her partner's name is Melanie Gunderson. She's a journalist. They live across the street from each other—both in downtown lofts."

"Not together?"

32

"To quote Cordelia, they each need 'a loft of their own.' It's an updated, more or less consumer-driven spin on Virginia Woolf's famous essay."

That made him laugh. "I think I've missed you two."

"You'd better call your credit card companies—report the thefts."

"Yeah." He sighed. "Unfortunately, I don't have the numbers with me. I'll have to get hold of my assistant back in Istanbul, have him make the calls." He slipped a cell phone out of his jacket.

Jane was surprised at how cheap it looked. Maybe he really did live a bare-bones life. "Better get you a pillow and a blanket."

"I owe you, Jane. I owe you so much."

"We settled all our scores long ago."

"I know. Even so, thanks."

5

Julia leaned toward the bathroom mirror, applying the finishing touches to her makeup, feeling a kind of grim resignation at the image staring back at her. Severe headaches had dogged her ever since her return to the United States. They'd gone away for a time but in the last few months had returned with a vengeance. Along with the headaches came a kind of continuous nausea. She'd lost weight, which she could hardly afford. She'd already lost too much as a result of the drug-resistant strain of TB she'd contracted while working in southern Africa. The AIDS crisis in that country had consumed her life for the last few years. She would probably still be there if she hadn't become ill. Her lungs were clean and healthy again, but she wondered if some of the vestiges of the disease—and the cure—weren't the cause of her current problems.

A doctor she'd begun to see had put her on a migraine medication that seemed to be helping, although the tests she'd undergone were inconclusive. Except for one. She didn't have a brain tumor. She'd been so busy starting up a free outreach clinic in downtown Minneapolis that she hadn't had the time to study the headache issue herself. She did know that migraines didn't come in clusters, the way hers did. Sometimes she would experience five or six headaches a day, lasting from a few minutes to a few hours. It was debilitating and frustrating when she had so much work to do.

Julia's medicine chest was full of medications, most of which didn't work. She was seeing the medical profession from a different point of view these days, and it wasn't pretty. Nevertheless, she had made progress on the free clinic, which was her primary goal at the moment, and that gave her a sense of accomplishment even in the midst of personal chaos.

Last February, Julia had rented a fully furnished Uptown penthouse loft. She'd been looking around for a place to buy but ended up subletting from a man who planned to spend the next couple of years working on a business venture in China. With spectacular, virtually unimpeded views of Lake Calhoun to the west and Uptown to the north, not to mention green building practices, it was everything she'd been looking for and more. She'd asked her lawyer to negotiate a clause in the rental agreement that allowed her first crack at buying the place, just in case the owner ended up staying in China.

Working in southern Africa for several years had changed her perspective on life and the world—and her values vis-à-vis that world. If she hadn't had some persuasive reasons for sticking around the Twin Cities, she would have returned. She'd never taken a salary while she was there. She couldn't. There were so many problems, so much pain and heartache, political corruption, and poverty, and yet the people themselves were generous, dignified, and deeply brave. They were also under the sway of religious traditions that gave them license to live dangerously when it came to HIV and prevented them from getting the help they so desperately needed. One day she would go back. She was sure of very few things these days, but that was a given.

36

After filling the electric teakettle in the kitchen, switching it on, and making sure the mugs and biscotti were set out on a tray, ready to take into the living room, she drifted over to the piano, pulled out the bench, and sat down. This was turning into one of her good days. Maybe it was the new medication, or maybe the headaches were calming down. Either way, her mood was positive, even buoyant.

The baby grand, stored for many years while she was out of the country, had once belonged to her father, a man she'd never known. Her mother and father had divorced when she was two. She'd inherited the piano after her mother's death. Just before the funeral, Julia had met a woman who would change her life forever. Everything, invariably, led back to Jane.

Julia's mother, a psychologist and therapist, maintained—in her endlessly self-analytical way—that she and Julia's father had never been compatible because they wanted different things. He'd been a free spirit, a musician, who didn't appreciate what it would take to settle down and raise a family. Her mother cautioned her, over and over, to be careful about relationships. She advised her only daughter to live her life deliberately, find out who she was. If she didn't know what was truly important to her, it would be impossible to fit into the puzzle of another person's life.

Julia listened. She always listened. However, unlike her mother, who had been deeply practical, not the least bit romantic, Julia believed in fate. It might not make psychological sense, or stand up to the rigors of reason, but she'd always known that when she found the right person, nothing on earth, with the exception of death, could separate them.

Julia had spent much of her young life searching for that special someone. By her late twenties, she'd come to the unhappy conclusion that, to have any relationship at all, she might need to settle for less. She'd been in exactly two relationships before meeting Jane, both with men, and neither successful. She'd been attracted to women ever since medical school but had never acted on it. When Jane came into her life, she couldn't deny her feelings, although it did take some time for her to see that this was the hand of fate beckoning her into her future. Roses, though, had thorns. She never would have guessed that wanting a life with Jane would ultimately mean that she would be forced to turn her back on the work she loved so much. At times, she found that she both loved and hated Jane, almost in equal measure—but the love always won out.

Swinging her legs under the keyboard, Julia adjusted the piano seat and then opened a book of classical solos. Music was a cherished solace. She was glad now that her mother had insisted she take lessons. The acoustics in the loft were so good that she felt as if she were on stage at Carnegie Hall. Placing her hands lightly over the keys, she closed her eyes and floated to Pachelbel's Canon in D. She might not be able to see fate's entire plan for her life, but it would eventually guide her back to Jane.

The phone rang just as Julia finished the final measure. She sat for a moment, breathing in as the bright high notes reverberated through the loft, then faded. She stood and walked purposefully over to the kitchen counter, where she picked up the phone.

"Julia? It's Peter. I'm downstairs."

"Hey. Glad you could make it."

"Your phone message made it sound important, whatever 'it' is."

"When you come into the building you'll see an elevator right in front of you. Take that to five. I'm the middle door. Five-B."

"I'll be right up."

Irina had been married to Steve for nine years. For a great part of that time, he'd been out of the country, fighting in Iraq. In many ways, he was a stranger to her, someone who appeared to prefer the dust, heat, and danger of a foreign battlefield to his life at home. She'd been pregnant three times in the years they'd been together.

38

The first pregnancy had ended in a miscarriage, the second in a still-born child. She had been forced by Steve's absence to deal with the second loss—and an almost overwhelming sorrow—by herself. She couldn't really blame Steve for being away, and yet, down deep, she did. After the birth of her son, Dustin James, in mid-April, her depression had finally lifted. Little Dusty made life worth living again. Chess was merely the icing on the cake.

Steve was an aviation engineer. He was a decent man. Not kind, but fair. He believed in what he was doing in Iraq, even if Irina didn't. She'd kept quiet about her opposition to the war, knowing that he needed her support and love. Gradually, though, that love had been eroded by time and distance, by forgotten birthdays, too few letters, phone calls and e-mails that always seemed rushed. When he'd been hit by shrapnel after a roadside bomb exploded outside Mosul last summer, he'd been forced home to nurse his wounds. Irina felt sure that this would be the end of his days in combat. Then yesterday, he'd dropped a bomb. He'd been approached by a private military contractor called the Brigade, who wanted to hire him to work for them in Afghanistan. In an unconvincing effort to include her in his plans, he'd asked her to drive down to Rochester with him, bragging that he would earn more working for the Brigade in a year than he'd make as an engineer in ten. There was a time when she would have argued with him, tried to get him to stay, but now, since Chess had come into her life, her feelings had changed.

"You going in to the gallery today?" asked Steve. He buttered a piece of toast and took a bite so big that half the slice disappeared into his mouth.

"Eleven to six," she said, pouring a second round of boiling water over the baby bottles in the sink.

"Smells like bleach," said Steve.

"I rinsed the bottles with it."

"Jesus, Irina, are you kidding me?"

39

She was used to his opinions, although they still hurt. "I rinse them thoroughly. There's no problem. By the way, my sister's coming over in a little while to babysit."

He dropped another slice of bread into the toaster. "Where'd you go last night?"

She looked up.

"You were gone for a couple hours."

She'd been absolutely positive that he'd been asleep when she left, that he never knew she'd gone. Now she had to think fast. "I just kept tossing and turning, so I went for a drive." They hadn't slept in the same bed since his return from Iraq. He wanted to resume their sex life, but because it had been a difficult pregnancy, she couldn't deal with it. It was partly an excuse, and they both knew it. To say that their marriage was on the rocks was an understatement, and yet, for some reason, she couldn't bring herself to completely let go. "You go for late-night drives all the time. I wasn't worried about Dusty because you were here."

He moved up next to her and stuffed the last tip of buttered toast into his mouth. "Honey, I know you don't want to hear this——"

"I don't. So just drop it, okay?" She hated it when he tried to be nice. It was just an act.

He began again. "If everything goes the way I think it will with the Brigade, I could be deployed to Afghanistan by the end of the month."

Her back stiffened. The man he'd talked to yesterday had promised him money, adventure, and another chance to serve his country. It was like throwing a steak to a salivating dog. "I don't understand you. We might be having problems, but doesn't Dustin mean anything to you?"

When he touched her shoulder, she pulled away. She was keenly aware of the disdain he felt for the way she'd been handling their little boy's health issues. Dusty had been born prematurely. His immune system hadn't developed properly. Because of that, Irina kept him away from people and worked hard to shield him from germs that might harm him. She couldn't risk the loss of another child. Steve thought she was overreacting, that she was too protective, had even gone a little crazy. Maybe she had, but in her mind, everything she did was a necessary precaution. As long as he was home, he was simply going to have to live with it.

Glancing over at him, Irina saw that he hadn't dressed yet. He was still in his pajama bottoms and V-neck T-shirt. He'd always been fastidious about his clothing and his personal hygiene, which she appreciated even more now that they had a child. He put on a clean white T-shirt every night before he went to bed and replaced it with a new one after his morning shower. He looked so different these days, now that his hair had grown out. Normally, he kept it shaved on the sides with the top a little longer. A military cut, he called it. Irina thought it made him look mean, very different from the shaggy-haired man she'd met twelve years ago. His time in the military had changed him in more ways than she could count. Most significant was the effect his service had had on his self-confidence. All the shyness and reticence had been burned out of him. Some might say the change was for the good. Irina thought the jury was still out.

"Honey," he said, trying again. "Just listen to me for a second. Have you thought any more about finding a therapist for us before I go?"

"What's the point of seeing someone now?"

"I was hoping that after I left you'd stick with it a while."

"Seeing a marriage counselor without you doesn't make any sense." He stepped closer. "A lot of this is my fault."

Tears welled in her eyes.

"I don't want to leave like this."

"You mean leave me all alone with a child to raise? At least my sister is here for me."

Irina worked two days a week at the gallery. Steve would occasionally stay with the baby, but most of the time he was either with his buddies or at work. He'd taken a part-time job with an aviation contractor. Misty, her younger sister, was just out of drug rehab and currently unemployed. Irina had been touched by how eager she was to take over as the primary babysitter. Without her help, Irina would have been chained to the house. "If you hadn't told my mother that she was no longer welcome in our home——"

"You know why I said that. Irina, look at me." He tried to turn her around, but she wouldn't budge from her place at the sink. "We need to talk about this."

"She doesn't support the war."

He moved around her, leaned on the counter, and looked up at her. *"Please."*

"Admit it. You hate her guts. She's a liberal. All liberals are un-American."

"I never said that."

"Maybe it's for the best that she doesn't come over. I was so sick of you two arguing."

"It's not like you don't see her, I've never prevented you from going to her condo."

"Prevented me? What's that supposed to mean? This isn't the 1950s. You don't tell me what I can and can't do."

"Fine. Invite her over all you want—after I'm gone. I was just trying to protect you."

"Protect me from my own mother?" She didn't want to get into it with him, but more and more these days, it was becoming impossible not to. They were like two caged animals circling each other, searching for an advantage.

"This is hopeless," said Steve. "I don't know why I even try."

"You're too sensitive about your military service. U.S. foreign policy wasn't handed down from God, you know. You're not right about everything."

Steve had always had a temper, but after serving in the military,

42

anything and everything set him off. She could see by the sudden redness flooding his face that she'd just stumbled over a trip wire.

"Your mom actually blamed me—*me*—for the looting that went on at the Baghdad Museum. That comment crossed the line, and you know it."

Steve had been in Baghdad in April of 2003. His unit had been fighting in another part of the city when the museum was looted.

"Since you mentioned it, I was in your office this morning." His fists rose to his hips. "You're doing research for your mom, right? On the looting in Baghdad? The Nimrud gold?"

"Mom's giving a speech in New York next month." Her mother had been asked to give a talk before the UN, but Irina's interest in the Nimrud gold had nothing to do with it.

"God damn it, why can't that woman just drop the subject. She doesn't have all the facts. She just wants to blame. To blame the U.S. To blame *me*."

"Steve—"

"No, you need to hear this. Our government *did* put the museum on a no-strike list. We knew it was important."

"Then why wasn't it protected?"

"Do you have any idea what it was like in that city? The compound had been filled with Republican Guard by the time we entered. There was a serious firefight in that area, one we didn't start. It was illegal, under international law, for Saddam to put his men inside those walls. It *made* the place a military target. The U.S. commanders showed great restraint."

"No units were assigned to the museum, Steve. Planners simply didn't believe the museum would be looted. That's unconscionable."

"Oh, so you're taking her side now. Okay, let's think about it. A unit gets assigned to the compound. The guys get there and find looters—and Republican Guard. So the unit commander does what he's required to do when someone starts shooting. He requests backup, tanks and mortars. But because the museum was put on a no-strike list, the commander's request would have been denied. What we've got now is a killing field."

Irina's head was beginning to throb. "Quiet a minute." She leaned toward the baby monitor she'd set on the kitchen counter. "Is that Dusty?"

"You're not listening." He grabbed the toast out of the toaster without buttering it and stormed out of the room.

"Don't wake the baby!" she called after him.

Just then, Misty sailed through the screen door. "Whoa," she said, coming to a halt next to the center island. "What did I walk in on?"

"Just more of the same."

"Something about Mom? If it is, I'm with Steve."

Misty, the classic bad girl who seemed to attract nothing but bad karma, had been at odds with their mother since she was a teenager. If the two of them weren't fighting about her drug use, her poor grades, or her spotty work history, or her generally snotty attitude, they were battling over her current boyfriend. Move forward fifteen years and nothing had changed.

"Put Dusty in his swing chair when I leave," said Irina, finishing her coffee in two quick gulps.

"Yeah, yeah." Misty set her purse on the counter and ran a hand through her bleached blond hair.

Irina was sad to see that her sister was starting to look hard, older than her years. Physically, Irina and Misty were opposites. Where Irina was thin and petite, taking after their mother, Misty was fleshy and tall, like their dad. Mom had married twice, once for love—her first marriage—and once for lust. Irina and Misty were the product of number two. Dear old dad was long gone. He'd been a worka-holic, a ghost in their lives, so they hardly missed him when he ran off with his secretary and settled in Argentina. Irina had been too embarrassed to tell any of her friends because it was such a pathetic cliché. After the second divorce was final, their mother quit trying. The gallery was her passion now. Men, as she often said, were too much trouble.

"You should be nicer to Steve," said Misty, pouring herself a mug of coffee. "He's sweet."

Irina glanced at her sister's tight hip-hugger jeans. The look might have worked for her once upon a time, when she'd been young and thin, but now she just looked cheap.

"And *you* should be nicer to Mom," said Irina on her way out of the room.

"Sure. Like that's going to happen. Did you hear the latest?"

Irina paused in the doorway and turned around.

"Mom wants me to come work at the gallery—part-time. I haven't had any luck finding a job. She thinks this is the answer."

"Maybe it's a good idea."

"Me and Mom? In the same room? Are you kidding me? It will be thermonuclear war."

"But you need to support yourself somehow."

"It's not fair. She's loaded. Why can't she just help me out?"

"She is. She's letting you stay at our old family house free of charge."

"Yeah, but I have to toe this stupid line or I'm out. I figure, hell, most of her money came from our dad anyway. I think some of it should rightfully be ours."

"That's not the way it works. We'll inherit after she dies."

"Can't happen soon enough for me."

"You don't mean that."

Misty's gaze dropped to the mug in her hand.

"Look, you're doing me a big favor by babysitting Dusty. I'll write you a check, something to help out. It's just . . . you're not—"

"What?" she snapped. "Using?"

"Are you?"

"No."

Irina worried constantly about her sister. She'd been in and out of rehab so many times that it seemed impossible to think she'd stay clean for more than a few months. Drugs were everywhere these days. Misty told her once that she could walk out of Irina's home and find just about anything she wanted in a matter of blocks—and this wasn't the inner city, it was Apple Valley.

"It's a dangerous world out there," said Misty.

"Tell me about it," said Irina, remembering the snapshot of Melvin Dial's bloody body lying behind his couch.

6

How long?" asked Chess, his right leg bouncing nervously. He was sitting on a wicker rocker on Jane's back porch, talking on his cell to a man in New Jersey who created and sold fake passports.

"A week to ten days," came the raspy voice.

"You can't do it any sooner?"

"I'm good and I'm cheap. You want fast, you go someplace else."

This was the only connection Chess had. You couldn't just call up a man like this out of the blue and expect him to talk to you. You had to do it through intermediaries. "What about the new driver's license?"

"I might be able to get that to you sooner, but I can't promise. I'm pretty backed up."

Chess was in the wrong line of work. "Okay. It's a deal."

"Money first. Then I start."

"I'll wire transfer it to your bank today." It was going to take virtually every dime he had left in his Swiss account, but it was money well spent. He needed a new passport, just in case things got too hot and he had to run.

"You've got all the info?" asked the man. "The routing number?"

"Yeah," said Chess. "And you've got Irina Nelson's address?"

"We're all set."

After hanging up, he sat for a few minutes looking at the backyard. Jane was still asleep upstairs. It was just after eight, too early to be awake after so little rest. With everything on his mind, he'd barely slept at all. He bitterly regretted his decision to return to the Twin Cities. When Irina called to tell him she'd found a buyer, he should have lied, told her the bull had already been sold. Instead, as usual, he let his curiosity, his need for money, and his lust for a woman lead him into a dangerous back alley.

It had taken weeks to get the bull into the country through Central America. He recalled one particularly horrible time, riding for three days through the Guatemalan jungle, the humidity beyond belief, spiderwebs sticking to his clothes, his hair, his face. He'd come up through Mexico, over the Texas border, and then, traveling back roads, finally reached Minnesota. If he couldn't sell it, it would take that long—or longer—to get it back out. It would also take money, which he no longer had.

Lifting Ed the Blackmailer's cell phone out of one of the pockets of his safari jacket, he willed it to ring. He wanted to talk to him, whoever he was, and see if he could renegotiate the price of his silence. Until the bull was out of his life, Irina was right. It was best to stay out of sight. Jane's house seemed as good a place as any to hide, although he wasn't sure how long she'd let him stay.

Thinking back on the first time they'd met, he remembered how bad he felt about lying to her—back when he still felt bad about lying. He wasn't gay. Cordelia had merely assumed he was, referring to him constantly as a "beautiful boy." He went along with it because he wanted the part in the play, and if thinking he was gay made her happy, and made it easier for them to be friends, that was fine with him. Only later had he seen it as a path to his inheritance. The irony and utter outrageousness of playing gay in order to fool his parents by marrying a lesbian at a wedding presided over by a Catholic priest appealed to him. Chess had always shaded the truth, when necessary, a tad more than he should. He often did it to make people happy, but he also lied to get what he wanted. The only real problem about making things up was that he would sometimes forget what he'd said. To be a successful liar you needed an ironclad memory.

Chess's mom had refused to speak to him after she learned the marriage was bogus. He'd been hoping that she would forgive him, but it wasn't in the cards. He'd left the country without saying good-bye because she refused to see him. He thought that, given enough time and distance, she would change her mind.

In fact, she had. Two years ago, when she was dying in a nursing home in Lake Forest, his older sister had e-mailed him and said that their mom had something she wanted to say to him—and that she wanted to do it face-to-face. Before he made the plane reservations, he received another e-mail saying she was dead.

Over the years, Chess had concluded that his original sin was failing to find a woman and live happily ever after. To Chess's way of thinking, there was no such thing as "happily ever after." It was a fairy tale, like Santa Claus or the Easter Bunny. Most people settled for something less than they wanted, or accommodated a partner's desires in ways that diminished them. Or they divorced. Chess had escaped all that heartache by simply admitting what most refused to see.

His parents had been a prime example. They projected the fantasy image of a happily married couple, but behind the doors of their home in Lake Forest the truth was far different. The fact that his mother and father had the audacity to tie his inheritance to what they knew was a lie infuriated him then, and did so still. Justify our existence by climbing into the same unhappy bed as we did and we'll reward you. It was absurd. Even so, his heart broke when he thought of his mother sitting alone in that nursing home, watching the last of her life fade to black. To come to the end of the road without a reconciliation with her youngest son must have seemed a cruel fate. During those final hours, she had reached out to him, but it was too late.

"Are you okay?"

Chess turned to find Jane standing in the doorway.

"You're crying."

"Am I?" He touched his cheek, felt the tears.

She opened the screen door wide and let her dog out into the yard.

"I was thinking about my mother. Do you remember her?"

"I actually liked her a lot."

He gazed out at the flower garden along the back fence. The sun hit the tops of a thick patch of iris, not as grand as *Le Jardin de Monet, les iris,* but close. "I never got a chance to say good-bye. She died a few years ago. We became estranged after . . . you know. It still bothers me."

She didn't say anything, just looked at him with those intense blue-violet eyes.

Although Chess had spent a lot of time with her, he'd never really understood what made Jane tick. She didn't talk about herself much, or pontificate on pet subjects. Instead, she asked questions and seemed genuinely interested in the answers. In Chess's experience, that was rare. He assumed that made her the beneficiary of more than one unsought confidence over the years.

She was dressed casually this morning in jeans and a red cotton shirt. Her lush brown hair spread loosely across her shoulders. She'd aged, for sure, most notably in the wrinkles starting to form at the edges of her eyes. He figured she dyed her hair, although if she did, she'd never admit it. She was as vain as the next woman. It would no doubt surprise her to learn that a certain amount of womanly vanity made her more attractive, not less. She could be generous, sometimes even kind, but at heart Chess saw her as a Gordian knot. Con-

50

voluted. Moody. Private. That's what had fascinated him years ago, and apparently still did. Someday, perhaps, someone with the skill of an Alexander would forgo trying to untie her and instead take a sword to the workings of her heart. He wished he could be around to see it.

"I suppose I should get out of here, let you have your house back. I want to thank you again for letting me stay last night."

"Were you able to get your stolen credit cards canceled?"

For a moment, he was thrown. "Oh, yeah," he said. He'd almost forgotten last night's lie. He touched the abrasions on his cheek. On the way over to her house, he'd found a brick in an alley and scraped his face, then rubbed some gravel in his hair. It added a note of authenticity to his tale of woe. "Everything's been handled."

"Are you hungry?" she asked. "I could fix you some breakfast."

"Are you still a great cook?"

"That's the prevailing opinion."

He sniffed the air. "Coffee?"

"It's set on a timer. Can't start the day without a caffeine fix."

"Sure," he said, smiling broadly. "Breakfast would be great."

"And if you need to stay another night, that's fine with me."

"Can I get back to you about it later in the day?" As he followed her into the kitchen, the phone in his hand—the blackmailer's cell—began to vibrate. "You go on," he said. "I've got to take this."

He flipped it open and said hello, pushing out the screen door and walking a few yards out into the grass.

"Morning." The words were spoken in a deep baritone, but it sounded fake, as if the guy were intentionally lowering his voice.

"Ed?"

"That's me."

"Who are you?"

"Just consider me a friend."

"Funny." He stepped over to a tree and stood with his back to the porch door. "I didn't kill that guy."

"Right."

"I'm not lying."

"Whatever you say. But I cleaned up your mess and I still want the money."

"We need to meet, talk this over."

"Nothing to talk about. You pay me or I send the photos to the police."

"I don't have fifty thousand dollars."

"Come on. You've traveled all over the world. You've got to be a man of means."

A conclusion he'd drawn, no doubt, from looking at the stamps on his passport. "No money unless we talk first," said Chess.

Silence.

"Did you hear me?"

"I heard."

"So?"

"How much money do you have?"

Chess relaxed a little. This guy wasn't a pro. "My financial situation is complicated. Look, whoever you are, I promise I'll pay you something. It's worth it to me. I didn't kill Dial, but you made a potential mess go away, and for that you deserve something."

"How much?"

"That's what I want to talk to you about. Meet with me and we can firm up a price."

"Is this a trap?"

"Absolutely not."

"Because if you try anything, those photos go straight to the police. You can't just walk away from a murder scene, you know."

Chess pressed a fist to his mouth to stop himself from laughing. The guy was such a pathetic amateur. "What did you do with the body?"

"It's safe."

"I don't care if it's safe. I want to know that it's gone. Buried in the woods where nobody will ever find it. Or weighted and dumped in a lake."

"I took care of it. I'm not stupid."

That remained to be seen.

"Listen, buddy, you don't tell me what to do. I tell you."

"I'm just trying to be helpful," said Chess. "Where should we meet?"

He hesitated. "If I agree, it has to be someplace public."

"The Witch's Hat." It popped out of his mouth before he'd even thought about it, probably because he knew the university better than any other part of town. The tower was in a park, high on a hill. Nobody could sneak up on him there. "You know where it is"

"You mean the water tower in Prospect Park? Over by the U?"

"That's the one."

More hesitation. "I suppose I could meet you."

"At eleven. Today. Eleven on the dot."

"Don't push me. I'm the one in charge here, not you."

"I'm aware of that," said Chess, working a little meekness into his voice. "So? Do we have a deal?"

The guy didn't respond right away. "Okay," he said finally, sounding less than sure of himself. "Eleven. I'll be there. But no funny business. Remember, I got those pictures."

7

Irina was running late. She'd managed to pull herself together after the fight with Steve, although it had left her stomach churning. At least her sister had arrived on time to take care of Dusty—one worry off her plate.

The Morgana Beck Gallery of Antiquities was located on a tree-lined street in the heart of St. Paul. Grand Avenue was thirty blocks long and ran from the Mississippi River all the way downtown. Irina described the area to customers as a mixture of the trendy and the historic, with neighborhood ethnic and big-city urbane tossed in for good measure. In fact, Grand Avenue boasted some of the best shopping and the best restaurants in town. Unlike the malls, most of the businesses were independent, one of a kind. Irina hated the burbs. Apple Valley had been Steve's idea. She much preferred the inner city, having grown up in a house not far from here—the place that Misty currently called home, thanks to the generosity of their mother.

The gallery was a restored redbrick Queen Anne duplex. Her mother's office was on the second floor in an octagonal turret. A duplex, as it turned out, was the perfect arrangement for them. The first floor held the galleries. The second floor had a fully stocked kitchen so they could grab meals on the run. Two of the three upstairs bedrooms were used for storage, and the third had been made into a shipping office. Much of their business these days came from online sales.

Irina parked her Saab in the small lot behind the gallery. As she slid out, she noticed that a planter on the back deck had been knocked over, spilling dirt across the wood planks and dislodging a huge hibiscus. Because of the wrought-iron bars on all the windows, they'd never had a break-in. She approached the rear door cautiously, righting the planter and kicking the excess dirt onto a small patch of grass that grew between the house and the blacktop. The door was locked, which Irina took as a good sign. Grand Avenue ran through a mostly residential area, so it could have been kids running around after dark.

Before Dustin was born, Irina worked four days a week. Now, because her mother thought she needed the time to take care of her child, she was down to two. Tuesdays and Thursdays were her days to open the gallery. Majid Farrow, a man she disliked intensely, mainly because her mother thought the sun rose and set on his abilities as an appraiser and a salesman, opened the other days.

Majid was from Texas—specifically, River Oaks, a suburb of Houston. His mother was Iranian born, a professor of Egyptian archaeology and philology, his father an American heart surgeon with a practice in downtown Houston. Irina's mother had hired Majid the day after he graduated from Macalester with an interdepartmental master's in Middle Eastern studies, Islamic civilization, and art history. That was seven years ago. He was a good fit for a gallery that specialized in Middle Eastern art and antiquities, but Irina felt that he enjoyed displaying his knowledge at her expense. Her degree was in art history, but nowhere near as specialized. She'd worked as hard as he had, if not harder, to become an expert in the field. Still, her mother seemed to prefer his opinions. He'd come late to his studies, which meant that he was six years older than she was. She thought of him as a peer. His avuncular treatment of her suggested that he thought otherwise. The less she worked with him, the better she liked it.

Mornings at the gallery were for light dusting, setting up the cash register, sorting the mail, checking e-mail, and finally opening the double front doors to the public at eleven. It was already after that. Instead of charging in, Irina thought it best to walk along the west side of the building to the front, scanning the windows for anything amiss. After checking the east side, she paused for a few seconds at the base of the wide front steps and looked in through the bay window. All the track lights were on. Something wasn't adding up. Her mother always turned off the track lighting when she closed the gallery for the night.

Turning to the street, Irina shielded her eyes from the sun and scanned the parked cars. She spotted her mother's pearl gray Audi Roadster halfway down the block. Feeling relieved that her mom had already arrived, she headed back to the rear of the house and let herself in. Her mother was probably fuming. Arriving late was a cardinal sin in her lexicon of business blunders.

Steeling herself for an argument, Irina walked into the main showroom but stopped under the arched doorway, her hand flying to her mouth to cover a gasp.

The glass counters had all been opened, the contents scattered around on the floor. Nothing, not a single relic, was where it should be. Masks had been torn down from the walls. Standing shelves had been knocked over, some of the ancient glass artifacts broken into a million little pieces on the polished wood floors. The doors to three smaller climate-controlled galleries were open, allowing Irina a full view of the destruction.

Rushing up the back stairs, she entered the second-floor hallway, her gaze traveling swiftly to the open doorway into the living room.

"Mom?" she called. "Are you here? Are you okay?"

The second floor had been ransacked, just like the first. The backs and seats of all the antique couches and chairs had been ripped open, with big puffs of stuffing scattered virtually everywhere. All the cupboards in the kitchen were open, their contents dumped.

Rushing through the chaos into her mother's office, Irina let out a scream.

Her mother was slumped face-first onto her desk. Under the chair was a thick pool of sticky dark red blood. Irina pressed the back of her fingers to her mom's cheek and was so startled by how cold the skin felt that she withdrew her hand as if she'd been burned. She moved around behind the chair, grabbed her mom by her shoulders, and eased her back. The front of her white angora sweater was stained the same dark red as the floor. Irina stood very still, feeling another scream well up inside her.

Do something, she ordered, backing up, horrified at the revulsion she felt at being in the same room with a dead body. It was her mother's body. She shouldn't feel that way.

She wanted to run, to breathe fresh air, to wipe the sickening image from her mind. Instead, she dove for the corner of the room and vomited. Shivering violently, she edged over to the phone, picked it up, and started to tap in 911.

"No," she whispered, letting the phone drop back on the desk. She had to think this through.

Across the river in Minneapolis, Chess paced under the tower. He couldn't get one of the comments the blackmailer had made out of his mind. *You can't just walk away from a murder.* Did that mean the blackmailer had seen him walk away from Dial's house? Could Ed be the neighbor, the chatty bald guy who'd called to him as he was leaving? Had he seen Chess and Dial arrive the evening before? Maybe he heard something—a noise, an argument, a cry in the night—and

58

decided to take a look in one of the windows to see what was going on. A neighbor might have a key.

Chess checked his watch. It was eleven fifteen. Whoever this asshole was, he was late. Feeling frustrated, he kicked a stone down the hill, scanning the park for anyone who might be walking toward the tower. With the exception of a mother and her two kids sitting in the grass on a blanket, and a man seated on a bench eating a fast-food burger, the park was deserted.

"So how long am I supposed to wait?" he muttered. As he slid the cheap cell phone out of his pocket, it began to vibrate.

"Hello?" he said, stepping into the shade.

"I can't come," said the blackmailer's voice. "We'll have to re-schedule." Without waiting for a response, he hung up.

"Wait. Hello? Hello?" Chess flipped the phone closed. What the hell? Before he could come to a decision on what to do next, his own cell rang.

"Yeah?" he said, unable, or more likely unwilling, to keep the ag-gravation out of his voice.

"Chess? Is that you?"

It was Irina. She sounded upset. "What's going on?"

"It's Mom. She's dead. You've got to help me. You have to come over here."

"Where are you?"

"The gallery. Mom's office. Someone *murdered* her."

His mind began to spin. "God, that's . . . God." He swallowed back his shock. "You need to stay calm. Can you do that for me?"

"I think so."

"Have you checked the entire gallery? Are you alone?"

"I never thought of that," she said, her voice rising. "What if the killer is still in the building?"

"Can you lock your mom's office door?" He heard it slam shut, then the sound of a bolt being thrown.

"It's locked."

"This is a more difficult question. Have you touched the—I mean, your mother? Is her skin cold?"

"Yes," she said, her voice sounding strangled.

"That probably means whoever did this to her is long gone. Have you called the police?"

"Not yet."

"Perfect. Just stay put. I'll be there in ten minutes."

"Hurry."

Chess bounded up the steps to the double front doors, relieved to find them open. As soon as he was inside, he turned and locked the doors behind him.

He'd only been upstairs once. Slicing his way through the shambles of the once elegant gallery, he bolted to the back stairway and took the steps two at a time.

"Chess, is that you?" came Irina's frantic voice through the closed office door.

"I'm here."

A second later, Irina emerged looking deathly white. She fell into his arms. "I thought you were never going to get here."

He held her, feeling her body shiver through her light cotton dress. "I need to see your mom."

She seemed grateful as she took his hand and led him into the office. Morgana's body, her eyes closed, the front of her fuzzy sweater gummy with blood, sat hunched against the back of her chair, her head lolling to one side. "Is this the way you found her?"

"No. She was slumped across the desk."

Chess took hold of Morgana's shoulders and eased her back down. "It looks like a gunshot. You saw the entrance wound, right?"

She gave a stiff nod.

"The front doors were open."

60

"They were?"

He looked around for a bullet casing but couldn't find one. The shooter could have used a revolver, or maybe he was just careful. Chess gave himself a minute to think it through. "The guy must have been standing in front of the desk. What's this?" He nodded to a file folder open on the desk. "Looks like a trust agreement. You know anything about that?"

"She did it years ago. She and her lawyer go over it every spring. If there are any changes in the documents, she talks to me about them, but there hardly ever are any. It's just a formality."

He crossed back to the door, staring into the living room. "What are these people looking for?"

"You think it's the bull?"

He didn't reply. Walking back out into the front room, he picked up a cushion and righted a chair. Irina stood in the doorway and watched.

"We're not safe," she said.

"Let's not jump to conclusions. Your mother was shot. Dial was stabbed."

"So what? They're both dead."

"It might mean the murders weren't related."

"But we don't know that."

"No, we don't. Whatever is going on here, we need to stay focused on getting rid of that statue. Listen." He moved back to the doorway and looked her square in the eyes. "There are a lot of artifacts from the Baghdad Museum floating around the black market— I've bought and sold my share—but nothing as big or as high profile as the winged bull. If someone *is* on our trail, that's the reason. We have to work quietly and quickly. Are you with me?"

Her eyes looked glazed, off center. She gave a weak nod.

"You've got to be sure. We don't have time to waste, Irina. We act decisively or we call it off."

61

"I'm in, Chess. All the way."

"You've got it hidden away?"

"It's safe."

He kissed her with a passion he didn't feel. She was far more skittish than she'd been when they'd first discussed the sale of the bull in Istanbul last August. She'd turned into a woman who had to be coaxed along, handled with care. If she'd shown that sort of temperament earlier, he never would have cut her in. He'd been in a bind, though. He needed her, needed her connections. Greed motivated her, but it wasn't her bottom line. She tried to hide it, but after the buy was made, Chess was the prize she wanted. That meant he had to keep her happy until the bull was safely disposed of and the money was in the bank.

"You're going to be fine," he said, his arms encircling her, his fingers kneading the muscles in her neck.

She burst into tears. "I feel so guilty," she said, choking on her sobs. "My mom is dead and it's all because of me."

"We don't know that." He held her tighter. "You have to be strong, have to think of the future." He stroked her wispy blond hair, kissed her forehead. "You can be strong, can't you?"

She backed up and brushed the tears off her cheeks.

"It's time to call 911. Can I get you anything first? A glass of water?" He eased her down onto a chair, then leaned over her.

"Do you love me, Chess?"

He crouched down, took her hand in his, and pressed it to his chest. "With all my heart."

8

He's back," said Jane as she stood at the head of the wooden stairs leading down to the lake in front of her restaurant, holding her cell phone to her ear. The lunch rush was over, so she was taking a break.

"Who's back?" asked Cordelia. She sounded impatient.

In the background, Jane could hear trombones. "Is the Allen Grimby doing an adaptation of *The Music Man?*"

"I can't hear you."

" 'Seventy-six Trombones'?"

"Nah, I think there are only two. And a tuba, a flute, and an oboe."

"Kind of an unusual band."

"What?"

"Can you go into another room or something?"

A door slammed.

"There, that's better," said Cordelia. "Now, *who's* back?"

"That itinerant preacher. The one dressed in the monk's cowl."

"Well, yippy freakin' skippy. It's really nice of you to keep me updated on the comings and goings of Friar Tuck, but trust me, it's not necessary."

"Chess stayed at my house last night."

"He did? Why?"

"He was mugged."

"Heavens."

"I'll tell you about it when we have more time."

"Did you manage to get all the deliciously licentious details of his love life?"

"A little more than we got at lunch."

"Excellent, Janey. Just excellent. Everything ready for the party tomorrow night?"

The catering wing of Jane's two restaurants was taking care of the food. Her house had undergone a thorough cleaning. The champagne was already chilling. Because of her father's heart scare last year, this birthday felt like a gift. She wanted to do it up right. "How many RSVPs have come back?"

"Forty-nine. Most are couples, so plan on around a hundred. If *moi* had been in charge, we would have needed to rent the Metrodome."

Thirty yards away, the preacher was reading from what looked like a personal journal. The crowd wasn't large, maybe a dozen people, but they seemed attentive. His voice was deep, and it carried well.

"What are you wearing?" asked Cordelia.

A question like that usually came with heavy breathing. "Right now?"

"Earth to Jane. No, dingbat, at the party."

"Oh. A tux and a tiara."

"Entirely brilliant. I believe I said something in the invitation about dress being optional, though essential. Oh, drat. The tuba player is throwing a hissy fit. I've gotta go. Later."

Jane trotted down the steps to the footpath, curious what the preacher could be saying. Keeping her distance from the crowd, she sat down cross-legged in the grass, her back against a sturdy elm.

The preacher lifted his head and made eye contact with each member of his audience. "'Blessed is the man who has suffered and found life. Jesus said, What you look forward to has already come, but you do not recognize it. Blessed are the solitary and elect, for you will find the kingdom. For you are from it, and to it you will return.'"

He turned a page. "'Jesus said to them, When you make the two one, and when you make the inside like the outside and the outside like the inside, and the above like the below, and when you make the male and the female one and the same, so that the male will not be male and the female not be female; and when you fashion eyes in place of an eye, and a hand in place of a hand, and a foot in place of a foot, and a likeness in place of a likeness; then you will enter the kingdom.'"

"That's not in the Bible," shouted a gray-haired man sitting astride a dirt bike.

"No?" said the preacher.

"Not in any Bible I've ever seen."

He closed the book and held it down at his side. "Let me ask everyone a question. How many of you have read *The Da Vinci Code*?"

Almost everyone raised a hand.

"Why doesn't that surprise me. Now, how many of you have read the Bible? Not just passages but cover to cover."

One woman raised a hand.

"I find that fascinating, don't you?"

"*The Da Vinci Code* had a better plot," called a teenaged girl.

A few people laughed.

The gray-haired man shot the girl an angry look.

"How many of you believe in God?" asked the preacher.

This time, everyone raised a hand.

"And how many believe the Bible is the inerrant word of God?"

"What's 'inerrant' mean?" asked a woman standing at the front.

"Incapable of error," said the preacher. "Perfect in every way."

Only one young man in the back didn't raise his hand.

"Then tell me this," said the preacher. "If you really believe the Bible was written by our creator, why wouldn't you want to read it? I honestly don't get it and would like someone to explain it to me. I would think people would be falling over each other to find out what the Lord of the Universe had to say."

"But that stuff you read," said the gray-haired man. "It wasn't from the Bible, right?"

"It's from the Gospel of Thomas."

"There is no Gospel of Thomas."

"Sure there is. There's also a Gospel of Mary, a Gospel of Peter, a Gospel of the Savior, the Gospel According to the Hebrews, the Infancy Gospel of Thomas, and the Gospel of Philip. All these books were understood by many early Christians to be sacred texts."

"That's garbage," said the gray-haired man. "I don't know what you think you're doing here, but if you people want my opinion, that guy is the devil in disguise." In a huff, he pedaled off.

The preacher's gaze traveled to Jane, stayed with her for a few seconds, then returned to the crowd. "Do you people think that early Christianity was any different from Christianity today? In the first, second, and third century, the variety of beliefs was every bit as great. The Bible developed out of that broad mix of ideas. It was assembled by the group who won the battle over what was and what was not correct belief."

"What's your point?" called a man in a business suit.

"Just that we have an oversimplified view of the Christian faith."

"God inspired the Bible," called a young woman standing to the side. "I don't need to know how it happened. That's just a waste of time."

Several people nodded.

The crowd began to disperse.

Jane found it an interesting exchange. Not the fire and brimstone she'd been expecting.

The preacher waited until his audience had all gone, then got down off his wooden box, picked it up, and trudged through the grass to the path around the lake. He nodded to Jane as he walked past. She nodded back. She had no personal animus toward him, but just the same, she hoped he wouldn't come back.

Around four, as Jane was working in her office, she got a call from Julia. "Hey, stranger," she said, clicking on her cell and leaning back in her chair.

"I'm calling to RSVP about your dad's birthday party."

"Can you come?"

"Wouldn't miss it."

"I thought maybe you were out of town. I left you a couple of messages."

"Apologies about that," said Julia. "I've been incredibly busy."

"Still working at that clinic in Uptown?"

"No, I've got something new in the works. Very exciting."

"You going to tell me about it?"

"Didn't Peter tell you?" She sounded disappointed that Jane didn't already know.

"What's my brother got to do with it?"

"I'll tell you all about it when I see you tomorrow night."

As they said their good-byes, Jane concluded that the phone call was even more proof that Julia wasn't trying to push her way back into Jane's life. Cordelia was simply wrong when it came to Julia and her intentions.

Jane left the Lyme House early that night. She needed to make sure everything at home was as ready as possible for tomorrow evening.

She said a quick good-bye to her manager just after ten and made her way up the hill. After the noisy interior of the pub, the sweet scent of late spring flowers was a welcome relief.

As she approached her front sidewalk, hands in her pockets, head down, making a mental list of the projects she would need to finish before she could take a week or two off to drive up to Blackberry Lake, she didn't see Chess sitting on her steps until she was almost on top of him.

"Evening," he said, standing up.

"Wasn't sure I'd see you again."

He sat back down and patted the space next to him. "The cement's nice and comfy. Why don't you join me?" He held up a white sack. "Unlike me, you've lost weight. Way too thin. I've decided that it's my calling in life to feed you."

That made her laugh. "How long have you been here?"

"Half an hour. Maybe a little more."

"You could've come to the restaurant."

"I know. Come on, eat something." He looked into the sack. "I've got a chocolate éclair, a coffee éclair, two English toffee brownies, a cream horn, and two slices of chocolate pound cake. Pick your poison."

"You pick."

He handed her the coffee éclair. "It's from a terrific bakery downtown."

She took a bite. "Very good."

"I always sniff out the best bakeries."

"So where are you staying tonight?"

"That's why I came back." He removed a brownie and bit off the corner, closing his eyes and groaning. "I'm addicted to chocolate." Chewing slowly, he continued, "This morning, before you got up, I noticed that you have an outside stairway that leads to a third-floor apartment. It looked vacant, so I walked up to check it out. I could only see it through the windows, but it seemed nice. If nobody lives up there, could I rent it from you? Just for a few days."

"I haven't used that space in years." She didn't need the money anymore, but mostly she didn't rent it because she'd had some bad experiences with renters.

"I can't pay you much," he said.

"I don't want your money. Why don't you just stay in the guest bedroom?"

"Is there any furniture up there? A bed? A couch?"

"Sure, it's completely furnished."

"But I'll bet the dust is an inch thick."

"I have my cleaning woman give it a once-over every couple of months."

"Clean sheets on the bed?"

"It's a single bed. Not as comfortable as the double in the guest bedroom."

"You know me. I like my privacy. I won't be around long. I have a business deal pending that requires me to be in the Twin Cities for another few days, and then I'll be out of your hair."

She eased down next to him. He smelled nice, like he'd just showered, shaved, and splashed himself with cologne. He didn't have any of his bags last night, but tonight a rolling leather suitcase sat in the grass. He must have gone back to "Robert's" house to get it. He'd also changed into a pair of tan canvas drawstring slacks, leather sandals, and a black linen shirt.

"Of course you can stay."

He leaned over and lightly kissed her cheek. "You're the best."

"I don't know about that."

"I have something for you. I wanted to give it to you right away, but I didn't want you to think of it as a bribe."

"You don't need to give me anything."

"It's not about need, it's about want." He dug into the pocket of his slacks, took out a small, square box, and handed it to her.

Inside she found a ring. "Chess, no. This looks expensive."

"It's a Roman snake ring from the second century."

"It's too much."

"I wore it for a while. Now I'm passing it on to you. It's just stuff, Jane. Old stuff, for sure, but stuff nonetheless. Nobody really *owns* something like this. It just gets passed around. Besides, I like giving people beautiful things."

She tried it on each of her fingers until she found the one that the ring fit perfectly—the index finger of her right hand. "What's it made of?"

"Gold."

She pulled it off. "I can't take this."

"Of course you can. You may not know this, but in Turkey, people celebrate special occasions by giving gold as a gift. Turks love gold. Not because they like to show off but because it's something tangible; it keeps its value in a world where currency fluctuates. This particular ring is worth around two thousand, give or take. In a good year, I sell hundreds of rings like this, and much more besides. I'm hoping to make a big profit from the sale of a piece of Mesopotamian art, but I always travel with jewelry to sell. It's what I do. Giving you a ring isn't much different from you treating me to lunch at your restaurant."

"There's a huge difference."

"Do you like it?"

She was touched that he wanted her to have it. "I love it."

"Good. I want you to wear it. Something you'll always have to remember me by."

9

The next morning, just after sunup, Chess crept down the long out-side stairway and slipped quietly into a waiting cab. He was carrying an orthopedic cane and wearing a snap-brim cap over a gray wig. He also wore the four heavy crew-neck sweaters he'd bought yesterday and an oversized sport coat. The clothing made him look a good thirty pounds heavier. The gray mustache and dark glasses put the finishing touches on an image he hoped would fool anyone watching the Hyatt Regency in downtown Minneapolis.

Having lived in the Middle East for most of his adult life, Chess experienced a jolt of culture shock as the cabby whisked him through the early morning streets. It seemed odd that there were no mosques, no minarets with crying male voices, calling people to prayer. There was no old city, no street bazaars, no riotous color. Just endlessly boring modernity.

Glancing out the back window, Chess searched the street to make sure nobody was following the cab. So far, so good.

Old, in the Middle East, meant ancient. In Minnesota, old barely stretched a century and a half. As a kid, Chess had dreamed of time travel. Going backward had always appealed to him far more than going forward. All his curiosity was centered on the ancient, which was science fiction enough.

He remembered begging his parents for books on archaeology. Later, in high school, he had read everything he could find on the ancient world, pouring over photos of archaeological digs, reading books on ancient art. He wanted to be an archaeologist when he grew up but discovered, much to his embarrassment, that he was too lazy to make the effort required.

When Chess turned forty, he finally found his way into the kingdoms of his dreams. *Antiquities.* People were insane to think they could own ancient artifacts. These treasures belonged to everyone and no one. If a few came into Chess's possession, legal or otherwise, who was he to give them away for free? He wasn't above using other people's obsessions to make a living. If anything, ancient cultures had taught him that time was the lord of all. Every life was a tiny speck on an endless continuum. The shortness of a human life argued for enjoying what you had while you had it.

Chess was particularly drawn to Babylon before the Persian conquest and to *ancient* Egypt, when the pharaohs ruled—not the newer Ptolemaic dynasty that took root after the death of Alexander the Great. It wasn't smart to admit to oddball beliefs, but Chess had undergone several hypnotic regressions. He already believed in reincarnation, and this merely cemented it. His first birth had come during the reign of Abieshu, the grandson of Hammurabi. He could still taste the saltiness and dust on his tongue, smell the sweet scent of burning herbs in an alabaster bowl.

"Ever think about time travel" Chess asked the cabby.

The guy turned briefly to stare at him. "You mean like *Star Wars?*"

"Forward in time or backward. Either one."

"I'd like to go back to eleventh grade, when I decided I didn't need to graduate from high school."

Chess studied each car as it passed, each driver, then swiveled again to see who might be far enough behind to look innocent but have the cab in his sights. When he returned his attention to the front, the Hyatt was just ahead of them.

Five tense minutes later, he was safely inside his hotel room. He was as positive as he could be—without the gift of divination—that he hadn't been followed and that nobody had noticed him arrive at the hotel. He rode up to the sixth floor alone, and nobody, not even a housekeeper with a cleaning cart, met him in the hallway.

Fumbling nervously in his pocket for his pack of Camel Turkish Royals, he lit one, inhaled deeply, and then, with the cigarette dangling from his lips, ripped off the sport coat and sweaters. Sweat soaked his undershirt, so he took that off, too. He didn't like this cloak-and-dagger shit but agreed with Irina that continuing to stay at the Hyatt was like walking around with a bull's-eye on his back. He could easily be tracked through his credit cards, so he couldn't use those either.

Flopping down on the bed, he stuffed a couple of pillows behind his head. He snatched a glass ashtray off the nightstand and set it on his stomach. Then he took another deep drag. He didn't plan to stay in the room for more than a few minutes, but he needed those few minutes to calm down.

As he blew a stream of smoke into the air, his thoughts turned grimly to his current problems. There was no arguing with probability. Based on the fact that Dial's house was tossed, as was the gallery, Dial's and Morgana Beck's murders had likely been the work of the same person, for the same reason. He and Irina had been lucky so far, but counting on luck was a fool's errand.

All the way along, Chess had been so careful, taking things slowly, being as sure as humanly possible about each link in the chain that had brought the bull into the United States. Caution had been the reason it had taken him so long to complete the job. Somewhere along the line, his defenses must have been breached. As he saw it, he had several major hurdles to leap, any one of which could make his decision to return to Minnesota end in disaster.

First, he had to stay alive in order to sell the statue. Was that two problems? Staying alive seemed axiomatic, so he set that aside. He had to sell the bull because he needed money. Through the gallery, Irina had access to some of the best connections in the country. The bull was in the United States, and so was Chess; thus selling it here would provide the quickest return. Not necessarily the safest, but safety was a questionable commodity just about anywhere these days. Irina, a woman who was eminently knowledgeable as well as romantically tractable, was his best hope to sell the bull fast.

If someone out there was after the bull, and Dial's and Morgana Beck's deaths were indeed connected, it appeared that nothing, not even murder, was too high a price to pay to get the ancient statue back. Poor Morgana had probably spent the last few moments of her life insisting that she knew nothing about it. Perhaps the murders had been committed by the much-talked-about foreign triumvirate hunting down looters from the Baghdad Museum. If Chess had to place a bet, he'd bet on them. Which led to another hurdle.

Irina was every bit as much of a target as her mother, or Dial, or Chess himself—but while Chess had found a place to hide, Irina was living in the open. How did he keep her safe? Should he urge her to go move out of her house? Find a hole to crawl in? If what she'd told him was true, her marriage was over, but hiding out with a baby in tow would be problematic. This, clearly, required more thought.

Another hurdle was the idiot blackmailer who seemed to think Chess had killed Dial. He had some ideas on how to handle that. He would follow through on them just as soon as he bought himself a set of wheels. That led to problem four. Money. Normally, it was problem one through ten.

Until he received the new fake passport, credit cards, and driver's license from the forger in New Jersey, all he had to live on was the cash and traveler's checks he'd brought with him. Subtracting what he'd spent last night on clothing, a shaving kit, a new suitcase, dinner, and cab fare, it came to about seventeen hundred dollars. Fortunately, he had an ace in the hole. He'd taken Dial's wallet, which had netted him just under two thousand dollars. Also, he still had a key to Dial's house. If he was able to screw up the courage to go back, he might be able to locate the PIN numbers for one or more of the old man's credit cards. That would give him unlimited access to Dial's credit for at least a couple of days.

The first order of business was to find a used car lot that sold wrecks for cash. On the way to the hotel, he'd spotted one on Lake Street south of Lyndale.

For the next few minutes, Chess repacked his suitcase. He lit another smoke as he worked to fold everything neatly inside. His laptop, as well as some ancient coins, a few rings, and two Babylonian cylinder seals, also stolen from the museum in Iraq, were what had driven him to take the risk of coming back to the hotel. But now that he was here, he was glad to retrieve all his belongings.

One other item on Chess's to-do list was to find a gift for Jane's father. Last night, as Jane was helping him make up the bed in the third-floor apartment, she had invited him to tonight's party. She'd been so helpful, so concerned that Chess had everything he needed. She brought up fresh ground coffee, making sure the coffeepot worked. She also stocked the cupboard with sugar, jam, bread, and a fifth of good bourbon. Into the refrigerator went cream for his morning coffee, orange juice, eggs, butter, and a six-pack of beer. She tried out the air conditioner to make sure it would cool him should he need it. He couldn't remember when his heart had been so warmed. Rarely did anyone ever give him anything without expecting something in return. Jane and Cordelia were both like that. They gave because they liked to give, and they liked him, for no other reason than friendship.

Chess was looking forward to the party. He needed a break from all the stress he'd been under, and he was curious to meet Jane's friends and family. The invitation, however, came with one proviso. Jane would introduce him as an old friend. The details of their true connection must remain hidden.

Chess had, of course, agreed. Still, the idea of making every jaw in the room drop was a tantalizing tableau.

"What should I get my father-in-law for his birthday?" whispered Chess.

He had so many trinkets. Then again, a quarter-million-dollar cylinder seal did seem a bit much.

10

Irina found a parking spot on Grand Avenue in front of the gallery but couldn't bring herself to go in. She sat in her car and talked on her cell.

"Where are you?" she asked, resting her elbow on the open window and leaning her head against her hand.

"Eating breakfast in a café just down the street from the Hyatt," said Chess.

In the background, she could hear voices, laughter. "I thought you weren't going back there."

"I had to. But don't worry. Nobody recognized me. I used to do a lot of theater, so I'm good at disguise. Now, tell me everything that happened yesterday after I took off. Don't leave anything out."

The yellow and black crime scene tape crisscrossing the front and back doors of the gallery was an image that would stay with Irina for the rest of her life. Because the police search of the main floor was complete, Irina had been given permission to start the cleanup, but the second floor was off-limits. The gallery was to remain closed to the public until the detective in charge of the case was satisfied the scene had yielded up all its secrets.

"You talked to the police, right?" said Chess. "I'm sorry I couldn't be there with you."

Irina had watched stoically as her mother's body had been zipped into a body bag and removed from the building to a waiting van. After the medical examiner left, she'd been interrogated by a middle-aged homicide cop, Kevin Lathrup. She tried to get through it, but the longer they talked, the more frantic she became.

"The whole thing was brutal," she said, covering her eyes. "I couldn't tell them the truth, that Mom was killed because of me."

"Stop saying that. We don't know what happened."

A cavernous pit of guilt had cracked open beneath her. "I can't seem to catch my breath."

"Just take it easy."

"I need you."

"I know, baby, but you've got to be strong. We can't be seen together."

Forcing herself to sit up straight, she looked across the street, mesmerized by the sight of a woman pushing a toddler in a stroller.

"Irina?"

"What?"

"Tell me more about what happened yesterday."

She closed her eyes. "The cop called my husband to come pick me up. Guess he thought I was too upset to drive."

"Did you tell your sister about—"

"She was babysitting at the house. God, I wanted a glass of wine so badly, but I couldn't, not in front of her."

"How did she take it?"

"With amazing stoicism."

"Is she always pretty stoic?"

"Mom and Misty weren't close." Irina gazed up at the second-floor turret, her mother's office. "I invited her to spend the night. I didn't think she should be alone. Steve didn't have the guts to act annoyed, not after what had just happened, but he was. He called a friend and then left. He said he wanted to go bring my car back home."

"At least that showed some concern."

"Concern, yeah. That's Steve." The anger she felt toward her husband centered her, made her feel more in control. It was only momentary. "I'm a mess."

"No you're not," said Chess. "You're just grieving. It's natural. Don't be so hard on yourself. What are your plans for the day?"

"I'm sitting outside the gallery. I had to come. I don't know what I'm going to do once I get inside, I just had to get out of the house. Can't we find *someplace* safe, where we can see each other?"

"Let me think about it. I'll call you later in the day. Everything's going to be all right, Irina. Just keep repeating that. I know this may seem crass, but you could use some of your free time to start calling your business contacts. The sooner we sell the bull, the sooner we can be together."

"I've started making a list."

"If there's any way I can help, let me know."

She remained in her car for a few more minutes, summoning up her courage, wondering how this would all turn out. Before leaving the house, she'd done something rash. She'd taken Steve's key ring and had gone into his locked gun cabinet, removing one of the pistols. A few years back, he'd shown her how to remove the clip, how to hold it with both hands when she fired, how to position her feet. He wanted to take her to a firing range, teach her to shoot, but she refused. Guns were ugly and heavy and dangerous. Guns and violence were his life, not hers. Now she wished she'd learned.

She'd looked the gun over, practiced dropping the clip into her palm, pressing it back into the handle. Steve always kept his guns loaded, but she had to make sure. When she left the house, the pistol was hidden in her purse, where it would remain. Walking up the steps to the front door of the gallery, she wondered if she'd ever feel safe again.

The sign in the window said CLOSED.

It struck her for the first time that she was now the owner. According to her mother's living trust, Misty would get a cash settlement, but the gallery was hers. Perhaps she and Chess could run it together. Why not? They could continue to travel. Chess would never be happy living in one place. They could spend part of the year in Istanbul and the rest of the time in Minnesota. She would fire Majid and hire someone new to manage the place. She was getting ahead of herself and knew it. Chess said he loved her, but that didn't mean he wanted to get married, or spend the rest of his life with her. Still, she needed a way out of her present nightmare, even if it was only in her mind.

Pressing the key into the front lock, Irina felt tears well again. She stood up straight, squared her shoulders, and went inside.

Across the room, Majid sat perched on a stool behind the main counter, staring into space. "Hi," he said, so softly she almost missed it. The only part of him that moved as she walked toward him was his eyes. They followed her, his face expressionless.

"What are you doing here?" she asked, setting her purse next to the cash register. "You got my phone message?"

He didn't respond.

"Majid?"

"I got it," he said, lifting a mug of tea to his lips.

"That's all you've got to say?" For just an instant, his eyes seemed to challenge her. She'd never seen him behave like that before. Then again, she supposed everybody dealt with death differently.

She hadn't been able to reach him last night. She felt bad not being able to tell him what had happened to her mother in person, but didn't want him to hear about it on the nightly news. She finally decided to leave a message on his answering machine. He hadn't called back, as she'd expected he would.

Twisting the mug around in his hands, he said, "I'm sorry, Irina. She was a special woman."

The offer of sympathy threatened her hard-won composure. "Thanks," she said, opening her purse and removing a tissue.

With his coffee-colored skin, long dark lashes, and thick black hair, Majid looked more Iranian than American, although his accent was pure Texan.

"I own the gallery now," she said.

Contempt rose in his eyes. He'd never allowed himself to show it so clearly before. Aiming his hard gaze out the front windows, he said, "Do the police have any idea who did it?"

"Not yet."

"I have a theory."

A shiver ran down her back. "You do?"

"Somebody was obviously looking for something. A cop came to my apartment this morning, wanted to ask me some questions. I told him I thought it was a robbery gone bad. The killer had to be looking for one of two things: either an artifact worth a whole hell of a lot, or something with deep historical significance."

"That's all we sell," she said irritably.

"No, you're missing my point. I think we might have bought something illegal. Those artifacts stolen from the Baghdad Museum are all antiquities dealers are talking about these days."

"Don't you think you're overstating it just a bit?"

"No."

She moved to the end of the counter, her body vibrating like an idling car. Was it just a wild guess, or did he know more than he was letting on?

"You've heard about that cabal, right? The ones going around shooting people up like cowboys in white hats, searching for what rightfully belongs to the Iraqi people."

"I don't think that's for real. It just makes a good story."

"No, it's real. Those folks are on a mission. My uncle in Espahan wrote to me about them."

Majid had spent a month in Espahan, the town in central Iran where his uncle lived, two summers ago. When he returned, Irina had detected a subtle difference in him. He seemed more sensitive about political issues, and he was even more dismissive than usual of her opinions and suggestions regarding the gallery. Never, of course, around her mom. He was too clever for that. She'd mentioned the change to her mom once, but Morgana had simply brushed it off, saying it was just Irina's imagination.

"The cop wanted to know where I was on Wednesday night. *Me.* As if I had anything to do with Morgana's death."

"Where were you?"

He turned to look at her. "At home. Studying. You knew I'm learning to speak Farsi, right?"

"Were you alone?"

"Of course I was alone."

Irina spied a pair of mirrored aviator shades resting on the far side of the cash register. She nodded to them and said, "Are those yours?"

He picked them up, looked them over. "Never seen them before."

They looked exactly like the ones Steve wore, but since he refused to set foot in the gallery, they had to belong to a customer, or one of the police officers. The style wasn't all that unusual.

"How long before the cops will allow us to open up?"

She found the remark insensitive. "I have no idea." She had the urge to tell him right then and there that he was fired, but reason prevailed. She needed his help to reorganize the displays and to get an idea of how much they'd lost.

"Do you want me to stick around?" he asked, his voice quiet, his tone flat.

"No need."

"Then I'll take off. Call me when you want to start the cleanup."

He stopped when he got to the front door and turned to face her. "You may not believe this when all is said and done, but I'm not your enemy, Irina. I never meant you any harm."

She found the comment unsettling. Standing rigidly behind the counter, she held her breath until the front door clicked softly behind him and he was gone.

11

Hattie slumped at the kitchen table, scowling at her tuna sandwich.

"Eat up," said Jane. "Yum yum."

"It doesn't taste right," grumbled Hattie. She picked at the crust, eyeing Jane with a lugubrious stare.

"What's wrong with it?" hollered Cordelia from the other room.

Just after eleven, Cordelia had phoned Jane and pleaded with her to come to her downtown loft, saying she'd been called unexpectedly to the theater and didn't have a babysitter for Hattie. Hattie's nannie, Cecily Finch, had announced just a month after Hattie's return that she and her latest boyfriend, Clyde, were leaving for Europe. After all this time, Cordelia still hadn't hired a new nanny. She was understandably picky. By relying on Mel, Jane, a couple of theater friends, and preschool three days a week, she'd been able to make it work.

"It tastes bad." Hattie's lower lip cranked out a good inch.

"What tastes bad, Peaches?" asked Cordelia, sailing into the room as she applied her lipstick.

"The stuff in the center."

Out of the side of her mouth, Cordelia whispered to Jane, "What did you put in it?"

"The usual. Tuna. Mayo. Celery."

"Ah, I see the problem."

"And that would be?"

"Capers and cornichons. They are a tuna salad essential in this loft." Running her hand through the little girl's golden tresses, she asked, "What kind of capers should we put in today?"

"What *kind*?" repeated Jane. "A five-year-old can tell the difference between one caper and another?"

"Hattie is a connoisseur."

"I am," agreed Hattie.

Jane forced a wan smile.

"So remix it," said Cordelia. She disappeared up a short stairway into her loft-within-a-loft bedroom.

"I want the capers with the salt. The me-ter—rian kind."

"Mediterranean."

"Yah."

Jane remixed the batch while eating the first sandwich. She prepared the second and then set the plate down in front of the unsmiling little girl.

"I'm not hungry," announced Hattie.

"Eat." There was a reason why Jane didn't have kids.

"No, thank you." Hattie had impeccable manners. Cordelia insisted on it. Climbing down from her chair, she bounced out of the room.

Jane followed her into the living room, plate in hand.

Right after Hattie's return, Cordelia had divested herself of all the Swedish modern furniture she'd bought at IKEA in favor of Oriental decor. The forty-by-eighty-foot loft was currently awash in early Ming—or whatever. Painted Chinese cabinets and accent chests, Chinese ceramic pots, blue and white china lamps, "Imperial Court" living room furniture, black lacquer chairs with dragon motifs, silk pillows, oodles of meditating buddhas and hand-painted wall hangings. The walls, those that weren't brick or glass, had been repainted fire-engine red, gold, or black. It was definitely not feng shui. In Cordelia's opinion, feng shui was *so* over.

Cordelia appeared a few moments later in gray dress slacks and a blue silk mandarin jacket with a stand-up collar, frog buttons, and a big black happiness icon embroidered on the back.

"Chess reappeared at my door last night," said Jane, fingering the ring he'd given her. "He asked to stay in the third-floor rental—just for a few days. He's in town on business."

"Maybe we can do dinner before he leaves."

"Something weird happened, though," said Jane, wondering if she should eat Hattie's second sandwich. It was a shame to let it go to waste. Was this how parents of small children put on weight? "While I was getting dressed this morning, I saw him walk out to the curb and get in a cab. I would never have recognized him if I hadn't heard him come down the outside stairs. He had on so many clothes that he looked fifty pounds heavier, and he was wearing a gray wig and a cap and carrying a cane."

Cordelia stopped her forward progress into the room, turned around, and cocked her head. "If it's some new kind of drag, I'd know about it. So there's got to be another reason."

"He's still in the closet."

"No way."

"It's true. Did I make a mistake letting him stay?" She picked up one of the sandwich halves, nibbled at the tip.

"Nah," said Cordelia. "There's no harm in a little dress-up. Did Hattie eat anything?"

"Nothing," said Jane, dropping the sandwich back on the plate. Waste or no waste, she didn't need two tuna sandwiches in her stomach.

"No dessert," cried Cordelia as she boogied over to a solid wall of small factory windows.

Hattie glanced up at Jane with an impish we'll-see-about-that look in her eyes.

Cordelia cranked open one of the small panes and called, "Mel, my dove. Talk to me."

Mel's head popped through a window in the loft across the street. "Yes, my sweet?"

"I'm leaving now. Jane is taking Hattie for the afternoon. We'll all rendezvous at Jane's house tonight at six. Party to start at seven. Guys ties, girls pearls."

"I'll be there," called Mel. "Love you."

"Ditto."

Jane couldn't believe they were still communicating by shouting out the window. It must appeal to some weird desire to explore the various possibilities of urban connection.

Twirling around, Cordelia said, "Now. Hattie, I have your backpack all ready to go. You have every stuffed animal you might possibly miss while you're away. Every piece of pink or black clothing you might require should you soil something you're already wearing. Several books. Your harmonica. Janey will take you to the Lyme House. Should you become hungry for anything remotely resembling food, a vegetable, a protein, or—"

"A fruit," said Hattie, finishing the oft-quoted sentence as she lay on the floor paging absently through a picture book.

"That's right. Only then can you avail yourself of the mouthwatering delights a five-star restaurant has to offer."

"It's not quite five-star," said Jane, flicking a tiny piece of cornichon off the front of her jeans jacket.

"Close enough." She adjusted the chopsticks holding up her mound of auburn curls as she proceeded to the door. "I will swing by the mother ship later today on my way to your place, Janey, and pick up our duds for the evening."

"The mother ship" was Cordelia's current name for her loft.

"Look," cried Hattie. She whipped her head around, pointed a finger in the air, then pointed it down at the floor. "A bug!"

Jane found it hilarious that Cordelia, a woman who loathed every form, every incarnation of creepy crawly critter, had a child inordinately fascinated by them. Cordelia had worked hard to make sure Hattie was grounded in all the arts—film, theater, music, dance, children's literature, fine arts, even some crafts; Hattie particularly liked Shrinky Dinks—but nothing compared to her interest in bugs, much to Cordelia's utter and continuing bewilderment.

"It's just a phase," said Cordelia.

"You hope," said Jane.

"Trust me. She's a Thorn. Thorns and bugs don't mix."

Jane held out her hand to the little girl. "Are we ready?"

Hattie scrambled to her feet and ran to her, hugging her legs. Jane smoothed the hair away from her face. She adored the kid, even if she did frustrate the hell out of her sometimes.

"Onward and upward," said Cordelia, thrusting the backpack at Jane. Like the good drum majorette she'd never been, she led the marching band of three out the door.

When it became clear that Jane would be expected to take part in babysitting Hattie, she sent away for something she hoped would engage the little girl, captivating her attention so that Jane could get on with some of her work. In her wildest dreams, she never imagined that Hattie would become spellbound almost to the point of inertia.

As soon as they arrived at the Lyme House, Hattie skipped down the basement hall to Jane's office. She waited impatiently, twisting her blond curls around her fingers, doing her special excited dance, sighing loudly, until Jane pushed back the door and turned on the light. Then, scooting as fast as her little legs would carry her, Hattie dragged a chair over to a small table Jane had set up in the corner.

The object of Hattie's adoration was an ant farm. Not just any ant farm. This one was a giant gel habitat. The translucent blue gel contained, according to the box the farm came in, all the nutrition and water the ants needed. Developed from a NASA experiment to study animal life in space, the gel ant farm had received a Teachers' Choice Award in 2006. It received the Hattie Thorn-Lester Award two months ago—a much more prestigious prize, in Hattie's humble opinion.

Jane had sent away for the ants. Her first inclination was to simply go outside and find a few, but the guidebook warned against it. Apparently, if the ants didn't come from the same colony, and especially if the ants differed in size, fighting would ensue. An all-out ant war, while it might be interesting to watch, wasn't what Jane had in mind. When the ants arrived in the mail—large, black, mean-looking critters—she and Hattie poked little holes into the gel. In rapt silence, they watched the ants burrow shafts. It was impossible to shelter the little girl from existential matters in the ant colony, so Jane didn't try. Amazingly, worker ants carried their deceased brethren to the top for easy cleanup. Hattie insisted that she be allowed to bury each ant in the flowerpot Jane had set next to the table for just such a purpose. It was always a very solemn moment when Hattie discovered a lifeless body. She insisted on a graveside service. Jane said a few words; Hattie patted the dead ant and then gently brushed some dirt over it.

The ant farm was better than a video game, better than a picture book or a playground, or even a hot fudge sundae. Hattie would sit for hours, transfixed, talking to them, encouraging them, singing to them, but mostly bossing them. Sometimes she would lose patience when they didn't listen to her. Jane tried to help Hattie understand that the ants didn't speak or understand language, but Hattie insisted Jane was wrong. They *were* talking. They just had very tiny voices. As Cordelia would undoubtedly say, for good or ill, *Even ants should obey a true Thorn.*

Jane worked until just after three, making progress on a project that had been on her desk for several weeks. In the current economy, the restaurant was doing a much bigger business in appetizers. Instead of ordering a full meal, people would choose an appetizer, a glass of wine, and, if they were feeling flush, maybe a dessert. Thus, the appetizer menu was in the process of being revised and expanded. Jane had worked up a special trial menu. For a fixed price, a couple would get three appetizers to share, a bottle of wine, a basket of fresh bread, and one dessert. They'd tested it out last weekend, and it was a hit. Now that she'd made a decision about driving up to the lodge, she had to sign off on the new menu before she left. The new offerings had to be costed out, keeping a specific price point in mind. It was tedious work. Leaning back, she stretched her arms over her head and looked over at Hattie, "Hey, sweetie. I think it's time to head back to my house."

Hattie was no longer sitting but standing on the chair. "This ant is dopey. He thinks he can get out. I pushed him back in the goo."

"That's good."

"Yah. I took care of it."

"Want to go feed the ducks?" This was Jane's only hope for prying Hattie away from the farm.

Her eyes lit up. "Yes!"

On their way out, they stopped in the kitchen for a sack of stale bread. Hattie hugged it to her chest as they made their way down the steps to the lake walk. The best feeding spot was a sandy patch a few hundred yards from the restaurant. As usual, Hattie dawdled, watching the ground for potential bug activity.

When they finally reached the log where Jane liked to sit, Hattie cried, "Look, baby duckies!"

Jane opened the sack and handed her a croissant. "Remember, small pieces."

"I know."

Hattie always approached the ducks with infinite care, talking softly to them, telling them she loved them. She would holler at kids who rushed at them, forcing them to fly away. Thankfully, they were alone on the beach today.

As Jane made herself comfortable, she assembled a mental list of everything she needed to do before the party tonight. Cordelia still hadn't received an RSVP from Peter. Maybe he thought, because he was family, that he didn't need to call.

Hattie rushed up to her. "More bread."

"Are you having fun?"

"I *love* duckies."

"I know you do, sweetheart, but we can't stay much longer."

"Five more minutes?"

Hattie had no idea how long five minutes was. "Yes, five more minutes."

She crept back to the shoreline, holding out a piece of baguette to a goose.

"Be careful," called Jane. Geese, in her opinion, were nasty critters. "Just toss the bread on the ground." Hattie didn't have much natural fear of animals. Oddly enough, the animals, birds, whatever, seemed to sense her benevolence and responded in kind. The goose stretched out her neck and nibbled the piece of bread away from Hattie's fingers.

"That kid's got a way with animals," came a man's voice. When Jane turned to see who had spoken, she immediately recognized the face but couldn't place it. Then it hit her.

"You're the preacher."

She hadn't recognized him at first because he wasn't wearing his cowl. He had on normal clothes—a light blue polo shirt untucked over a pair of white painter pants. While he had seemed stocky, even a bit fat, in his monk's attire, she could see now that it was all muscle.

He opened a sack of Wonder Bread and took out a slice. "She's a beautiful kid."

"Thanks," said Jane, adjusting her sunglasses.

"Different hair color, but she looks just like you."

Hattie didn't look a thing like her, not that Jane was about to discuss Hattie with a stranger.

The man stepped up to the edge of the water. He tore his bread into quarters and tossed them, making a clicking sound with his tongue. He kept a good distance from Hattie but glanced at her a couple of times and smiled.

"There's that asshole minister," called a boy's voice.

Two teenagers, one in a red tank top and baggy jeans, the other in a baggy black T-shirt and even baggier jeans, had stopped on the walking path.

"My dad thinks you're a freak," called the boy in the tank top.

"The devil," said the one wearing the T-shirt.

Jane watched in horror as the kid in the T-shirt picked up a rock and heaved it at the preacher. "Stop it," she yelled, rushing for Hattie and whisking her into her arms.

"What the hell?" called the preacher. He turned and lunged at the boys.

As they took off running, the kid in the tank top scooped up another rock and threw it, this time connecting. The preacher went down, holding his head and groaning.

Hattie pointed at the preacher and began to cry.

"It's okay, baby," said Jane, kissing her, holding her tight. "I won't let anybody hurt you."

Jane waited, shielding Hattie, until the kids were out of sight. Then, hurrying over to the man, she crouched down, still holding Hattie in her arms. "Are you okay?" she asked.

He lifted the hand from his face, revealing a gash less than an inch away from his right eye.

"That kid could have blinded you," said Jane.

Spitting sand out of his mouth, the preacher said, "If I ever see those two little turds again, they're toast." He took out a handkerchief and pressed it to the wound.

The words didn't sound very preacherlike. "You need to get to a hospital, have that looked at."

"Nah, I'm okay."

"If you need a ride—"

"I've got a car."

"I wish *I* had a car," said Hattie coyly, playing with a button on Jane's shirt.

"You do?" The preacher rolled over, pulling himself to a sitting position. "Where would you drive it?"

"China. To see the panda bears."

Jane and the man exchanged amused glances.

"I have a first aid kit," announced Hattie, poking Jane in the chest. "It's in my backpack."

"Really?" said the preacher, eyeing her with growing amusement.

"You can use it for your owie."

"That might not be a bad idea," said Jane.

They all moved back to the log, Hattie talking in a long stream about an owie she got on her elbow once.

"That must have hurt," said the preacher.

"I cried and cried. I almost *died*."

"Did you?"

"Uh-*huh*." Hattie scrambled out of Jane's arms.

Jane found the first aid kit in a side pocket. She grabbed a few antiseptic towelettes and an antibiotic cream and handed them over.

"You've both been a big help," said the preacher, wincing as he applied the towelettes. "What's your name, little one?"

"Hattie."

"My name is Lee. I'm very pleased to meet you."

Hattie lowered her eyes, glancing up at him shyly. "Yah."

Jane didn't know if it was a first name or a last name. Whatever the case, Lee had a broad face, a gap between his front teeth, a strong, sturdy body, and hands the size of center cut pork loins.

After he finished applying the antibiotic cream, Jane handed him an adhesive bandage.

"All better," said Jane, grinning at Hattie.

"Can I feed the duckies more bread?"

"Just for another minute."

Jane dug around inside the sack and came up with a couple of dinner rolls.

"I could fucking kill those little dirtballs," seethed Lee under his breath as soon as Hattie had scampered off.

"Are you a minister?"

"Me? Hell, no."

"But I thought—"

"Nah. I used to be a cop down in Chicago—until I had a little disagreement with my sergeant. I'd always been interested in religion, so I spent a year in seminary, thought maybe I should become a minister. Found out it wasn't for me. That's when I took a job working as a security consultant in Atlanta, worked there for ten years. Finally quit last March."

"So now you go around wearing a monk's cowl and preaching from books that never made it into the Bible?"

"The cowl's just for show. It helps me get people's attention. And no, I'm not really preaching. Just reading. I've been traveling around for the past few months. I guess you could say I'm looking for a place to call home—and while I'm looking, I'm having a little fun. You religious?"

Jane took off her sunglasses and began to clean them with her shirttail. "Not really."

"Believe in God?"

"Yeah, some kind of god. What about you?" It was a crazy question. Of course he believed in God.

He glanced up as two ducks soared over the trees and skidded into the water right in front of them. "John Lennon once said that God was a concept by which we measure our pain. I think he was dead-on. Our pain, our guilt, and our fear."

"So why go around talking about the Bible?"

He shrugged. "People are too complacent. They don't really give their beliefs much critical thought. They need some shaking up. And hell, I love to argue religion."

Jane slipped her sunglasses back on. "Then you're in the right country." It was a one-liner worthy of David Caruso on *CSI: Miami*. "Listen, would you consider doing me a favor? If you're planning on any more biblical street theater, could you take it someplace other than right under the deck of my restaurant?"

He looked back at the log building rising above the trees. "You own that place?"

"I do."

"The food is incredible. I had the pan-roasted pheasant the other night, the one with pine nuts and caramelized orange. It came with this great polenta. Oh, and the pub burgers are terrific."

"If you like the place, then take pity on me. Your sermons—and your audience—aren't exactly good for business."

He touched the bandage on his face. "Point taken. I'll move over by the grandstand. Or maybe I'll go back to Lake Phalen. I liked it over there."

"Hattie," called Jane. "It's time to go."

"*One* more minute?" Hattie called back, holding up a finger.

"Okay," said Jane. "One."

"Since we've got *one* more minute," said Lee, smiling at the little girl, "there's something you should know. You've got a couple guys watching your restaurant. I've seen them around for the past three days. I don't know if they're casing the place, hoping to find a way to break in, or if they're staking it out for another reason. Anyway, you should be aware of them."

Jane was thrown. She hadn't noticed anyone.

"Like I said, I have a lot of experience in private security. It's second nature for me to notice stuff like that. Just a word to the wise."

"Could you describe the men to me?"

He sat forward, picked up a pebble, and tossed it from one hand to the other. "Let's see. One is big, maybe six-three, always wears a baseball cap—I assume to hide his red hair. Midthirties. The other one is shorter and thin, long dirty blond hair. He sometimes wears it pulled back into a ponytail. Midtwenties. Most of the time he's out in the parking lot sitting in a Jeep, keeping an eye on both entrances. I've seen the other guy in the bar a couple of times, chatting up the bartender."

"I don't get it."

"Maybe you have an enemy. Or, like I said, they could be casing the place, looking for a way in. Have you had any drug problems?"

She raked her hair away from her face and held it, turning his words over in her mind. "Only once that I know of, but that was a while ago. I suppose I'd better call the police."

"Won't do you any good. These guys haven't done anything wrong. The cops would just brush it off."

"Then—"

"It was me, I'd buy myself my own security. Do you have a guard?"

"Never thought I needed one."

"I'd offer to do it myself, but they've seen me a couple of times. Of course, they've probably pegged me as a preacher, just the way you did, which could be an advantage—or not. Hard call. If you like, I can recommend the names of some private security firms in the area. They won't come cheap."

"I'll have to think about it."

"Don't wait too long. You and your little girl, you've been nice to me. I don't forget things like that. Watch out for those two. They're up to no good, you can count on it."

12

Chess drove past Dial's house that afternoon in the new used ratty and rusted '93 Cadillac Eldorado Sport Coupe he'd just bought. The tacky gold paint on the exterior was bad enough, but the interior, though in reasonably good shape, was a deeply humiliating fire-engine red. He'd dickered over a better-looking '91 Ford Bronco, but because it had two hundred and twenty thousand miles on it and was five hundred dollars more, he'd opted to deal with his humiliation and buy the pimp-mobile.

Sailing past Dial's place, he discovered another problem he hadn't anticipated, although he should have. The mail was piling up in the box to the right of the front door, spilling onto the steps, where a couple of packages had been stacked up behind two tightly rolled newspapers. It wouldn't be long before the neighbors became suspicious and called the cops—if they hadn't already.

Chess sped down the block, turned the corner, and parked in the shade of an oak. The door creaked and grated as he pushed it open with his foot. When he slammed it shut, he held his breath, waiting for one of the bumpers to fall off.

"Piece of crap," he muttered, heading for the alley. He would approach Dial's house from the rear, enter the yard through the back gate. Once again, the privacy fence would save his ass. All would be fine if he could just make it inside without being seen.

Guitar riffs from Bachman-Turner Overdrive's "Takin' Care of Business" kept repeating inside his head like a skip in an old vinyl record. It was pure, unadulterated rock and roll, perfect for the occasion.

As he hurried up to the garage directly behind Dial's, a voice called, "Thanks, Jer. I'll bring it back in the morning." A bald man carrying a post-hole digger emerged into the alley. For just an instant, Chess wondered if he could duck behind something—a garbage can, a hedge—but the man turned and smiled.

"Hi."

"Ah, hi," said Chess. It was the neighbor, the one who'd caught Chess leaving Dial's house. In fact, this was just the man Chess had come to see, although this wasn't the way he'd pictured the encounter.

"Hey, you're that guy I saw coming out of Melvin's door the other morning."

Should he deny it? Didn't seem likely to work. "Yeah, that was me."

"I've been wondering," said the man, setting the post-hole digger down. "Has Melvin gone somewhere?"

"London." He studied the guy's reaction, evaluating every shift, every fluctuation or variation in his body language, hoping he would give something away. Was he Ed the fucking Blackmailer or wasn't he? "He'll be gone about a month."

Adjusting his shades, the guy stepped a few paces closer. "Really? He usually tells me when he's planning a trip. I water the plants, pick up the mail."

So the guy did have a key to the house. Bingo. "You're Ed, right?"

"Ed? No, the name's Glenn. Glenn Smith."

"Then who's Ed?" asked Chess.

The man thought about it, shook his head. "I don't know any Ed."

"No?" He let the question hang in the air. Sometimes silence worked better than an outright demand to push an opponent off balance.

"Look, I'm just concerned. The mail is piling up outside on the front steps. That's a dead giveaway that the house is empty. Somebody might see it and try to break in."

"I'll take care of it."

"Because I'd be happy to do it. You know. Like I said. Pick up the mail, water the plants."

"Melvin asked me to handle it this time."

Glenn gave him an appraising look. "You one of his antique dealer friends?"

"Why would you ask that?"

"I don't know. Just guessing. He buys a lot of strange stuff. But then, if you're his friend, you'd know that."

"You think I'm lying to you?"

"No, no. Just making conversation."

"Come on, let's not quibble about names. We both know you wrote the note."

"What note?"

Confusion was a simple attitude to fake. "Don't make this difficult."

Glenn pulled the post-hole digger in front of him.

Another gesture that was easy to read. He was attempting to put something solid between them, something threatening.

"I have absolutely no idea what you're talking about," insisted Glenn.

"You're sure?"

"Look—" The neighbor glanced over his shoulder. "I think there's been some kind of a mix-up here. You've got me confused with someone else. I'm not Ed, I'm *Glenn*. I lost my job fourteen months ago, so I've got nothing but time on my hands right now, and I like to think of myself as a good neighbor. That's why I offered to help Melvin out with the mail and his plants. I've done it four or five times. It was his idea to pay me, not mine. He knows how tight things have been for me and my wife. If he asked you to take care of the house this time, then fine. Whatever."

The guy needed money—interesting—and if he *was* the blackmailer, he was just the kind of novice Chess had pictured. Still, it wouldn't be smart to push him, and if he wasn't Ed, Chess would be giving away information best kept private. "I think we understand each other." The comment was vague enough to obscure the real meaning.

"Yeah. I think so. But just to be sure—you'll be taking care of Melvin's place while he's gone, right? You'll take in the mail?"

"Absolutely." While he was at it, he would look around for those credit card PIN numbers. Once he was done, he'd drive to the nearest post office and get the mail stopped.

"Do you have a name?" asked the neighbor. "A phone number where I could reach you if something comes up?"

"Like what?" asked Chess.

"I don't know. If smoke starts coming out one of the windows."

"If that happens, call the fire department."

"But you know what I mean. Something unforeseen."

"My number's unlisted. Sorry."

"Right," said Glenn. "Right."

"You betcha," said Chess.

It seemed obligatory to say that phrase at least once while in Minnesota.

13

The oak tree in Jane's backyard caught the last orange rays of the evening sun. As she sat on a teak bench, sipping from a glass of pinotage, she reminisced with one of the first guests to arrive at the birthday party, a woman who had worked on her dad's gubernatorial campaign last fall, and in the process become a friend. Above their heads, paper-thin yellow and black Chinese lanterns glowed in the deepening twilight. If Jane had been allowed to put in an order with the universe, she couldn't have asked for a more perfect night.

"Hey, Janey," called Mel from the porch door, waving the cordless phone. "It's Nolan."

She excused herself, cut across the grass, and went inside. Mel, looking festive in the jade green mandarin jacket Cordelia had bought her for the occasion, handed over the phone, then hoisted Hattie into her arms and carried her off into the dining room. The kitchen was humming with activity, so Jane retreated down the rear hall to her study and closed the door.

"Hi," said Jane. "You got my message."

After returning to the house with Hattie, Jane had given Nolan, her PI buddy, a call. She wanted to run the information Lee, the preacher, had given her by him to see what he thought.

Nolan was a former homicide cop, a friend, who had invited her to apprentice with him. Over and over again, he insisted that she had great instincts when it came to solving crimes, that she was a natural. He had a PI business that he wanted to pass on to her as a legacy, but before that could happen, she would need to put in enough time to get her own investigative license. A year ago, she'd almost agreed to step away from the restaurants for a while to work with him. That was back when she thought she could have her cake and eat it, too. She couldn't, though. She had to make a choice. In an economy like this, the restaurants had to come first. In fact, as far as she was concerned, she was done with "sleuthing," as Cordelia called it, altogether.

"I'm on my way over to the Lyme House as we speak," said Nolan. "I thought I'd see for myself what's going on."

"I owe you. Honestly, I'm not sure how upset to be about these two guys."

"Depends on what they're after. Anything unusual going on that I should know about?"

"Can't think of a thing."

"I'll call you later, let you know what I find."

"But you're coming to the party, right? We can talk when you get here."

"Fine, but I expect your help on this one."

"Nolan, I can't."

"What do you mean you can't?"

"Let me hire you. I'll pay you your going rate."

"That's crazy. This is another chance for me to teach you."

"I'm too busy right now." It was true, and it was a lie. She had to bite the bullet, tell him she'd made a decision, but that conversation would require a better venue than a birthday party. "We'll talk."

"Right." He gave a disgusted grunt and rang off.

Jane heard a burst of laughter and clapping. Confident that it heralded the arrival of her father, she left the room and headed for the front hall. Sure enough, her dad, accompanied by his girlfriend, Elizabeth Piper, were receiving a warm greeting from the crowd. For the first time in over a year, her dad looked rested. He and Elizabeth had just returned from a monthlong vacation to Cape Cod.

After hugging them, Jane ushered them into the dining room, where her catering staff had set out the food on the long mahogany table. She'd made sure all her dad's favorites were on order: chicken and beef satay with a spicy peanut sauce; tiny French tomato tarts with gruyère, Dijon mustard, and fresh basil; several whole charred beef tenderloin filets, sliced thin and served with horseradish sauce; crab cakes with roasted corn and bacon; and a particular favorite, traditional Southern-style buttermilk biscuits, hot from the oven, resting next to a chafing dish full of sausage gravy. In the backyard, several charcoal grills had been fired up and were churning out miniature pizzas, another front-runner for her dad's favorite appetizer.

"There's a bar in the back porch," said Jane, this time just to Elizabeth. Within the space of a few seconds, her dad had been drawn into a heated conversation with a couple of his golf buddies. "We've got a special petit verdot, a wonderful pinotage, soft drinks, sparkling water, but mostly we're pushing the champagne."

"My mouth is watering." She picked up an empty plate and got in line. "The house looks wonderful, and so do you. That tux fits you like a glove."

"I have them specially made."

"Because you wear them at your nightclub. Yes, I know." She selected a couple of the tomato tarts and then stepped away from the table. "That huge Happy Birthday sign out front really touched your father. He was tickled to death that you and Peter wanted to throw him this party."

Jane wasn't sure where they got the idea that Peter had anything to do with tonight's celebration. Not that she intended to clarify. "I'm glad. I want this to be a special night for him."

"He's got terrific kids, that's for sure. I know he feels blessed."

An hour later, as Jane was standing with Chess and Melanie in the backyard, finishing the last bite of a slice of grilled pizza, Cordelia opened the screen door and waved to get her attention. In her orange sequined evening gown, she looked like a giant traffic cone.

"Peter," she mouthed.

Jane excused herself and joined Cordelia in the kitchen, where she found the conversation much louder and mixed with blats of live music.

Cordelia had surprised everyone by hiring a small orchestra for the occasion, the same group Jane had heard practicing in the background a few days before when they were talking on the phone. A tuba player, an oboist, a flutist, a saxophonist, a trumpet player, two trombonists, and an upright string bass player had set up in the living room and were working their way through everything from classical gavottes to ragtime to klezmer dance tunes to an oddball sort of New Orleans jazz. The group would never have been Jane's first choice—or any choice at all—and yet they added a definite note of gaiety, if not downright hilarity, to the gathering.

Following Cordelia into the front hall, Jane found Peter hanging Sigrid's coat up in the front closet. Mia, their eleven-year-old daughter, stood with her arms held stiffly at her sides, her eyes locked on the floor. Sigrid bent down. Talking slowly and deliberately, punctuating her words with hand signs because Mia was deaf, she gave her some last-minute instructions. Mia didn't smile or look around, just stood still, her expression solemn, too solemn for a child her age. She'd lived in a mixed bag of foster homes for most of her young life. With Peter and Sigrid's marriage on the rocks because of Peter's decision to find Mia, the child Sigrid had given up for adoption, it couldn't be all that much easier for her even now.

106

Jane hadn't seen or talked to her brother—or Sigrid, or Mia—since the first week in November, the night of the election, when they'd gathered together with a crowd of staff and supporters in two hotel suites at the Maxfield Plaza in downtown St. Paul to wait for the results.

Mia had shot up at least an inch or two since then. The freckles that spread across her nose and cheeks, once so prominent, had faded. The fact that Jane had missed all these changes stunned her. For the first time it truly penetrated how completely her brother had cut her out of his life. But as soon as the thought engaged her, she realized there was something wrong with it.

Peter wasn't the only one who had backed away. Jane was as guilty as he was. He'd never prevented her from contacting Mia, from developing a relationship with her. Jane had allowed that to happen all by herself. The problems she had with Peter didn't need to leak over onto Mia—but they had. Jane had stopped calling or dropping by because she didn't want to run into her brother. He'd changed—and not for the good. Jane wanted him to see that his actions had consequences, not just for himself, but for others. Every time they got into it, though, he would turn the tables, try to convince her that she was in the wrong, that she was a sorry excuse for a sister, someone who only wanted to blame. Jane figured the truth was probably somewhere in the middle.

Crouching down and holding out her hand, Jane said, "Hi, Mia. Remember me?"

The edges of Mia's mouth turned up. She inched forward a few paces but continued to keep her distance. "Ha," she responded. With her platinum hair, blue-gray eyes, and strong, athletic frame, Mia was a mini Sigrid—but a Sigrid without the feisty self-assurance.

"I'm glad you could come."

She gave a stiff nod.

Sigrid looked pretty much the same as she always did, although her sardonic smile, usually in evidence, was noticeably absent. Peter was the one who had changed the most. His thick brown hair, worn in a defiant buzz cut for over a year, had finally grown out. He wore it pulled back into a short ponytail tied at the nape of his neck with a piece of twine. The scruff was gone as well, and the beard was back. He looked so handsome, more like the brother she remembered. When he turned around and found her a few feet away, he flashed her a brittle smile.

"I didn't know if you were coming tonight," said Jane.

"You didn't?" said Sigrid, placing her hands over Mia's shoulders. "Peter told me he RSVP'd last week."

"Never received it," said Cordelia, the subject of another one of Peter's strained smiles.

"Hey, don't gang up on me," he said. "I thought I'd done it."

Everyone glanced up as Hattie thumped down the stairs wearing a pair of black satin ballerina slippers several sizes too big for her feet.

On arriving at the house, Cordelia explained to Jane, sotto voce, that Hattie had begged for the shoes, insisting that her feet would get *really* big *really* soon. Tomorrow or the next day, for sure. That since they were invited to a special party, she needed something fancy to match her Ziegfeld Follies hat. Ultimately, Cordelia had relented, partly because she was so amused, but also because she remembered a similar pair of shoes she'd wanted as a little kid, a pair her mom had refused to buy.

Hattie clumped up to Mia. "Hi," she said. "Wanna play?" Mia was the only other child there. Her sudden appearance must have seemed like manna from heaven.

Peter lifted Hattie into his arms and gave her a kiss. "You remember me, don't you?"

"Uncle Peter!"

This time his smile was real. "I heard you were back. Welcome home, sweetie."

"Thank you," said Hattie, using her best manners. She lifted the hat off of her head and dropped it on top of his.

"Say, Hattie," said Peter. "You haven't met my little girl. Her name is Mia. She's deaf. Do you know what that means?"

Hattie pressed a finger to her chin and shook her head.

"It means she can't hear. If you talk to her, she can sometimes understand if she's looking at your mouth. So speak very slowly and clearly to her, okay? Make sure she's looking at you when you talk."

Hattie patted his beard. "Okay."

As soon as he set her down, Hattie tugged on Mia's hand. "We can draw with chalk on the sidewalk. It's fun."

"It's getting kind of dark," said Sigrid.

"I'll turn on the light over the front steps," offered Cordelia. "Come on, you two, let's go get the chalk." Cordelia knew sign language, so she signed to Mia as they walked back through the dining room.

Peter touched the satin lapels on Jane's tux. "Nice threads."

"Thanks. Nice headdress."

He pulled Hattie's hat off and was about to hand it to her when he thought better of it and put it back on. "Goes perfect with my clothes, right?"

He'd come to the party wearing a purple and gold Vikings football jersey tucked into a pair of worn jeans. He looked like he'd lost weight.

"Very stylish," said Jane.

"Where's Dad?"

"Last I saw, he was in the backyard."

"I gotta go wish him a happy birthday."

As he waded into the crowd, shaking hands, slapping people on the back, Jane turned to Sigrid, who had moved over to the living room archway to listen to the mini orchestra.

"How are you and Peter doing?" she asked during a lull in the music.

Sigrid folded her arms over her chest and leaned against the arch. "We should probably talk."

"When?"

"I'll call you."

"Is everything okay?"

Sigrid eyed her for a moment. Returning her attention to the band, she said, "Yes. And no."

"At least tell me *something*."

"Oh, all right. How's this for a headline? Peter and Sigrid are back together."

Jane's face must have registered surprise, relief, eagerness, disbelief, or all of the above. Whatever Sigrid saw, it was enough to make her sardonic smile return.

"That's wonderful," said Jane.

"That's amore," Sigrid responded dryly.

"Where are you?" demanded Irina, worry tightening her stomach as she stood in the bathroom of her home, rifling through the medicine cabinet, searching for the bottle of Excedrin.

"At a party," came Chess's voice.

She heard music in the background, people talking, having a good time. "How can you be at a party at a time like this?"

"I'm at a friend's house. She's letting me stay for a few days."

"*She?*"

"She's gay, Irina. It's her father's birthday. I had to come."

She found the Excedrin bottle, tapped a couple into her palm, swallowed them down without water. "You were supposed to call me. I thought we were going to try to get together. I can't handle this all by myself."

"But if someone's watching you—or me—it's not safe."

"I don't care. When I got home tonight, Steve was packing. The people he's hoping to work for called him, asked him to drive back down to Rochester. He'll be gone overnight. That means I'm home alone. What if something—" She stopped. She couldn't go there. "You've got to come stay with me. It's starting to get dark. The house, it's so big, and I hear noises."

"What sort of noises?"

"I don't know," she snapped. "Creaks. Scary sounds."

"Turn on some music."

Was he nuts? "It has to be quiet so I can hear if someone's trying to break in."

"No one will break in, Irina. You'll be fine."

She sank down on the edge of the bathtub. "You don't know that. Why are you treating this so lightly?"

"I hardly view our problems as light."

"Two people have been murdered because of us. I'm not sure I can live with that."

He sighed. "Yeah, I hear you. I'm getting cold feet, too. Maybe we should call it off. Money doesn't mean much if we're dead. As it is now, we're sitting ducks. The safest thing to do would be for me to just take the bull and go."

"No, you can't go."

"Irina—"

"Because I may have found another buyer."

"You did? Why didn't you say that right away?"

"We had a brief phone conversation this afternoon."

"And he's definitely interested?"

It annoyed her that he assumed it was a man. "It's a woman. And it's not a done deal, but I think we can bring her along. It may take some time. I can't do it without you."

"What's her name?"

She made it up on the spot. "Diane Middleton. She's unlisted."

"When can we meet with her?"

"Early next week."

"Why wait?"

"She's going out of town with her boyfriend this weekend, but Monday, we'll get together at her house."

"Fantastic. We have to hang on, just a little while longer. Call your sister. Maybe she can come stay with you."

Irina already had. Her sister didn't answer, and Irina saw no point in leaving a message. "Just a minute," she said, pulling the phone away from her ear. She thought she heard Dusty crying. She'd been playing with him for hours, hoping to get her mind off the growing dark. He was back in his crib now, but it was time for his bottle. "Misty's not home."

"Okay, so go around and check all the windows, all the doors. Make sure they're locked. Call me when you're done."

"But you're so far away."

"Keep your cell with you. Call 911 if you have to. The police can get to your place in a matter of minutes."

At least she had the gun. It was in Dusty's bedroom, under the pillow on the double bed. She planned to sleep there tonight.

"I love you," said Chess.

"Do you?"

"Oh, honey, just hang on. We'll make this work. You believe me, don't you?"

Her lips parted in a grimace. "Yes."

14

Julia had no intention of arriving at the party at the same time as all the other guests, thus diluting her impact. When Jane saw her, after so many months apart, she wanted it to be a special moment, uncluttered by anything else.

Waiting until just after ten, Julia opened the side gate and strolled casually into the crowd. Jane was standing about fifteen feet away, her face lit by the glow of a Chinese lantern.

"Hey," said Julia, carefully angling past several of the guests.

"Hey yourself." Jane gave her a friendly hug. "I thought maybe you weren't coming."

"I couldn't miss Ray's birthday."

Jane's reaction was subtle, just a slight widening of the eyes, a slight lifting of the eyebrows, but Julia caught it. It made her smile.

"Dad will be glad to see you."

Julia had chosen to wear clothes that looked virtually the same as the ones she'd been wearing on the night they first met: dark pleated pants, a boldly striped vest, a white blouse, and a wide silk tie, all the pleats and tucks accentuating her slimness.

"You look great," said Jane. "Can I get you something to drink? A glass of champagne?"

"Don't you have anything more lethal? Brandy? Bourbon? Strychnine?"

Jane's smile lit up her face. She gave a slow wink and then said, "I'm with you. Be right back."

Julia found a vacant bench and sat down. She swiped at her eyes with the back of her hand and attempted to put a mental choke hold on her feelings. She hadn't expected to be quite this emotional.

Jane was back in record time with two tumblers of bourbon. She handed one to Julia and then sat down. "If you're hungry, there's food in the dining room, and pizza on the grills out here."

"Thanks, but I think I'll wait a bit." She took a sip. She rarely drank anything but wine—and lately, because of the headaches and the mix of medications, she rarely drank even that. Tonight, however, she needed something stronger.

Jane fingered the gold necklace at her throat.

Julia had seen the necklace before, but the snake ring on her index finger was new. "That's a beautiful ring."

Jane drew her hand down to look at it. "It's Roman. Second century. A friend gave it to me."

Not good news. Julia wanted to ask who the friend was but restrained her curiosity. "What's it made of?"

"Gold. So, you were going to tell me about some new venture you're involved in. Something to do with Peter?"

Julia read the abrupt change of subject as another bad sign. "Sure. He came to my loft the other day. I guess I'm surprised he didn't tell you."

"Loft? You've moved? You're not still living in White Bear Lake?"

"I've sublet a place not far from here on Lake Calhoun. It's got spectacular views. You'll have to come see it."

"I'd like that," said Jane.

Julia wasn't sure she meant it.

"But what about Peter?"

"I'm in the process of developing a free clinic in downtown Minneapolis. I hope some of my ideas will become a template for starting similar free clinics in other cities around the country."

"That's a pretty tall order."

Julia crossed her legs and turned toward Jane, closing some of the distance between them. "I've already got seven retired doctors on board. They've committed to donating chunks of their free time to the clinic. With so many people out of work, and more losing jobs and health insurance every day, the need is greater than ever. I've got a lot of connections, know a lot of people. With luck and hard work, I plan to get this up and running by the end of the year."

"That's wonderful," said Jane. "Really. But what's Peter got to do with it?"

"I've hired him to film a documentary. I want to use it as a teaching tool. I need a way for others to see that what I'm doing is possible. I've hired a writer, and I've got a director in mind. I'll be producing it myself."

"Always the dedicated professional—and you're branching out. Very impressive."

This was going better than Julia had expected. She swirled the ice in her drink, took another swallow. "I'm hoping to sign a contract with Peter in the next week or two. I thought he might have said something to you about it. He seemed pretty excited."

"It's really nice of you to use him."

"Peter is exactly what I was looking for. And it's the way the world works, right? Friends help friends."

Jane nodded, falling silent.

"Something wrong?"

Before she could answer, a heavyset man in an expensive-looking double-breasted suit walked up. "Jane," he said, eyeing Julia briefly, "the culinary powers that be want you in the kitchen. It's time to serve the birthday cake. The head guy thought maybe you'd like to be the one to carry it in."

Jane stood. "I had no idea it was this late." She introduced the man as Chess Garrity, an old friend, and then said, "I'll catch you both later."

"We'll mix and mingle," called Julia to her retreating back. The bourbon had eased some of the tension in her muscles. She felt better now, more centered and in control.

"Nice party," said Chess. He eased down next to her, unbuttoning his coat.

The suit hid his girth well. It was probably handmade. If she had to guess, she'd say it was Italian. "How do you know Jane?"

"We go way back."

"To the cradle?"

He laughed, tapped a cigarette out of a pack, and offered her one.

"No thanks."

"I actually met Cordelia first," he said, bending over a silver lighter, lighting the tip, and blowing smoke over his shoulder. "You know her?"

"Where *is* the dragon lady?"

"Dragon lady?"

"The Mad Carlotta? The Wicked Witch of the East? Typhoid Mary? Take your pick. They all apply."

"Not a fan, huh?"

"Pretty much not. Do you live in town?"

"No. Istanbul. When I'm not in Amsterdam. I deal in antiquities. Mainly ancient Mesopotamian and Egyptian art."

Julia cocked her head, deciding to take a wild guess. "Are you the friend who gave Jane the snake ring?"

"Guilty."

She found herself grinning. "It's a striking piece."

"She's worth it."

Curiouser and curiouser. "And you're here because—"

"A buying trip. Jane's letting me stay in her third-floor apartment for a few days."

Jane never let anyone stay up there anymore. "How did you two first meet?"

He took a deep drag off the cigarette, blew smoke out the side of his mouth. "That's kind of a long story."

"I'm not going anywhere."

He laughed easily and stretched an arm along the back of the bench behind her. "Jane and I lived together once—just for a few months. We were pretty young. I think she'd just graduated from the university."

"I thought she moved in with her girlfriend, Christine, right after college."

"Oh, sure. I knew Christine. She was a wonderful person. Funny, smart, athletic—if you're into athletic. I never have been."

She didn't doubt it.

"What about you?" he asked. "What do you do to pay the rent?"

"I'm a doctor. An oncologist. I specialize in HIV."

"In the Twin Cities?"

"I spent the last few years in Africa. I'll be going back to Johannesburg for a few weeks next fall. The government is honoring me with a humanitarian award."

He raised his eyebrows. "Congratulations."

It was bragging, but she'd never been averse to a blatant show of self-regard. "I'm hoping to start a free clinic here in Minneapolis sometime within the next year."

"You are an admirable woman."

"I've never aspired to ordinariness."

⌣

117

He wiped a hand across his mouth. "I can see why you and Jane are friends. Unless—are you more than friends?"

"No."

"Then I'd say she's missing out. And you live—"

"A loft on Lake Calhoun. If you know the city, it's right across from the concession stand."

"That new building? I drove past it today. Looks incredible—and expensive. It's harder and harder these days to know where to put your money, don't you agree? Real estate used to be a good option, but you've got to be careful today. That's one positive for my line of work. Antiquities are verifiable pieces of real property, not just something on paper. They don't lose value."

Julia was always interested in a good investment, although her interest in Chess went well beyond that. "I'm a wealthy woman, Mr. Garrity."

"Call me Chess."

She removed her iPhone from the pocket of her slacks. "I'd like to hear more. Do you have examples you could show me?" She punched a couple of keys, then swiped her finger down the screen, bringing up her calendar.

"Sure."

"How about tomorrow? I have a meeting at eleven. You could come by the loft, say, nine?"

"It would be my pleasure." He waited a beat. "What price range were you interested in?"

"Price is less an issue than the object itself. I'm interested in something unique, an object that will maintain its value. And, of course, beauty."

His eyes lingered on her. "I've got several pieces that should interest you. One in particular. Although it's expensive. Possibly too expensive."

118

"Bring whatever you have. No promises, of course—but it never hurts to look."

Irina perched on a chair in the back bedroom, rocking the crib with her foot, her arms cradling her stomach. Her son's eyes fluttered every few seconds, but he was definitely in dreamland. She'd held him for the longest time, giving him his bottle, rubbing her cheek against the soft fuzz on his head, humming to him until he fell fast asleep. She didn't want to put him down, but finally had. Now, easing back, she switched on the small boom box behind her, the one she'd loaded with a Disney lullaby CD. It seemed so peaceful, so safe, cocooned in this room with only a tiny night-light to illuminate her baby's face, as if nothing could ever touch either of them or do them any harm. She'd taken a couple of Xanax, which made the world feel much more manageable. If they could navigate safely through the next few days, find a buyer for the bull, everything might still work out okay.

She called her sister again, and this time she left a message.

"Misty, hi, it's me. Don't know where you are, but I thought you might want to come by, spend the night. Steve had to drive back down to Rochester. He won't be home until late in the day tomorrow. Let me know. Or just come over if you can. 'Bye."

She watched her sleeping baby. She'd let him stay up too late, but rationalized that being with him soothed her, and he could sleep as long as he wanted in the morning. He was such a good little boy. He was her future. She pressed a finger gently against his little fist, wondering if Steve had noticed that his baby didn't look a thing like him. That was a card she hadn't played yet, one she wanted to reserve for just the right moment. *We're all liars,* she thought. *We keep secrets.* Lying wasn't always wrong when survival was the issue.

Irina crawled into bed around eleven, listening to the silent house, thinking about her mother, the funeral that would need to be planned.

Once the police released her mother's body, she would go to the funeral home, make all the arrangements. If Misty wanted to come along, fine. If not, she'd do it herself. She'd spent so much of her life alone that this wasn't anything new.

She was almost asleep when her eyes popped open. Was that a noise? She couldn't be sure. Thinking that it was her sister coming in the front door, she got up and walked out into the hallway.

"Misty?" she called. She froze when she saw a beam of light sweep over the living room. Rushing back to the bedroom, she closed and locked the door, then dove for the cell phone in her purse and hit 911. A man's voice answered. She whispered her address and told him that an intruder was inside her home. He asked her to leave the phone on, said a squad car would be dispatched. He wanted to know more, but Irina tossed the phone on the bed.

She felt around under the pillows until her hand hit cold metal. Rising up, she backed up all the way to the window, spread her feet, and with both hands pointed the gun at the door.

The door handle moved one way and then the other.

Her hands shook.

The handle moved again.

"Get out," she screamed. "Get the hell out of my house."

Dusty began to cry.

She squeezed the trigger. Once. Twice. In the darkness, the muzzle fire looked like a flame. She kept firing, through her baby's cries, through her own screams. "Get out! I'll kill you! I will kill you!"

The gun kept jumping in her hand. The room smelled like the Fourth of July. Then, as suddenly as it had begun, the upper part of the gun slammed back and there were no more bullets.

She stood very still, not even breathing, realizing with a raw dread that she was out of options.

15

The grandfather clock in Jane's living room struck one in the morning as the party wound down to a few last stragglers. Jane's father and Elizabeth had left just after midnight. So had Cordelia and Mel, announcing that they had to get Hattie into bed. Julia was gone. Chess was out in the backyard eating the last of the pizza and talking to Sigrid.

Jane stood at the front door, thanking people for coming and wishing them a good night as her catering crew finished cleaning up the dining room. She was tired, but elated that the celebration had gone so well.

At last, drifting back into the living room, she picked up a couple of empty plates, but instead of taking them into the kitchen, she sat down to think. Peter had kept his distance all evening. She was hoping they could talk for a few minutes, if for no other reason than to break the ice between them, but it had never happened. Still, there was one thing she had to do before he and Sigrid left.

Grabbing a pen and a pad of scratch paper from her office, she spent the next few minutes looking for Mia. She found her in the basement rec room, curled into the corner of the couch, reading under the light of a floor lamp. Mouse was sleeping on the floor next to her. He adored kids, couldn't get enough of them. If there was a kid in the house, that's where you'd find him. Maybe it was his need to protect, or his love of play. He and Mia had bonded within moments of meeting each other.

Sitting down next to the little girl, Jane wrote on the pad, "Did you get some of the birthday cake?"

Mia nodded.

"Did you like it?"

This time, her eyes widened when she nodded.

Jane wrote, "Mia, will you forgive me? Your Dad and I aren't on very good terms at the moment, but I shouldn't have let that keep me away from you. I want to be part of your life. I want you to be an important part of mine."

Mia took the pad and the pen and wrote, "It's okay."

"No it's not," wrote Jane, "but if you'll give me another chance, I want to make it up to you."

Mia kept her eyes averted, gave a shrug.

Jane wrote, "Tell me what you like? Your five favorite things to do." She handed Mia the pad and pen.

The little girl thought for a few seconds. She flipped to a clean page and wrote, "I like to draw, mostly horses, but sometimes flowers and people." She chewed her lower lip. "I like going for hikes in the woods. I like reading stories about girls. I like looking at picture books of artwork. I like to make cookies and bake them in the oven." She read it over, counting each "like" on her fingers. "Fah," she said out loud.

Jane smiled. Mia had given her a lot to work with. She wrote, "Have you ever gone to the Institute of Arts here in Minneapolis?"

Mia shook her head.

"I think you'd like it. It's a big building full of paintings, drawings, and every kind of artwork. Would you go with me sometime soon?"

She gave a guarded nod.

Jane continued to write. "Have you ever gone for a hike up near Taylors Falls? It's very beautiful."

Mia shook her head.

"Do you have good hiking shoes?"

Mia wrote, "Dad bought me boots."

Jane grinned and wrote, "Then we'll do a hike, too. I'll talk to your mom and dad tonight before you all leave so we can nail down a time that would work."

Mia reached for the pad and pen. "Would it be just you and me?"

Jane wrote back, "Would that be okay?"

Mia looked up at her, gave a shy nod.

"Can I give you a hug?" wrote Jane.

Another shy nod.

Jane gathered the little girl into her arms, kissed her hair, held her tight, and tried her damnedest to live in the moment for once. She hoped she'd made a breakthrough. Now she had to follow it up with more than just good intentions.

The next morning, as Jane was pouring kibble into Mouse's bowl, the landline rang. She used the remote to turn down the TV and said hello.

"It's Nolan."

"You never made it to the party last night. I saved you some cake."

"Thanks, but I thought this was more important. Nobody was watching the restaurant. I stuck around for several hours."

"So that's good news." She found some chicken scraps in the refrigerator and added them to Mouse's bowl. He was already in his "sit" position when she set the dish down in front of him.

"Not entirely. I drove to your house after I left the restaurant, in-

123

tending to come in, but found a guy sitting in a Jeep two houses away holding a pair of binoculars. I'd say you're the one being watched, not the restaurant. When he saw me, he took off. I chased him, but a truck pulled in between us and he got away."

"Did you get the license plate?"

"Already ran it. It's a rental. Rented to a man named Eddy Redzig, a resident of Toronto. Far as I can tell, he doesn't exist. It gotta be an alias."

She sat down. "Did you get a look at the guy who was driving?"

"He was blond. Long hair."

"Sounds like one of the guys Lee described to me." She'd never seriously considered that she might be the target. "What do you think I should do?"

"Work with me. We'll figure this out."

"We already talked about that."

"You know, Jane, one of these days I'm going to stop asking."

How could she make him understand? "I have to make the restaurants my first priority. Especially in this economy."

"Fine. I never said you couldn't do both."

"But that's just it. I can't."

"You're afraid that if you get involved in real investigative work, it's all you'll want to do."

"My restaurants are my life."

"Your passion."

"Right."

"They were once. Are they still?"

If she wasn't a restaurateur, who was she?

"I think you should give it more thought. In the meantime, I'll dig a little deeper. Keep your eyes and ears open."

After hanging up, she sat at the table, watching Mouse nose his favorite green tennis ball around the room. So often these days she wished she had his life. Good food. Lots of love. A comfortable place to live. No financial or relationship worries. "What if we traded places for a while?"

He gripped the ball in his mouth, carried it over, and dropped it in her lap.

"You want to go outside and play catch?" she asked, rubbing his ears. "I suppose we can do that for a few minutes." As she stood, she saw the words BREAKING NEWS crawl across the bottom of the TV screen. She turned up the sound.

"Early this morning, a jogger found the body of a man in a remote area of Minnehaha Park. The name of the victim has not been released, but police are looking for a second man in connection with the suspected homicide—Chester Garrity."

When a picture of Chess flashed on the screen, Jane felt as if she'd touched a bare wall socket.

"If you know this man, or have any information about him, please contact the Minneapolis Police Department."

Rushing to the door, Jane called over her shoulder to Mouse, "I'll be right back."

She burst out into an overcast, sticky summery day and charged up the outside steps.

Banging on the door, she shouted, "It's Jane. Come on, Chess, open up." She banged harder. "Wake the hell up. I need to talk to you." He had to be inside. She hadn't heard him leave. Checking her watch, she saw that it was just after nine. She'd slept in, something that always put her in a bad mood. She hated getting a late start to her day.

Cupping a hand over her eyes, she peered though one of the screened windows. The interior was dark. The small TV set across the room was off.

Swearing under her breath, she charged down the steps, returning a few minutes later with a key. She opened the door and went in, not caring if he was asleep, dead drunk on the couch, or naked in bed with another man.

"Where are you?" she called. His suitcase was open on the floor next to the drop-leaf kitchen table. Clothes littered the living room. The remnants of his breakfast—half a frozen burrito and a partially filled glass of orange juice—sat on the draining pad next to the sink. Crossing into the bedroom, she found the bed unmade.

"Dammit," she shouted to the empty room, her mind flashing to the men who were watching the restaurant and her house. She had no proof of a connection, but she also had little doubt. "What are you mixed up in? What the hell have you got *me* mixed up in?"

Five stories above Lake Calhoun, Chess sat in Julia's loft, drinking a cup of French pressed coffee and eating a chocolate pistachio biscotto. He couldn't believe his good fortune. Running into a rich narcissist was always a stroke of luck, but to find one with the door to her heart hanging open was like winning the lottery. He figured it was best to let her steer the conversation.

"You brought something for me to see?" she asked, her warm smile muting the frank appraisal in her eyes.

He nodded to the leather case next to him.

She sat down, arranging herself in a Bauhaus-inspired chair by unbuttoning the classic gold-buttoned blazer she wore over a pair of precisely creased tan slacks. "I have to admit that I'm curious about you," she said.

"About my relationship with Jane?"

"We can start there."

As if there were anything else she wanted to know. "You said that you two were just friends."

"We've dated in the past."

Unrequited love. Too good to be true. He'd seen the way she looked at Jane last night, part possession, part yearning.

"Jane never told you about me?" he asked.

"Not that I recall."

126

"I hope you don't find this too forward, but I admire you, Julia. I pride myself on being a good judge of character. You seem like someone I can trust." He'd come to the conclusion that she was smart, even clever, but not terribly subtle. What he'd said was blatantly disingenuous. Even so, her eyes flickered with interest. "Twenty-one years ago next week, Jane and I were married."

Her mouth opened. She was silent for a good half minute. "Married," she repeated, the word coming out guttural, harsh. "Are you still—"

"I flew to the Dominican Republic and got a divorce." He explained the essentials without lingering on the particulars. "I still care about her, as she cares about me." He paused, mostly for dramatic effect. "This episode in our lives isn't something she likes to talk about, so if you'd keep it to yourself—"

"Don't give it another thought," said Julia, a little too quickly.

"I'm worried about her," continued Chess, leaning forward and helping himself to another biscotto. "She seems lonely."

"You think so?"

Actually, he didn't think so, but it was the right thing to say. "She needs someone to love, someone to take care of. Maybe that's old-fashioned, but it's the way I see it."

"No, I agree. I suppose we all want to find that one special someone."

"You two seem perfect for each other."

The look in Julia's eyes was nothing short of ecstatic, but she stayed cool, didn't comment.

Chess sighed. "You've probably already got someone in your life."

"No," she said hesitantly.

"But the love is gone. You've moved on."

Her eyes drifted to the grand piano. "Since we're being honest, maybe—oh hell, why not. I might as well tell you the truth. I'm still in love with her."

127

Chess set his cup on the coffee table. "I thought so."

"Is it that obvious?"

"A little. I also formed my opinion from watching Jane. She's still carrying a torch for you, that's pretty apparent, even though she's fighting it."

She sat up straighter. "Did she say anything to you about me?"

"Just that you're a very important person in her life."

"She actually said that?"

"Exact words. Then again, you know Jane. She's very private. She didn't elaborate."

"Something I admire about her."

"Oh, yeah. Me, too."

She ran her fingertips along the arm of the chair.

"To be honest," said Chess, eying yet another biscotto, "I'm a romantic at heart. Do you believe in love at first sight?"

"Unreservedly. If you're fated to be together, you will be."

Fate. Perfect concept for a besotted narcissist. "Sometimes fate needs a bit of a shove."

She laughed at that one. "You have a point."

"I also believe in past lives. Reincarnation. I've experienced it personally. I know that may sound strange to a doctor, someone who's used to dealing with facts, reason, objective reality."

"You're talking about hypnotic regression?"

"I've undergone several."

"You're right to think I don't give that theory much credence. Even so, I'm always willing to listen. It's not like we've discovered everything there is to discover." She poured them each more coffee.

She might be a manipulative narcissist, but under other circumstances, he would have enjoyed getting to know her. "I think it's time to look at what I brought."

She nodded, seeming far more eager and open to him now that they'd shared a juicy secret.

He pulled the case in front of him. "Let's start with the least expensive." He removed a cloth, set it on the table, and drew back the folds. "These are Roman gambling dice, first century A.D. They were carried by soldiers. Each one is hand-carved from a single piece of animal bone. This particular set was discovered at a Roman military site near the Danube River. I have all the paperwork. Everything I sell has a documented provenance."

"How much?" asked Julia, picking one up.

"Three hundred and eighty-five dollars. That's a very good price."

"They're intriguing, but I guess I'm interested in something a little more dramatic."

"Of course." This time he took out a box. Opening it, he handed her a four-inch Egyptian blue scarab. He explained that it was made somewhere between 1000 B.C. and 700 B.C., between the twenty-first and twenty-fifth dynasties. "Eighteen thousand," he said.

She turned it over in her hand. "I've always liked scarabs. I gave Jane a scarab ring once."

"What a lovely gift."

"I doubt she ever wears it anymore."

Next he removed an Egyptian inlaid steatite pectoral. "This was placed on the breast of a mummy, outside the wrappings. It's from the New Kingdom, probably around 1300 B.C. There's a chip on the lower right corner, otherwise it's in mint condition. I could sell this for—" He hesitated. "Thirty-five thousand. A piece very much like it sold at Christie's in New York last month for forty-eight thousand." He could tell he hadn't found her price range yet. None of the artifacts had hit her sweet spot.

"Just in case none of those catch your fancy, I've brought you something truly special," he said, removing a rectangular wooden case. He opened it and handed her a small, mottled brown piece of carved rock. "This is a cylinder seal. It was used to authenticate tablets before paper was invented. The man who owned this would roll it over the wet clay to make his mark. It was his seal, his signature if you will. It's at least two thousand years old, possibly older."

Her eyes finally lit up. "What's it made of?"

"Steatite, which is considered a precious stone. It's actually a compact form of talc. In a way, I think it's fair to say that it's a voice from the cradle of civilization."

"What would something like this sell for?"

"Two hundred and fifty thousand. I couldn't let it go for any less."

She nodded, mulling it over.

"I do have another, utterly extraordinary piece," he said. "I don't have it with me because it's too precious to carry around."

"What is it?" she asked.

He felt a rush of anticipation. If she bought the seal for two hundred and fifty thousand, he'd be a happy man. If he could sell her the bull, he'd be over the moon. "It's called the Winged Bull of Nimrud. Nimrud was the capital of ancient Assyria—in the Bible it was called Kalakh. It's located south of Nineveh on the Tigris River. The Nimrud gold, which is roughly two thousand eight hundred years old, has been called the most significant archaeological discovery since the treasures of Tutankhamen were discovered in 1923. I can assure you, very few of these pieces have found their way into private collections."

"Do you have a picture?"

He removed one from the breast pocket of his tan cashmere sport coat. "You can keep it."

She studied the photo. "It's incredible," she said, awe in her voice. "The face. The wings. The craftsmanship."

"It's very special."

"How big is it?"

"Approximately four inches long by six inches wide—wing tip to wing tip. Five inches high."

"How much—"

"It's out of most people's price range. I just wanted you to see it."

"Tell me the price."

"One million two hundred and fifty thousand dollars."

She bit her lip, continuing to stare at the photo. "If I bought this, I would need to have it appraised."

"Are you seriously considering—"

"It's perfect. A one-of-a-kind piece—art and history combined."

"If you are serious, there's a very fine, internationally recognized gallery of antiquities in St. Paul. I'm sure someone there could provide an appraisal."

"You have all the paperwork?"

"Everything. But, Julia, I think you'd better give this a bit more thought. Owning an artifact like this is a significant responsibility. You'd need to insure it. Protect it. Make sure the environment in which you display it is temperature, light, and humidity controlled. In essence, you would need to become a curator."

"I want it," she said, suddenly, firmly. "I'd also like to buy the cylinder seal. But only after I have them appraised."

"Are you positive? My advice would be to wait, think it over. "

"Do you have other potential buyers for the bull?"

"Yes. One."

"Something like this only comes along once in a lifetime."

"That's true."

"I would need to pass this by my financial manager."

"You should—and you should take his or her advice." He could tell by the gleam in her eye that he'd hooked her deep. It wouldn't matter what anyone told her, she would know better.

"When could I see the statue?"

"I'll have to make some arrangements. Possibly tonight."

"Perfect."

The cheap cell phone in Chess's pocket buzzed. "I need to take this," he said.

"I'll clean up our coffee. My first appointment got moved up. So I really need to get going."

He stood by the windows looking down on the concession stands along the northeast shore of the lake. He'd parked his rust-mobile just down the street.

"It's me," came the voice he heard now in his dreams. "Your buddy, Ed. We're finished, man."

"Finished?"

"I don't want the money. I don't want anything to do with you."

"I don't understand."

"You're poison."

He pulled the phone away from his ear and checked the screen. The call had ended. What the hell was going on? As he slipped the phone back into his pocket, he saw a man in a business suit walk across the street to his car. The man kept looking over his shoulder, glancing around to make sure nobody was watching. Crouching down, he put his hand under the front fender. Then he was up and walking away.

It was a tracking device. It had to be. Somebody had found him.

"Say, Julia?" He turned toward the open kitchen. "Where's your car parked?"

"In the lot under the building."

Perfect. "And where's your appointment?"

"Downtown Minneapolis," she said, closing up the dishwasher and switching it on.

"I wonder if you could give me a lift. You can drop me anywhere along Hennepin or Marquette."

"Don't you have a car?"

"At the moment, I'm relying on cabs." He picked up his case. "Let's plan on taking the items over to the gallery in St. Paul sometime in the next day or two. Once you have the appraisal, we can talk about how you want to pay for them."

"A check? Money order? Cash? Whatever you like."

He wasn't cheating her. What she was about to buy was worth every penny of the price.

If it made them both happy, what was the harm?

16

Half an hour later, Jane was inside Cordelia's cacophonous downtown loft, attempting, with little success, to listen to three simultaneous conversations—Hattie's, Cordelia's, and Mel's. She'd come to tell Cordelia about Chess but needed to wait until they were alone.

Melanie was getting ready to take Hattie swimming at the Y. Cordelia had commandeered the kitchen to prepare everyone breakfast to order, since no two people wanted to eat the same thing. She hollered like a fry cook when an order came up.

"Fluffernutter sandwich," she called.

Jane, expediting orders, brought the plate to Hattie, who was sitting on the floor in front of the TV, struggling to put on a pair of socks while watching Animal Planet.

"Change the channel," hollered Cordelia.

"To what?" Jane hollered back.

"Turner Classic Movies."

"No," whined Hattie. "I want to watch the baby beavers."

Cordelia stepped out of the kitchen. "No whining and no blaming.

Those are the rules in this loft. I want you to have a well-rounded education, Hatts. There's an old Cary Grant, Myrna Loy movie on right now. *Mr. Blandings Builds His Dream House*, 1948. It's a classic."

"But I want to watch the *beavers*," she cried.

Melanie picked up her flute and started playing. "I have so little time to practice these days," she lamented. "Do you like flute music, Jane?"

"Love it. Can't live without it."

"Ham and eggs," hollered Cordelia.

"That's me," said Melanie, grabbing the plate from Jane's hand and making herself comfortable at the kitchen table. "That was a wonderful party last night. Had a long talk with your brother. Great guy. And Julia. I don't know why you all hate her so much. She's fascinating."

"Jane?" said Cordelia, turning around to look at her, spatula in hand. "What about your breakfast needs?"

"How about a stiff shot of vodka."

"I see," said Cordelia.

Jane nodded to the toaster. "Your order is up."

Blanche, the matriarch of Cordelia's cat colony, had hunkered down next to the toaster, looking both bored and earnest—an emotional sleight of hand only a cat could manage.

"Ah, my Toaster Strudel. Ambrosia."

Hattie flew into the kitchen. "Deeya, we have to pack."

"Pack?" said Cordelia, slathering sweet white goo on the strudel.

"Right now." She jumped up and down. "Right now. Right now. Right now."

"Honey, I'd like to eat my breakfast."

"But I want to go live in a mud house. We have to *pack*."

"A. Mud. House," deadpanned Cordelia.

"We need to bring lots of clothes. And my puppets. And pudding."

"See what happens when she watches that nature crap," said Cordelia out of the side of her mouth.

"A mud house might be interesting," said Melanie.

"Well, then, just friggin' *sign me up*," cried Cordelia. "Let's grab the Easy-Bake Oven and we can all go."

"Deeya, come on," cried Hattie, yanking on her arm. "I want to go live with the beavers."

Jane gave Hattie an understanding smile. She sat down at the kitchen table and pulled the little girl into her arms. "You know, kiddo, if you and Deeya are going to go live with the beavers, you'll need to learn how to be a good swimmer. I think it makes sense for you to go to the Y with Melanie this morning."

Hattie twisted a lock of hair around her finger. "I can swim."

"But not very well."

Rolling her eyes, she said, "Oh, all right."

"Go finish your sandwich," said Cordelia. "And turn off that wretched Animal Planet."

"Oh, look, elephants," cried Hattie, rushing back to the TV.

"I swear," said Cordelia, wiping a hand across her forehead, "I'm going to put a childproof lock on that channel."

Jane sat and listened to the back-and-forth, the arguing, the coaxing, the pleading, the yelling, then the kisses, the hugs, the waves, the long good-bye-bye. Hadn't Raymond Chandler written a book with that title?

"I'm exhausted," said Jane after Mel and Hattie were gone. The loft was a disaster. Toys and clothes everywhere.

"Tell me about it," said Cordelia, lifting the dirty plates over to the counter. "I love it, though. Not every minute, but Hattie's back home with me, where she belongs."

"You could sure use a nanny. Or an army."

"I'm working on it."

"Someone specific?"

"An ex-nurse from Sacramento. We're dickering over compensation."

"You going to let her live here, like Cecily did?"

"All part of the negotiations."

"What's her name?"

"Val Brown."

"I suppose she could move in across the street, like Mel. There are still some lofts that haven't sold. Maybe you should think about installing a tightrope."

"Ha ha." Cordelia poured herself a glass of grapefruit juice and crooked her finger, inviting Jane to join her in the living room. "So, what was so important that you had to rush right over?"

Jane collapsed onto an armchair and explained about the breaking news.

"Heavens," said Cordelia, nearly choking on the juice.

"Do you think he did it? Murdered that poor guy?"

"Not the Chester I know."

"That's just it," said Jane. "Do we know him? I thought we did. Now I'm beginning to wonder." She could see that Cordelia was resisting the idea. "I told you about the guys watching my house and my restaurant, right?"

"What guys?"

Jane gave her the down and dirty. "I think they're watching Chess, not me. He's mixed up in something bad—and he's got me mixed up in it, too."

"We have to talk to that boy, after which we must line up all our little gray cells and go a'sleuthing."

Jane shook her head. "I'm done with that. Nolan's looking into it for me."

"Done with sleuthing? *Out* of the question."

"Anyway," said Jane, "I can't find Chess. I tried his cell, left a couple of messages, but he hasn't returned them. Do you think I should tell the police that he's living in my third-floor apartment?"

"We know nothing about the man who died. What's his name?"

"The newscaster said the cops hadn't released it yet."

"Janey, we're a team. We've solved so many mysteries I can't even count them all."

"Remember what happened when we got involved with that murdered woman down in Iowa last fall. It nearly got Peter killed, and it caused a rift in our relationship I'm still trying to repair. No, I'm done with all that. I just want to keep my head down, run my restaurants, and lead a safe, quiet life."

"You'd be bored stiff. *You*, dearheart, are an adrenaline junkie, just like I am."

"I am not."

"Are too."

"We sound like two-year-olds."

Cordelia tossed the rest of her juice back and set the glass down next to her. "Look, let's do this much. Let's go back to your house and wait for Chester to come home. We can interrogate him together. Good cop, bad cop."

"I suppose we owe him a chance to explain."

"Damn straight."

"Maybe, if we both talk to him, we can get the real story."

"I am a human lie detector, Janey. Never fear. Besides," she added, rising and hanging her fringed sack purse over her shoulder, "when you're down, you need your friends to stick by you."

Irina crawled around on her hands and knees, scrubbing the wood floor with a hard bristle brush and Murphy's Oil Soap. Dusty was a few yards away, strapped into his car seat. She'd purchased it before he was born, thinking that she'd need it. She never had—until last night. After the police left, Misty had driven Irina and Dustin back to the house where they both grew up. It felt familiar, and yet strangely foreign to be back. Then again, she had nowhere else to go.

Nothing was clean enough. Irina insisted that Misty go out first thing and buy an air purifier, a new portable crib, baby bottles, formula, diapers, and new sheets and baby blankets. The air purifier now resided in the corner of the bedroom, hissing out recycled and decontaminated air. The crib had yet to be assembled, yet to be rubbed down with disinfectant wipes. Dusty had fallen asleep, but after last night, he was restless, crying at even the smallest noise. The constant hiss of the purifier was a steady sound that muted the world around them. It was a godsend.

Majid had phoned shortly after eight, saying he wanted to spend the day cleaning and detailing what was lost at the gallery. He suggested that he also start the reorganizing if he had time. The police had removed the crime scene tape from the front and back doors but left it on the back stairs leading to the second floor, which was still off-limits. The gallery would need to remain closed to the public until further notice. Irina told him she had other matters to attend to but agreed that he should go ahead and start without her. She asked him to concentrate on the main room and to make sure he photographed the damage. He seemed annoyed that she didn't offer to help.

"My mother just died," she told him.

"I know that."

"I need some time to grieve." She wasn't about to let him in on what had happened last night.

"And I need to work."

"Fine. Have at it."

Irina finished scrubbing the bedroom floor, wiping the last of the water and soap up with a bath towel. When she walked out into the living room, she found a disheveled man in ratty black jeans, a Nirvana T-shirt, and a black leather vest, sitting with one leg draped over the arm of a chair.

She shouted at him, "Get out of here! Take that filthy cigarette with you."

Misty came out of the the kitchen with a beer in her hand. "You can't order my friends around."

"I can and I will. Get him out of here," she said, kicking at an empty taco chip sack.

The guy made a circling motion next to his head with his finger.

By now, Irina was used to the implication, but she wasn't about to take it, not anymore—and not from him. "Leave now or I'll call the police."

"You can't call the police," said Misty. "I live here and he's my friend and I get to have my friends visit me."

"Leave," she yelled at him, balling her hands into fists.

Moving with infinite slowness, the man stood. He took a drag off the cigarette and blew a couple of smoke rings. "She's a freakin' nutcase," he said to Misty. "I'll catch you later."

Misty glared at Irina as the guy left. "I spend the last two hours at Target buying all that crap for you and *this* is the thanks I get?"

"I never want to see that man in this house again. Not as long as Dusty and I are staying here."

"You don't tell me what to do. You don't own this place, I do."

"Not until the trust is executed." Looking at her sister, at the hurt in her eyes, she softened her expression. They had to stick together, be a family, help each other. "I don't want to fight with you, but I can't have people smoking in this house. You know why."

"You're a freak, that's why."

"If calling me names makes you feel better, then go ahead. I'm only protecting my baby. People bring germs with them. I'm fighting a battle, Misty, for my son's *life*. If you love me, you need to help me."

Her sister let out a shriek and threw herself on the sofa.

"Let's not fight. I'm drained. I'm scared." Irina lowered herself down on the oak coffee table in front of her sister and nodded to the can in her hand. "You told me you weren't using."

"It's just a beer." She tipped the bottle back and finished it off.

"It's alcohol."

"No kidding."

"I care about you."

"I care about you, too. That's why you need to see a shrink. This," she said, pointing at the hallway into the bedroom, "it's not right. You need help."

The cell phone in Irina's purse trilled. She didn't have the energy to answer it.

"I'll get it," said Misty, heaving herself up. "It's probably Steve. I talked to him a little while ago, told him what happened. He's driving back. Maybe he's already home." Flipping the phone open, she pressed it to her ear and said hello. She listened a moment, then said, "It's somebody named Chess."

"Tell him I'll call him later."

Misty relayed the message, then listened a couple more seconds. "He says it's really important."

Irina's gaze rose to the ceiling. She just didn't have the steam to tell him about last night. He should have been there, should have protected her. "Do me a favor. Tell him what happened. I just can't do it, but he needs to know."

"Who is he?"

"A business friend."

She stretched out on the couch, closed her eyes, and listened to Misty tell Chess that someone had broken into her house last night, that Irina had called 911 and then fired sixteen shots into the bedroom door. She ended by saying that when the cops arrived, whoever had broken in was long gone.

Misty held the phone away from her ear. "He wants to talk to you."

She breathed out, held out her hand. "Oh, all right. Will you check on Dusty?"

Misty groaned. Oozing attitude, she handed the phone over and then stomped out of the room.

"Are you okay?" asked Chess, his voice an octave higher than nor-mal.

"That's kind of a dumb question, don't you think?"

"You're upset with me."

"I have a right to be."

Silence. "Do the police have any idea who broke in?"

"Of course not, but I do. It was the same people who murdered Melvin and my mother. They're after me now. And when they find you, they'll be after you, too."

He didn't say anything for several seconds. "I have a buyer for the bull."

That got her attention. She sat up. "You do?"

"I told her that I'd bring it by tonight. That means we have to go get it."

"How much did you ask for?"

"A million and a quarter."

It was a good price. "She's got the money?"

"She's loaded. If she buys it, we don't have to string along that woman you told me about. This will be so much quicker. I told her about the gallery, said you could authenticate it and give her an ap-praisal. She wants one of the cylinder seals, too. Two hundred and fifty thousand. We're just about home free, baby. Once the money's in the bank, we can get out of here for good."

Her heart sped up. "We?" He'd never said that before, not di-rectly. She wasn't sure how she could travel with Dusty. She wouldn't risk his life, not for Chess or all the money in the world. She had the gallery to think about, too.

"Of course, *we*. I know there are details we need to figure out, and we will, I promise. As long as we're a team, everything's possible. When can you pick me up?"

"I left my car at the house in Apple Valley."

"Doesn't your sister have a car?"

If Irina had to leave the house, Misty would have to babysit, so she wouldn't need it. "Tonight," said Irina. "I need to get some sleep first."

"What time and where?"

"Where are you now?"

"The Caribou Coffee at Ninth and Second."

"I'll pick you up at six."

17

Jane and Cordelia waited for Chess to return to Jane's house, but by two, Jane couldn't wait any longer. She had a meeting with her head chef at the Xanadu Club. Cordelia extracted a promise that Jane would call if she learned anything new. Several hours later, as she was standing at the Xanadu's bar pouring herself a cup of coffee, Nolan returned a call she'd made to him.

"Boy, you sure know how to get yourself in trouble," he said without preamble.

"What can I say? I'm blessed with interesting friends. Were you able to find anything out about the man who was murdered in Minnehaha Park?"

"He wasn't murdered there," said Nolan. "He was dumped. Name's Melvin Dial, a retired businessman."

Jane took her coffee and moved to a far stool. "What sort of business?"

"CEO of a medical software company until he retired about ten years back."

"Any idea how he died?"

"Knifed, according to my source. They found your friend's passport in the grass about ten feet away. The police think it fell out of his pocket when he dumped the body."

Jane turned to look out the window. It was rush hour in Uptown. Traffic was starting to back up along Twenty-eighth. "Should I be afraid of him?"

"Yeah, you should."

"I suppose I should call the police, tell them I know where he is."

"That would be my advice. And then I'd kick his ass to the curb. You don't need friends like him."

"What if he's innocent?"

"Apologize later. Put your safety first."

Jane had already come to the same conclusion. "I'm about to head home."

"You need me, you call. Anytime, day or night."

The doorbell rang just as Jane was letting Mouse into the backyard. Hoping that it was Chess, she rushed back through the house to the front door. She looked through the peephole before opening it, finding a plainclothes cop standing on her front steps. He detached the badge clipped to his belt and held it up.

"Jane Lawless?" he asked, looking her over.

"Yes?"

"You Ray Lawless's daughter?"

"That's me."

"Thought so. I voted for your dad."

"Wish more people had."

He was black, like Nolan, though not as tall or barrel chested, and he was younger. Jane glanced over his shoulder and saw a dark blue Crown Vic parked in front of the house. She supposed there was a reason cops drove that kind of car, but she couldn't, for the life of her, think of one.

"I'm Sergeant Kevante Taylor. I need to talk to you. Won't take long."

She led him into the dining room. "Actually, I was about to call you guys."

They each took a seat at the shiny mahogany table. Jane offered him a soft drink, but he shook his head. "How come you were about to call us?"

"Chess Garrity. That's why you're here, right? You're a homicide cop?"

He hesitated for just a second before saying, "Yeah."

"How did you connect us?"

"My partner's been digging into Garrity's past. We found a marriage license database with your name—and his—on it. Since you're the only Jane Lawless in the Twin Cities, I took a chance and drove over."

It was the last thing she wanted to hear. She needed that part of her life to remain buried. Now, with Chess's name on the front burner because of a possible murder charge, it would be a miracle if it didn't make the papers and the local nightly news.

"So tell me, are you married to this guy, because I'd heard—"

"We're divorced," she said, cutting him off before he could say any more. This was a bad dream coming true. She wondered what he was reading in her face.

"You have any idea where I could find him?"

"He's living upstairs in my third-floor apartment."

The cop's eyebrows shot up. "My LT said this trip would be a waste of time."

"Guess your LT was wrong. I just got home, so I'm not sure if he's here. I left him a couple of cell phone messages, but he hasn't returned them."

"Not surprising. He probably knows we're looking for him."

147

"You're welcome to go up and see if he's there. I'll give you a key. If nobody answers, you have my permission to go in."

"That's great, thanks."

She might as well be cooperative. She had nothing to lose except her sterling lesbian credentials. She waited at the table while he ran up the outside steps. She heard him bang on the door. Heard no response. He returned a few minutes later.

"Not home. I went in and looked around, but nothing jumped out at me. I'd like to come back with my partner."

"No problem."

He sat back down at the table. "Maybe you can fill me in on some background information. The passport we found indicated that Mr. Garrity lives in Istanbul. That right?" He removed a notepad from the inside suit-coat pocket.

"He's here on a business trip—he buys and sells antiquities."

Taylor made a few scratches on the pad. "You been in touch with him since the divorce?"

"We were only married a few months. We stayed friends for a while, but I haven't heard from him or seen him in over twenty years. Not until he showed up at my restaurant on Wednesday afternoon."

"Wednesday." He thought about it, then nodded. "Did he give a reason for the sudden appearance?"

"Just said he was in town and wanted to say hi. I was surprised to see him after all these years, but he seemed like the same old Chess. He's a friend, Sergeant. I have a hard time believing he's a murderer."

"That's understandable. We're just beginning our investigation."

"Chess is gay. Apparently, his boyfriend here in town kicked him out. He was mugged coming out of a gay bar in downtown Minneapolis and showed up on my doorstep Wednesday night with scrapes on his face. I felt sorry for him."

"The guy's *gay*?" asked Taylor, giving her a quizzical look.

Jane was determined not to go there. Catching sight of movement out the dining room window, she rose from her chair. A cab was pulling up to the curb.

"There's Chess," she said, watching him get out and hand the driver some cash.

"Ask him to come inside."

Jane crossed into the front hall and opened the door. "Hey, Chess," she called, sounding friendly. "I need to talk to you for a sec."

"Sure," he called back, flashing her a smile. He breezed in through the door and gave her a peck on the cheek. "Hot day. What's up?"

Taylor stepped out of the dining room, drawing his suit coat back to reveal his badge. "Sergeant Kevante Taylor, Mr. Garrity. We need to talk."

Chess's smile disappeared. He looked from Taylor to Jane and then back to Taylor. "What about?"

"You haven't heard the news?" asked Jane.

"News?" repeated Chess, his expression growing wary.

"Do you know a man named Melvin Dial?" asked Taylor.

Chess hesitated, then shoved a hand in the pocket of his dress slacks. "Ah, yeah, I do. What about him?"

Jane read the hesitation, and the attempt at a casual gesture, as guilt. She figured Taylor did, too.

"His body was found in Minnehaha Park this morning."

"Are you saying he's dead?"

"They found your passport in the bushes, not far from the body," said Jane. "He was murdered."

Chess looked away. He appeared to be absorbing the shock, or trying to figure out what to say. "Are you here because you think I had something to do with it?"

"Can you explain how your passport ended up in the grass?" asked Taylor.

"I, ah—" He ran the back of his hand across his mouth. "I need a minute. Jane?" He nodded for her to follow him into the living room.

149

Everything he'd said and done since coming in the front door, the sweat forming on his upper lip, and the complete disintegration of his usual bonhomie, only added to her confusion—and her growing anger. "What are you mixed up in?" she demanded.

He leaned toward her and whispered, "I can't talk to him."

"Why not? Did you murder that guy?"

"No."

"Then why can't you answer his questions?"

"Because I need a lawyer. I swear, Jane, I never touched Dial."

"But you know something."

"Yeah, I do, and when I explain what happened, it will look bad for me. That's why I'm going back in there and telling that guy that I refuse to talk to him without my lawyer present."

"Who's your lawyer?"

His eyes flicked to her and then away. "I don't have one. Not here, anyway. I was hoping, could you call your father? You're my last hope—you and your dad."

"Jesus, Chess. What am I supposed to think?"

"I may be a lot of unsavory things, but I'm no murderer. You have to believe that. You *have* to."

She needed more than just his word and a plea for trust. "How did your passport end up in Minnehaha Park?"

He slumped against the back of the couch.

"Tell me the truth, Chess. You're not a very good liar."

When his eyes cut to her, she had no idea how to read his expression.

"Fair enough. Here it is. I was playing poker with Dial on Tuesday night—at his house. I admit I was pretty drunk, so I don't remember all the details, but I always carry a couple of hundred-dollar bills in my passport. I took it out because I needed them. I stood up, set the passport on the mantel, and then sat back down. When I left that night, I forgot to take it with me."

150

"You're saying Dial was alive and well when you left?"

"He was. I never thought about my passport again until I was looking for it the next day. I went back to his house. The door was open. I thought it was strange, but I went in. Nobody was around. I swear, Jane. Not a soul. I looked for the passport on the mantel, but it was gone. I figured he'd found it and put it somewhere safe. I mean, I felt funny being in there. I don't know—it was like, I knew something was wrong, otherwise why was his door unlocked? When I left, his neighbor saw me go. We exchanged a few pleasantries. He can vouch for the time. And then, as I was coming around the lake, I saw your restaurant and decided to check it out, see if it really belonged to you. I could never have done that if I'd just murdered a man. You said it yourself. I'm not a good liar."

She recalled that he'd seemed distracted on Wednesday afternoon, but nothing extreme, nothing out of the ordinary. If he'd lost his passport, that would account for it. "How did the passport end up in the park?"

"I have absolutely no idea."

On the one hand, she wasn't sure what to believe; on the other, it wouldn't hurt to call her father. Maybe he could help get to the bottom of things. "Okay, I'll call him. But I want you out of my third floor. Today."

"Sure, I understand. You've been more than kind."

The cop was sitting at the dining room table talking on his cell when they returned to the front hall.

"Are you here to arrest me?" asked Chess, stepping in front of Jane.

"Just to talk." He flipped his phone closed and stood up to face them.

"Okay, but not without my lawyer present."

Taylor switched his gaze to Jane, then back to Chess. "If that's the way you want to play it. It would be a whole lot easier if you'd just answer a few simple questions. Cooperation goes a long way."

"Like I said, I want to cooperate, but I need to speak to my lawyer first." Turning to Jane, he said, "Would you phone him?"

"Your father?" asked Taylor.

She nodded, watching the expression on his face harden.

"We'll do it downtown," said Taylor.

"What if I can't reach my dad?"

"Then we'll do it when he's available. But it better be sometime today. Otherwise, Mr. Garrity will get a chance to be a guest of the MPD sooner rather than later."

18

Chess stood outside the Caribou Coffee in downtown Minneapolis, finishing a cigarette and waiting for Irina to pick him up. It was going on six fifteen, which meant that he most likely had another fifteen minutes to wait. Irina was rarely punctual. Next to him on the sidewalk were his two suitcases and his leather briefcase. He'd done as Jane asked, moved out of her third-floor apartment. Even if she hadn't asked, he was planning to do it anyway. The only reason he needed to come back to the house at all was to get his things. If someone had followed him to Julia's apartment this morning and put a tracking device on his junker car—without checking the car, he couldn't be one hundred percent positive that's what it was, but he was sure he was right—they'd found his hiding spot. He needed another. Besides, he didn't want anybody observing his comings and goings, especially not now, with the way everything was coming together for the sale of the bull.

After an abortive meeting with Sergeant Taylor and his partner, Sergeant Hellickson, down at city hall, Chess had been released;

much to his relief, Ray had arrived and given the police an ultimatum: Arrest him or let him go. On the advice of counsel, no questions would be allowed. Chess shook Ray's hand and thanked him profusely, but in response received nothing but the evil eye. Ray made it clear that the police considered Chess their number one suspect. They made a date to get together tomorrow to talk about his legal options, but legal options or no legal options, once Chess had the money from the sale, he would leave the Twin Cities—without Irina—never to return. He had to use his wits and his lawyer to forestall any action by the police.

Irina pulled up to the curb in a beat-up cherry red Mercury Cougar ten minutes later. She popped the trunk so that Chess could stow his bags.

The first thing she said after he flipped his cigarette away and got in was "Tell me about this woman you've been staying with."

He hid his smile behind a feigned cough and told her that she had nothing to worry about, that *she* was the love of his life.

"What's her name?"

"Oh, come on."

"Tell me."

He gave a tired sigh and snapped on his seat belt. "Jane Lawless."

Irina frowned and then turned. "Raymond Lawless's daughter?"

"How do you know Ray Lawless?"

"He ran for governor last year."

"Oh, yeah. Someone mentioned that to me. But look, she's just a friend. I'm not lying to you."

"I read an article about her that said she was gay."

"Was and is. Can we drop this now?"

Last summer, after spending an intensely romantic week with Irina when she was in Istanbul on business, he actually thought he might be in love with her. During the time they'd been apart, she'd changed. The sexy, fun-loving woman he'd gotten to know had morphed into a walking, talking bag of nerves—and a bag of bones. She'd lost so much weight that her clothes hung on her. Worse yet, every time he saw her, she seemed more strung out, her eyes sunk deeper in their sockets, her mouth held more tightly.

Chess reached for her hand, gave it a squeeze. "How are you feeling?"

"I had a nap, so a little better."

"I assume you heard about Dial."

She kept her eyes on the road this time. "What about him?"

"His body was dumped over by Minnehaha Falls. A jogger found him this morning. It made the local news. Unfortunately, so did my name."

She gripped the steering wheel, her knuckles white with strain.

He explained what had happened. "The cops aren't done with me. I'm apparently their number one suspect."

"But what happened to the blackmailer? I thought you were working something out with him."

"He called me this morning and announced that he's out, that he wants nothing more to do with me. Didn't want my money. Didn't want anything. I imagine the body was already in the park by then. I don't understand it either, but what's done is done—and I'm on the hook."

They drove in silence until they reached the freeway entrance.

Turning the air conditioner on, Irina said, "You're not the only one with problems."

Chess found the comment just this side of arctic. Were they trying to one-up each other on the disaster scale?

"Someone tried to kill me last night, so what does my loving husband do?" She pointed the car at the freeway and accelerated, cutting off a guy in a plumbing truck, causing him to hit the brakes and his horn. "Does he come home and comfort me?" she asked, paying no attention as the truck swerved around her and the guy

155

gave her the finger. "Not Steve. I'm not even sure he believes there was actually someone in the house. He went ballistic when he saw the damage I'd done to the bedroom door. He's insisting I come back to the house tonight, but that's not happening. I'm staying put with Misty."

"You think that's wise? With the baby and all?"

"What the hell would you know about babies?"

In the space of a few minutes, she'd gone from jealous to sulky to simmering.

"Misty's a slob, which means I had to scrub out the bedroom this morning. Before I go back there tonight, I need to stop at a drugstore to buy a couple of those disposable white masks. I'm going to insist that Misty wear one around Dusty. I'm extra careful about my hygiene, but she's drinking again, and hanging out with some real lowlifes. I'm just being cautious, you see that, don't you?"

In an effort to reconnect, to soothe her bruised feelings, he said, "Absolutely." What he understood was that she was becoming absolutely wacko when it came to her son.

"So where are we going?" he asked. He needed another cigarette, but Irina would never allow it, not even in Misty's car.

"The gallery."

"Why?"

"I hid it down in the basement after the gallery was ransacked. What safer place could there be? I discovered some loose bricks in the wall a few years back. I gouged a space out behind them. It's a perfect spot. Nobody knows about it but me."

Chess looked straight ahead, grinding his teeth. "You told me you'd put it in a safety deposit box—in a bank."

"I did, but I took it out."

"I am *not* a happy man."

"You're always telling me to calm down. Now it's your turn. It's more accessible this way. We can get at it anytime, day or night."

156

He wasn't convinced. The statue meant everything to him—more than Irina could ever understand.

In the summer of 2005, while visiting an old friend in the ancient city of Halab, Chess had been taken to an ancient antique shop on a narrow, winding back street, where he'd come upon the winged bull. He'd heard rumors about it but never expected to actually run across it in his travels, least of all to learn that it was for sale at a time when he had the wherewithal to buy it. The winged bull had an aura. He commented on it, described it, but nobody else could see it. The craftsmanship was of the highest order. When he ran his fingers to the tips of the wings, he saw an inner vision of another hand touching it, this one covered in jewelry set with precious stones, a man's hand with polished nails and smooth skin. He understood immediately what it meant. He'd owned it in another life. In that instant he realized something profound: He hadn't found it, *it* had found him.

Half an hour later, creeping down the back steps to the gallery basement carrying his leather attaché case, Chess let Irina take the lead. Her mood had improved now that she had a task to perform.

"We don't store anything down here except for shipping boxes and supplies. Whoever tossed the gallery didn't do much damage."

Packing boxes had been knocked around, probably to ensure they were empty. The cement floor had been swept clean, although Chess noticed that the corners were full of cobwebs.

"It's right here," said Irina, carefully removing a brick about a foot above her head. She removed three more bricks next to it and then reached inside. "What the—" she said, standing on her tiptoes, trying to see inside.

"What is it?" Chess set his case on a wooden table.

"It's gone."

He rushed over and sank his hand into the hole. For his effort, all

157

he got was scraped knuckles. Turning on her, he grabbed her by the shoulders.

"You're hurting me."

"Where is it?"

"I don't *know*."

"I don't believe you."

"Why would I take it?"

He wanted to make her feel *real* pain, make her pay for her incompetence. Instead, he walked around kicking boxes, venting his fury on something inanimate. "How could you be so stupid? This is the worst place in the world to hide something like the bull." It had been a mistake to let her take it, even for a few days. *She* was a mistake.

She burst into tears.

"Stop it. Just *stop* sniveling."

"You hate me. You never loved me."

"Do you have any idea what you've done? How important that statue is to me?"

"Yes," she spat back at him.

"Who has a key to the gallery?"

She dropped down on a bench. "Just me and Majid." She looked up at him, light dawning in her eyes. "It has to be Majid. He spent the day here cleaning."

"Where does he live?"

"A few blocks away. In an apartment."

"You've got the address?"

"What are you going to do?"

He thought for a moment more. "I need money. Cash. How much do you have with you?"

"I'd have to check. A couple hundred, maybe."

"I need more than that. Do you have an ATM card?"

"Tell me what you're planning."

He moved back to the hole, felt around inside again. Placing the bricks back into their slots, he eyed the wall from various angles, try-ing to see if the loose bricks were apparent. He came to the conclusion that they were, but only slightly, probably not enough to tip someone off that something was behind them. "Whoever took the bull knew about the hiding place. Have you ever hidden anything else behind those bricks?"

She gave a diffident shrug. "Yeah."

"What?"

"Pot."

"You kept a stash down here?"

"Sometimes."

"What else?"

"I kept a journal for a year or so back in '05. Didn't want anyone to see it."

"Anything more recent?"

Another shrug. "The love letters you sent me here at the gallery so Steve wouldn't see them."

"God, Irina, I told you to burn them."

"I couldn't," she said weakly, her chin sinking to her chest.

He felt suddenly like the gold standard against which the notion of *patsy* was judged. Yet, lame as it was, it touched him that she couldn't bring herself to burn his letters. She was a mess, but she wasn't malevolent—and at the moment, she was the only ally he had.

"Okay, here's what we do. I'll phone Julia, tell her I can't bring the bull by tonight. I'll make some excuse. But I need to get her over here tomorrow so you can appraise the cylinder seal. How does your morning look? Say, ten?"

"Do you forgive me?"

He wasn't willing to go that far. "If Majid did take it, I'll get it back."

"How?"

"Leave that to me."

"But you didn't answer my question."

He walked over, took her hands, and drew her up into his arms. She was shivering, still fighting back tears. Could a heart break minimally? Microscopically? If so, that's how his broke for her, although even that puny amount embarrassed him. She was a human wreck. How could he be drawn to that? "Of course I forgive you. We've got to stick together if we're going to make this work." It wasn't true, of course, but it placed him back on home turf. Pity wasn't his style. Nor was undying devotion. He couldn't do happily ever after as a young man, and he sure as hell couldn't do it now. If she was looking for that, from him, she was in for one hell of a letdown.

Yet the certainty he felt that he could never give her what she wanted made him unaccountably, mystifyingly, unfathomably sad.

19

Late Saturday night, Jane was hard at work in her office at the Lyme House, completing the pub's summer weekend music schedule. Her concentration was continually broken by thoughts of Chess, what he'd done or hadn't done, what his real reason was for coming to the Twin Cities and how his sudden reappearance had set in motion a series of damaging reverberations through her own life. Every so often she would shake herself out of a reverie, only to realize that she'd been staring into space for several minutes, completely unaware of the passage of time. It was during one of those reveries that she received a call from Sigrid.

"Hey," said Jane, dropping her pen on the desktop and leaning back in her chair, glad to change the channel in her brain, if only for a few minutes.

"Thought I'd see if you were free Monday afternoon."

"If I'm not, I'll make myself free."

"Excellent. I wanted to stop by, have that conversation I

promised—the one about me and Peter, and other various and sundry earth-shattering issues."

"Did we firm up a date yet when I can take Mia to the Art Institute?"

"We're thinking next Thursday. How does that sound?"

"Perfect. Maybe I'll take her out to lunch first."

"You know, this is really nice of you. In the mood she's been in lately, she could use another adult in her life."

"I should have been there all along. What time on Monday afternoon?"

"Peter's meeting with Julia over at her loft at four. He's bringing Mia with him because he says the view is incredible and wants her to see it. He'll be there about an hour. Thought I'd swing by after dropping them off. Maybe we could share an adult beverage and talk."

"It's a date. By the way, Julia told me last night that she's hired Peter to film a documentary."

"He's had a couple of offers in the last month. He's really pumped about it. Life is good, Jane. Really good. Anyway, gotta run. See you Monday."

Life is good, thought Jane, repeating the comment to herself as she rose from her chair and walked down the hall to the pub. As she was about to go inside to grab herself a beer, she saw Cordelia and a woman she'd never seen before barrel down the stairs from the first floor.

"You're here," said Cordelia, her expression full of enthusiasm. "I have someone I want you to meet." Turning to the woman next to her, she said, "Jane, this is Val Brown. I'm on the cusp of hiring her to be Hattie's new nanny."

Jane held out her hand. "You've got a big job ahead of you."

"I love kids," said Val, glancing over Jane's shoulder into the bar.

"Cordelia said you're from Sacramento. What made you move to the Twin Cities?"

"To be closer to my girlfriend."

From Cordelia's startled expression, Jane figured she hadn't done a particularly thorough job interview.

"She lives here?" asked Cordelia.

"No, in Fargo."

"Then why didn't you move there?" asked Jane.

"Ever been to Fargo?"

"Actually, I haven't."

"My girlfriend's a sheep rancher, lives about forty miles out of town."

"A . . . sheep . . . rancher?" said Cordelia, raising an eyebrow.

"Does she run the ranch herself?" asked Jane.

"Her six kids help."

"*Six* kids?" repeated Cordelia.

"It's a lot of work. That's why she's decided to sell and move to the Twin Cities. I figured your loft would be a perfect place for all of them to crash while she looks for an apartment. It's big, open. Close to the bus line. Oh, and First Avenue. A couple of her boys are really into music—mostly heavy metal."

Cordelia swallowed hard, squared her shoulders. "Val, dear, I've thought of a few more questions I need to ask before I make a final decision. Why don't I buy you a beer."

"Sure," said Val, looking eager to get inside. "Nice meeting you, Jane. I'm looking forward to getting to know you better."

As they walked into the bar, Cordelia turned and drew a finger across her throat.

Jane left through the downstairs door just after midnight and headed up the hill to the back parking lot, where she'd parked her Mini. She was engaged in a one-way conversation with her brother when she heard the slap of footsteps. She spun around, catching a glimpse of a man with long blond hair. He grabbed her and forced her face-first against the rear fender of her car.

163

Twisting her arm behind her back and up between her shoulder blades, he said, "Tell me where he went."

She tried to turn her head, to get a better look at him, but all she got for her effort was her face smashed against the trunk. Stars spun around her in the darkness. The coppery taste of blood trickled into her mouth.

"I'm not playing games," said the blond guy in a low growl. "Where'd your husband go? Tell me where he is or I'll break your fucking arm." He shoved her arm higher.

She grimaced, gritting her teeth. "I don't know," she said, the pain triggering tears. "I'm telling the truth."

"Bullshit. You're protecting him."

Her shoulder felt like it was about to pop out of its socket. "Okay, okay." Nothing mattered except stopping the pain.

He eased up a little.

"He left town."

"Where'd he go?"

"Chicago. The Drake Hotel. It's where he always stays."

"What about the bull?"

"The what?"

"Hey," shouted a different voice, this one from farther away. "You there. Get the hell away from her."

"What the fucking fuck," said the blond guy, releasing her.

She stayed where she was, sprawled across the trunk, breathing hard, trying to catch her breath, all the while listening to the second guy shout a string of obscenities at the blond man. Easing her arm around in front of her, she rubbed her shoulder, still half leaning on the fender.

"You okay?" called Lee, rushing up.

She stood, turned around, and half slid, half fell to the ground.

Lee helped ease her down, then propped her back against the tire. He got down on his hands and knees, cupped his hand around the

164

back of her neck, and studied her face. "This hurt?" he said, touching the bridge of her nose.

She groaned and pushed his hand away.

"I thought it might be broken, but it seems okay. Just bruised."

She felt her upper lip, touched the blood oozing from her nostrils.

"Here," he said, removing a handkerchief from his back pocket. "My mom always told me these would come in handy."

"Lee to the rescue."

"I wish I'd gotten here a few minutes earlier."

"Was he the blond man you told me about?" she asked, her voice sounding nasal and stuffy.

"Yup," he said, sitting down cross-legged on the pavement directly in front of her. "I've been watching the restaurant on and off. The boys were gone last night, I have no idea where, and then gone most of the day today. But on the way over to my soapbox on the other side of the lake tonight, I noticed the blond guy loitering by the wooden stairs that run down to the lake. I decided to stick around. I was over listening to the band concert earlier. I'd pretty much decided to call it a night and was heading back to my car when I saw him jump you."

"I owe you my arm," she said, using her tongue to search inside her mouth. She wanted to make sure all her teeth were where they should be.

He surveyed the parking lot. "You need more light back here. If you want, I'd be happy to give you a free security appraisal. I'm not selling anything. You can take my advice or leave it, no skin off my nose."

"I'll think about it."

"Those guys aren't going to leave you alone, you know. Just a gut instinct on my part, but I'm right. What did he want?"

"He thought I knew where someone might be."

"And do you?"

She shook her head.

"This someone—he, she important to you?"

"Not really. Someone I knew a long time ago."

He was silent for a few seconds. "I get it. It's this other person that's the target. These people are trying to find him or her through you."

"Him. And yeah, that would be my guess."

He scratched the side of his face. "I hate to bang the same note again, but you could use better security."

Jane was grateful he didn't press her for more details. She drew his handkerchief away from her nose. "I'll wash this and get it back to you."

"Keep it." He looked up at the sky. "Can't see many stars in the city. Gotta get out in the country to really appreciate the night sky."

"What did you preach about tonight?" She didn't feel like getting up yet, mainly because she wasn't at all sure her legs would support her.

"Read from the Epistle of Titus. That always inserts a note of terror into a romantic Saturday night."

"You really do enjoy annoying people."

He shrugged.

"How's your search for home coming?"

"The more I see of the Twin Cities, the more I like it."

"Wait until winter."

"I lived in Chicago. Can't be much worse than there."

She finally garnered the courage to touch her nose again.

"Feel solid?"

"Feels swollen."

"Maybe I should take you to the ER."

The throbbing in her arm had subsided to a dull ache. "Help me up," she said, using her good arm to push against the pavement.

Once she was standing more or less upright, she leaned back against the fender to get her bearings. And then she started to cry.

"Hey, there."

It was suddenly just too much. Getting beat up. Chess. Her brother. She didn't cry easily or often, but tonight she couldn't seem to stop.

She was about to crumple to the ground again when she felt his arm catch her.

"You're gonna be fine, Jane. Just fine."

She buried her head against his shoulder.

"Everything will work itself out. You'll see."

She was embarrassed and needed something to say. "Look, stop in for dinner anytime you want. Order champagne. Lobster. Anything you like."

His bushy brown eyebrows dipped. "Really?"

"It's on the house."

"Well, hell, you feed me and I'll do just about anything."

She tried to smile, but her nose hurt too much. "I'll keep that in mind."

20

Majid held a small flashlight between his teeth as he dipped under the yellow police tape attached to the doorway leading up to the second floor. Shining the light on the stairs, he headed up to Morgana's office. He'd worn a pair of soft deerskin gloves because he didn't want to leave fingerprints.

The full moon looked as if it had been hung in the sky right outside the unshaded windows in the octagonal turret. Its weak light bathed the room in silver. Switching off the flashlight, he pulled out the desk chair and sat down. The room reeked like a chicken that had been forgotten in the back of a refrigerator and gone bad. On the blotter, as well as under his feet, the moonlight turned the bloodstains an inky black. He hadn't expected anything quite this visceral to remind him of what had happened. He sat for a moment, composing himself, buttoning back his emotions.

He'd always wondered what it would feel like to sit in the queen's chair, to lean back and gaze around the kingdom—not to pretend to be in charge, but to actually *be* in charge.

Majid drew back the top middle drawer and let his fingers trail lightly along a row of antique fountain pens. He selected the one Morgana had used most often—a 1916 Parker with a hand-carved full gold overlay. He removed the cap, inspected it, made a few lines on the edge of a piece of stationery. Almost like a paintbrush, the nib had lots of flex and allowed the ink to flow smoothly, evenly, with no scratchiness.

"A scepter," he whispered.

Morgana had loved pens. He didn't understand this minor obsession, although he liked this pen well enough. He clipped it inside the pocket of his leather jacket. She also loved the color purple. The fountain pens were all filled with purple ink. The heavy permanent markers she used to write on her file folders were purple. Even the ballpoints she insisted he buy for use in the downstairs gallery were ordered with purple ink.

Majid's father had warned him years ago about women who favored purple—or lavender, or violet, or any incarnation thereof. He always seemed to work the question of a favorite color into conversations he had with women. He felt the answer "purple" was like a neon sign flashing the words BALL-BUSTING BITCH. Women who loved purple were imperious, his father had said, despotic, thought of themselves as goddesses. In many ways, Morgana fit the bill. She had lots of idiosyncrasies. Some of them were appealing, even fascinating. Some not so much.

The top drawer on the right side of the desk was filled with the usual office paraphernalia—a box of paper clips, a box of staples, tape, scissors, a few purple felt-tip pens. The middle drawer contained stationery and envelopes. In the bottom drawer he found a bottle of premium Scotch and several shot glasses. He knew the bottle would be there, unless one of the cops had taken it in for questioning.

On more than one occasion, he'd been offered a shot or two after the end of a "wicked long day," as Morgana liked to call them. He lifted the bottle out, set it on the desk, and stared at it, his eyes dry, his hands clammy under the gloves. Unscrewing the cap, feeling the moment like a heaviness in his bones, he tipped the bottle back and took a swallow. It burned his throat and began, if ever so slowly, to untie the knot in his stomach. He held the bottle up to the moonlight, saluting the oil portrait of Morgana hanging on the opposite wall.

"May Allah give you an easy and pleasant journey and shower blessings on your grave. Salaam."

He took another swallow, and then another, and another, until a good third of the nearly full bottle was gone. He wiped the top off with his glove and set the Scotch down on the floor next to the chair. Why put it away when he might want more?

He opened the top drawer on the left side—the only drawer on that side—and discovered a treasure trove of Morgana's personal cosmetics: lipsticks, powder, eyeliner, perfumes, other various and sundry potions and war paint. The perfume wafted lightly toward him, and for just a moment, he felt as if she were there, standing next to him . . . but the chicken stink was too strong. It overpowered the vision and dissolved it.

Why did he feel so deeply? How had he let this happen?

Leaning forward, Majid picked up a framed photograph Morgana always kept on her desk. It was a snapshot of Irina and Misty when they were kids. They sat together on the driver's seat of a pontoon, arms around each other, mugging for the camera, with a shoreline covered in the confetti of fall foliage in the background. It was an idyllic photo. Happiness, wealth, health, family. Irina couldn't have been more than ten, Misty a few years younger. He tried to see the future in their eyes, struggled to divine from their faces if they had any inkling at all of what life had in store for them. The answer, of course, was no. No one knew what life would bring. Humans were at the mercy of providence, the stars, chance, luck. The future was nowhere written in stone, although the past certainly was, cast as a sinful pillar of salt for all the world to see and revile.

Carefully, with a sense of great vigilance and solemnity, he set the frame back on the table. Then, with one lighting-swift sweep of his arm, he pitched forward and sent everything on the desk crashing to the floor.

"God forgive us," he whispered, his voice raw with anguish. "God forgive us all."

21

Irina patted Dusty's back as she walked around the bedroom, waiting for the little burp to signal that it was safe to put him down for his morning nap. He'd been bathed, powdered, cuddled, and dressed in a clean organic cotton Onesie. She lifted him off her shoulder and kissed his forehead, then placed him on his back in the crib and covered him with a thin cotton blanket.

"Mummy will be right back," she said, smoothing his cheek with the backs of her fingers.

She walked briskly down the hall to Misty's bedroom and threw back the door. "You promised you'd babysit Dustin this morning." She felt no desire to be nice. With beer cans littering the carpet, scuzzy people sitting around outside the house all day, and the constant late hours that caused Misty to sleep until noon, she was driving Irina bananas.

"Chill," mumbled Misty, rolling over and pulling the covers up over her head.

Irina found her sister's morning mellowness intolerable.

"Get up," she demanded. The ashtray on the once flawless night-stand overflowed with butts. The room smelled foul—sweat mixed with smoke mixed with garlic mixed with the stale smell of beer.

"Sure thing, Kemo Sabe," came Misty's muttered response.

"This is important." She yanked the blanket off her sister, let it drop to the floor.

"Jesus, are you nuts?" said Misty, pulling up a sheet to cover her nakedness. "Why are you being such a nasty-ass bitch?"

"I put Dusty down for his nap. I need to use your car again."

"Sure, take the car. Take my credit cards. Take whatever you want. You seem to think you own the world." She sat up in bed and ran a hand through her tangled hair. Smacking her lips, she muttered, "I feel like hell."

"You look like hell."

She stifled a belch. "I never signed on for this crap. Did you call Steve?"

"No, and I don't intend to."

"I won't babysit unless you call him."

"I can't," said Irina, breezing out of the room. "I'm running late."

"You never answer your phone, so he calls *me*," Misty shouted after her.

Irina was in the kitchen now, drinking a glass of orange juice.

"I'm getting sick of it," said Misty, stomping into the room. "I mean it. I won't take care of your little . . . *problem* unless you promise to call him back."

"All right, fine," she said, setting her dirty glass in the sink. "I should be back in a couple of hours. Be sure to wear one of those white masks around the baby. And don't smoke around him, understood?"

"Yeah, yeah, yeah."

Jane stood on the front steps of her father's house, touching her nose and hoping the makeup she'd used would cover the worst of the bruising. It wasn't as black and blue as she'd thought it would be, but it was still visible.

The information she brought with her, the conversation she was about to have, made even the minimal breakfast she'd eaten condense into concrete inside her stomach.

"Lord, what happened to you?" said her dad, a pained look crossing his face.

"Someone jumped me last night as I was about to get into my car."

"Where?"

"At the Lyme House."

He held the door open. "Are you okay? Who did it? Did you get a look at him? I assume you called the police."

The questions came out so fast that for a second she felt like she was on the witness stand and he was interrogating her, even though she knew it was concern. Digging her hands into her pockets, she said, "I'm fine, Dad. Why don't we sit down."

"I thought we'd talk in the sunroom."

"Where's Elizabeth?" she asked as they walked through the house, the home where she'd grown up.

"At church. If you want coffee, I just made a fresh pot."

Jane had called her father late last night, telling him she needed to talk to him this morning. He replied that he had a golf date, but that if it was important, he could always cancel. Something in her tone must have betrayed her. They knew each other too well. He guessed that it was about Chess even before she said his name.

Settling herself on one of the two Morris chairs facing a series of multipaned windows overlooking the back garden, she waited for her dad to resume his favorite glider. From the newspaper sections scattered around on the floor, she assumed that he'd been reading, drinking his morning coffee, and eating his usual toast and orange marmalade, a habit he'd developed when the family had lived in England.

After he lifted his feet up on an ottoman, his eyes narrowed into a tight, concerned focus.

First things first, she decided. "I have something I need to tell you." She seemed unable to find a comfortable position in a chair she'd always found so comfortable.

"About Chess?"

"It's not something I'm proud of."

She started slowly, telling him how Cordelia and Chess had become friends after Chess got a part in a play she was directing. It didn't take long for the entire story—the marriage, the money, the lies—to come tumbling out.

Through the telling, her father sat motionless. She said everything that came into her head, saying too much, too quickly, her explanations turning into rationalizations. She finally stopped—just stopped herself, too embarrassed to go on.

Her father remained silent for a few seconds, lacing his fingers over his stomach. "I wish you'd never met that man. He's a user. He used you then, and he's using you now."

"He swears he had nothing to do with Dial's murder. You're meeting with him this afternoon, right?"

Her father picked up his cup of coffee, held it to his chest, but didn't take a sip. "Quite honestly, Jane, I don't know that I'm willing to represent him. I didn't like him when I met him at the birthday party on Friday night. I liked him even less yesterday. And now, after what you've just told me—" He shook his head. "If he was a friend of yours, I would, of course, make the effort, but he's not."

Jane couldn't exactly disagree.

"Also, as much as you may not want to hear this, he may be guilty." Looking down into his cup, he continued, "I got a call a few minutes ago. Seems the police have been sitting on something. I don't know what it is, but it's big. I'll still meet with Chess this afternoon, but unless I hear something new, which I very much doubt, I'm going to recommend he find another lawyer."

"He doesn't have any money."

"Not my problem. And it's not yours either." Tapping his nose, he nodded to hers and said, "Are you going to tell me about that?"

She cleared her throat in preparation for a brave leap into a subject sure to upset her father even more. "Someone's searching for Chess. I got caught in the cross fire." She explained about Lee spotting two men watching the Lyme House. "Nolan saw one of them sitting in a car outside my house. He even chased the guy, but then lost him. Seems that these men think I'm still married to Chess."

Her father's frown deepened. "I don't want you anywhere near that guy, is that clear? I'm going to demand that he never contact you again. With any luck at all, he'll be in jail by tomorrow on a murder charge. Then let's pray these people, whoever they are, leave you alone. He's bad news, Janey. *Very* bad news. Are we on the same page?"

She raised her eyes to meet his. "Same page, same paragraph, same line."

22

Irina was relieved that Majid had made such great strides in reorganizing the first-floor gallery yesterday. If he hadn't, she would never have been able to meet with Chess and Julia Martinsen this morning. Unless Ms. Martinsen wandered into the smaller galleries—the three bedrooms that had been turned into climate-controlled exhibition spaces—she would never know that anything was wrong. To that end, Irina made sure those doors were locked.

Sitting on the stool behind the front counter, feeling fortified after downing half a Sausage McGriddle and a Diet Pepsi, Irina flipped open the cell phone that had been shrieking at her from inside her purse.

"Hello?"

"Honey?" came Steve's tentative voice. "It's me. How are you?"

He didn't sound angry, he sounded concerned. She could have dealt with anger, but not this. She wanted to hang up. "I'm okay."

"Are you? Really?"

"Aren't you still angry at me for shooting up the bedroom?"

"Not after I saw where the guy got in. He cut the back door screen. Broke the window and threw the dead bolt. I'm proud of you for what you did."

"You are?"

"You're a brave woman. You're even a pretty good shot. Most of the bullets actually hit the door."

His comments caught her off guard. "Just a mama bear protecting her young."

He remained silent for a few seconds. "I love you. I don't want to lose you."

"Or Dustin?"

"Or . . . Dustin."

He knew. Maybe he'd known all along.

"Come home."

"I can't."

"Why, Irina? If you're frightened, I can protect you."

"But you're leaving."

"I won't go."

She wanted him to go. She wanted the chance to build a new life with Chess and their son. "I need more time."

"Don't freak on me, okay? Go ahead. Stay with Misty. Until we can, you know, get things resolved. Oh, there's something I need to tell you. A woman from the medical examiner's office called about an hour ago. Your mother's body will be released tomorrow afternoon. They need the name of the funeral home you're using. They said they'd make the call and arrange the transfer."

Irina had so much to do—relatives to call, an obituary to write, the entire funeral to plan. Steve repeated the woman's name and number while she wrote it down on a piece of scratch paper.

"And your mom's lawyer called last night," continued Steve. "Something about getting you and Misty together to discuss the terms of the trust. Do you have his number?"

Irina didn't think any further discussion was necessary. She and Misty had both read the trust agreement many times. Getting together was a formality she could live without. "I'll take care of it."

"So, I mean, could we have lunch or something? Tomorrow?"

"I'll call you."

"Will you?"

His concern touched her. He had to know that their marriage was past the point of repair. Then again, a few days ago, she'd been waffling herself, wondering what to do. Now her path was clear, as clear as little Dusty's warm brown eyes. Her future was with Chess.

"Something wrong?" asked Julia.

Chess seemed on edge this morning. He turned and looked behind them as she pulled her Porsche into a parking space across the street from the Morgana Beck Gallery of Antiquities.

"Wrong?" repeated Chess. He fixed her with a smile of great warmth. "Nothing's wrong." After hesitating a moment, he added, "Well, to be honest, I thought I saw David's car behind us."

"David?"

"Let's just say he's an ex-lover and leave it at that."

Now she got it. "Someone who lives here in town?"

"Alas, yes. It's much too long a story and much too convoluted."

He didn't want to talk about his love life. Fine with her. She already had the beginnings of a bad headache brewing. "Say," she said, switching off the motor and removing the key, "speaking of exlovers, have you had a chance to put in a good word for me with Jane?"

This time his smile fairly twinkled. "We had a long talk last night. All about you."

"Really? And?"

"She's torn."

"About what?"

"Oh, you know Jane. She keeps so much inside. But I got the feeling that she believes she had her chance with you and she blew it."

"That's putting it mildly."

"I think, if you want to get your relationship back on track, that you need to do a little old-fashioned romantic wooing. Take it slow and easy. We all know Jane doesn't like to be pushed."

She was impressed that he understood Jane so well. They must have remained close, although if they had, Julia found it curious that Jane had never mentioned his name. "So, what do you think? Should I bury her office in flowers?"

"No, no. That's too overt. Try inviting her to dinner so she can see your new loft. I guarantee that if you don't make a pass at her, it will drive her nuts. Then find something only she can help you do. Reel her in inch by inch. Be sweet, caring, giving."

The approach he suggested was exactly what she had in mind, and yet it was good to learn that Jane was open to something more than the bare-bones friendship they currently enjoyed—or didn't enjoy, as the case might be.

"You'll keep working on her, right?" asked Julia.

"Count on it."

"She must trust you."

"I don't want to overstate my influence, but yeah, I think she does."

"Did you tell her I'm buying the seal and the bull from you?"

"No," he said, opening the passenger door and looking around before getting out. Facing her over the hood of the car, Chess added, "I keep all business private."

Just what Julia wanted to hear. Information was power—and power led to getting what you wanted, what you deserved.

They waited for the traffic to thin and then dashed across the street. Julia hadn't expected the gallery to be in an old duplex, although it shouldn't have come as a shock. Lots of businesses along

Grand in St. Paul were located in houses. This one was a beauty, well maintained, an antique in its own right.

The sign in the window said CLOSED, but the door was open. Carrying his leather briefcase, Chess led the way through dozens of tall freestanding displays to the back of the room. The walls were covered with lighted and mounted curio cabinets, paintings, masks, and every sort of ancient art. Classical music set an intimate, cultured tone. Julia was impressed.

A petite, thirty-something woman in a black sheath dress, a gray linen blazer, and a bold black and white scarf tied in a French twist around her neck stood behind a long glass counter. Chess introduced her as Irina Nelson, the daughter of Morgana Beck. Without the high-fashion clothes and discreetly applied makeup, the woman would have been plain as a stump, even mousy. Her hair was wheat blond, straight, and wispy—not quite lank, but not far from it. She was actually rather pretty if you looked carefully, but the deep circles under her eyes made her appear ill.

They shook hands, and then Chess removed the cylinder seal from the small wooden case. Irina took it from him and began her examination.

"This is quite fascinating," she said, her tone a mixture of surprise and reverence.

"Babylonian," said Chess.

"No, even older, I think. Sumerian." She carried it over to a desk, sat down, and turned on a small halogen light. Holding the seal under an enlarging glass, she studied it for several minutes, then removed a book from a shelf next to her and began to page through it. It took a while, but she eventually appeared to find what she was looking for. Before she returned to the counter, she measured the seal, made notations on a legal pad, and then took several Polaroid snapshots and a few digital pictures.

"Babylonian cylinder seals are mostly presentation scenes," she said, setting the seal on a black velvet display pad. "Earlier seals were much more creative, with a wider range of subject and theme. This one is somewhere between twenty-five hundred and three thousand years old. It's an extraordinary piece. Flying birds in rows, a temple gate, and what looks like a goddess picking fruit from a sacred tree. The tree is obviously a palm, not an apple tree, but many scholars believe this is where the origin of the forbidden fruit story in Genesis first came from. The palm was sacred in Mesopotamia and the Persian Gulf. For many reasons, civilization wouldn't have been possible without it."

"So, what's it worth?" asked Julia, running a finger along the carved surface.

"Two hundred and fifty to three hundred thousand. You could always take it over to the Institute of Arts, talk to a curator over there if you want a second opinion."

Julia was relieved that Irina was the one to suggest a second opinion. It put some of her worst fears to rest. "Do you have any sort of accreditation as an antiquities appraiser?"

Irina turned and gestured to a framed document hanging above the desk. "I'm an active member in good standing of the ISA, the International Society of Appraisers. I completed their accreditation program in 1999. I travel regularly to international art fairs, such as the BAAF in Basel, Switzerland, and in Brussels. My specialty is Holy Land antiquities. You can find all my credentials and more about me on our store Web site. Again, if you have any concerns, I would urge you to get another appraisal." Looking up at Chess, she asked, "How much are you asking for the seal?"

"Two hundred and fifty thousand."

"Then, in my opinion, Ms. Martinsen, you're getting a deal. Are you a private collector?"

"Not really. Although if I buy this, perhaps I can say it's the beginning of a collection."

"A worthy start," said Irina. "If you have the money, it's worth every penny." Glancing at Chess, she added, "May I see the provenance papers?"

Chess removed a manila envelope from his briefcase and handed it to her.

"Ms. Martinsen, do you have a card with your name and address on it? I need that information for the paperwork."

Julia slipped one from a thin hammered-brass card holder.

Irina appeared to know what she was doing. Even so, Julia studied her for anything that seemed false. As Woody Allen once said, *Paranoia is knowing all the facts.* Words to live by.

"Do you two know each other?" asked Julia, trying to make the question seem entirely casual.

"We met last year when I was in Istanbul on a buying trip," said Irina, sitting back down at the desk to read through the papers.

"At a cocktail party," said Chess. "It's a big world, but the antiquities community is relatively small. If you don't know the major players, at least you've heard of them."

For the next twenty minutes, Julia drifted around the gallery, examining everything on offer, from bronze axes to Roman amber glass cups to rings and bracelets and necklaces and beads. She was examining a Gnostic magical amulet when she felt a stabbing pain behind her right eye. She knew the signal. She would be spending at least part of the afternoon in bed.

Announcing that she was done, Irina stood again at the glass display counter and slid the provenance documents across to Julia along with her authentication and a two-page appraisal. She'd signed at the bottom and dated it. She asked Chess to sign on the line under her name.

"If you decide to buy the seal, you can sign right here." She pointed to the line next to BUYER. "I wish you the best of luck," she added, unsmiling.

"May I borrow your pen?" asked Julia, removing her checkbook from her purse.

Chess touched her arm. "Have you talked to your financial adviser about this?"

"He advised me to wait and think about it, talk to a couple of his friends who are collectors. But that's not necessary. I know what I want, and I want this." She signed the document with a quick scribble. "If you won't take a personal check, I'd be happy to go to my bank in the morning and get you a cashier's check."

"No, a personal check is fine," said Chess.

Julia wrote it out, feeling a surge of excitement.

Chess put the check in the breast pocket of his gray linen sport coat. He patted the pocket and then grinned. "I'm thrilled for you."

"Next up," she said, smiling broadly, "the Winged Bull of Nimrud."

23

Sunday afternoon didn't go quite the way Chess had expected. After Julia dropped him off at the Caribou Coffee on Forty-sixth and Nicollet, he planned to take a cab to Solera, a Spanish restaurant in the heart of downtown Minneapolis, which, according to everything he'd read in the local press, had the best tapas and traditional paella this side of Madrid. He wanted to celebrate the sale of the seal, and what better way to do it than with fabulous food.

However, instead of veal meatballs in a spicy honey glaze, piquillo peppers stuffed with goat cheese, and chorizo-stuffed dates with smoked bacon, he received a call on his cell from Ray Lawless. Ray explained that the police wanted to talk to him again downtown. Unlike yesterday, Ray urged him to make a show of cooperation. He said that he'd sit in on the interrogation and that afterward they could find a quiet corner and have a more complete conversation.

So, less than an hour later, Chess was seated in a small, airless room with Jane's dad, waiting for Sergeant Taylor to enter and start the grilling.

"Do you know what this is all about?" asked Chess, tapping his thumb and little finger rhythmically against the tabletop. The gesture betrayed his nervousness, but he couldn't stop himself. He felt keyed up. Apprehensive. The stony look on Ray's face didn't do much to alleviate his worry. The silver hair and kindly expression made Jane's dad appear approachable, even grandfatherly, but he seemed far less friendly today than he had yesterday.

"No idea," said Ray. "We'll just have to wait and see."

"Are you sure this is smart? Talking to the police, I mean."

"If the questions are general, your cooperation will help to establish your innocence."

Sounded like the party line, not what Chess expected from the man who was supposed to be his advocate.

Taylor entered a few minutes later, pulled out a chair, and sat down. He was so robust, his muscles so pumped, his manner so vigorous, that simply looking at him made Chess feel old.

Taylor flipped a file folder open, studied it for a few seconds, then placed his arms on either side of it and looked up at Ray, then at Chess. "Mr. Garrity, I have some questions I hope you can help me with. First, I want to thank you for coming down this afternoon."

Chess couldn't exactly say it was a pleasure, so he said nothing.

"Tell me how you met Melvin Dial."

He glanced over at Ray.

Ray nodded, giving him the go-ahead.

Forcing himself to remain calm, he said, "I deal in antiquities. I work for a broker in Amsterdam—Jan Ostrander. I believe I first met Dial through Jan."

"Antiquities," repeated Taylor, chewing the word over. "Are you familiar with the Morgana Beck Gallery of Antiquities in St. Paul?"

"Sure."

"Ever done business with Ms. Beck?"

"A couple of times."

"Do you know her well?"

"She's a business acquaintance."

"Did you see her this trip?"

"No reason to." He didn't like the direction this was headed but figured he'd play along. At some point, if Ray didn't stop him, he'd stop himself. Lawyers didn't know everything.

"The night Mr. Dial was murdered, where were you?" asked Taylor.

He looked at Ray again.

Ray nodded for him to continue.

Chess had already told a bunch of lies to Jane. He decided he might as well stick with them. He explained briefly about playing cards with Dial at his house on Tuesday night, how he needed more cash because he was losing. So he took out his passport, where he always kept a couple of extra hundred-dollar bills—but then what? He couldn't remember what he'd told Jane he'd done with it. On the fly, he made up another story.

"The card table had a small drawer in it. I slipped my passport into the drawer, just for safekeeping." Again he admitted that he was pretty drunk but stressed that when he left the house, Dial was fine. It wasn't until the next day that he realized his passport was still back at Dial's house. He went to get it around noon, found the front door open, and walked inside. Dial was gone. He thought it was strange that the door was unlocked but figured Dial had just forgotten. He looked in the drawer, but the passport wasn't there. He figured Dial had put it somewhere else, somewhere safer. He wasn't worried because Dial had said he'd call on Wednesday afternoon so they could set up another time to play. He jokingly called it a revenge match.

"Dial was being magnanimous," added Chess with a grim smile. "Said he'd give me a chance to get my money back."

"How much did you lose?" asked Taylor.

"A thousand, give or take."

"Were you good friends with Melvin Dial?"

"Cardplaying and drinking buddies."

"But never business?"

That was a tricky question. "Sure, over the years I'd sold him a few things. He was a collector. You probably already know that."

"Why are you in town, Mr. Garrity?"

Chess shrugged. "I'm from the Midwest, born in Chicago, went to the U of M for a few years. I wanted to come back and see what my old stomping grounds looked like."

"A walk down memory lane."

"If you like."

"That's all?"

"I'm always on the lookout for interesting antiquities." He wasn't sure, but he had the sense that Taylor was fishing.

Glancing back down at the open folder in front of him, Taylor turned a page and then looked up. "Are you aware that Morgana Beck was murdered on Wednesday night, the night after Melvin Dial was killed?"

Chess used every ounce of his acting skills to look shocked. "I had no idea."

"Where were you that night?"

He scratched the side of his head, looked down. "I went to a movie at the Riverview Theater. *Slumdog Millionaire* was showing. Seems everyone has seen it but me. It started around seven. I came out about nine." That much was true. He'd needed something to do that night until he could meet up with Irina and get back into Dial's house. "I ended up having dinner at a Mexican restaurant right next door. Sorry, I don't remember the name."

"Pepito's. Do you have a credit card receipt?"

"Paid cash. I didn't think I'd need an alibi," he added, salting the statement with just the right amount of disgust. "Are you suggesting I murdered both Dial and Beck? You think I'm some sort of serial killer?" He glanced over at Ray for support.

Ray's eyes bored into his.

Taylor straightened the file in front of him and then folded his hands on top of it. "So, you had nothing to do with Melvin Dial's death. No part in dumping his body in Minnehaha Park."

"None."

"He was fine when you left him Tuesday night."

"He walked me to the door, shook my hand, slapped me on the back."

"You were both feeling no pain."

"True."

"Was Dial feeling so little pain that he let you take his billfold with him when you left? All his credit cards? His driver's license?"

Oh God, thought Chess, slamming against a truth he couldn't talk his way out of. He'd been in such a hurry to leave Jane's house that he'd forgotten.

"I think we'd better stop there," said Ray.

"You told Dial's neighbor that you'd taken him to the airport and that you were watering his plants for him while he was gone."

"No, I—"

"Why did you say that?" demanded Taylor. He didn't wait for a response. "I'll tell you why. You knew he was dead because you killed him. The neighbor noticed that his mail was piling up, and you had to tell him something to make him think everything was okay."

"No, no—"

"But you made a couple of big mistakes. First, you dropped your passport in the grass when you dumped his body, a passport that had Dial's blood on it. Second, you removed Dial's wallet after you knifed him. We found the wallet taped to the back of a mirror in Ms. Lawless's third-floor apartment, the apartment you've been staying in for the past couple of days."

Chess felt all the blood drain from his face. He'd been hiding it from Jane, just in case she came up to snoop through his stuff. In all the chaos of packing so quickly, he'd never given it another thought.

"I had no reason to kill Dial. None. What was my reason? Tell me."

Ray placed a hand on Chess's shoulder. "Unless you're arresting Mr. Garrity, this conversation is over."

Taylor closed the folder. A uniformed officer entered the room.

"Stand up," ordered Taylor.

"What's happening? Ray?"

The uniformed officer handcuffed Chess's hands behind his back.

"Chess Garrity," said Taylor, his voice flat, "I am arresting you on a probable cause warrant in the murder of Melvin Dial."

"You mean I'm going to jail? I can't. Ray, tell him."

Instead of coming to his defense, Ray removed his hand.

While Irina was giving the appraisal, Majid had been sitting on the basement steps watching a spider build a web at the edge of the doorway. He didn't want her to know he was there. He hadn't expected her to show up on a Sunday morning, so thought it was safe to spend some more time cleaning. As soon as she'd left and locked up, he stood, removed a dust rag from his back pocket, and squashed the spider, sweeping the web away.

Crossing into the showroom, he sat down behind the desk. The papers were still spread across the top, so out of curiosity, he switched on the halogen light to examine the Polaroids. The image of the palm tree caught his eye.

Turning to the bookshelf next to him, he examined a series of reference volumes until he found what he was looking for. He paged through an exhaustive index and finally located the words "Kings of Sumer," then drew his finger down until "Adab, Dynasty of" appeared.

"What are you up to now?" he whispered, absorbed immediately by his search.

24

Unable to concentrate at work, Jane came home early on Sunday evening to cut the grass. She was relaxing on the back steps, cooling off with a cold beer, when her father walked in through the backyard gate. By the solemn look on his face, she knew he hadn't come with good news.

"Hi," she said, easing off the steps, brushing grass off her jeans.

"Don't get up."

"Want a beer?"

He leaned an arm against the iron railing. "No thanks. How's the nose feel?"

"I think it will live." She sat back down.

Mouse, who'd been rolling on the grass under the oak, tore himself away long enough to trot over and bury his muzzle in her father's hands, demanding a scratch.

"Hey there, big guy." He rubbed him energetically, from fore to aft.

"He's putty in your hands," said Jane, tipping back the beer bottle.

She hadn't had much to eat today, so one beer had given her a nice buzz.

Her father took off his sport coat and folded it over his arm, then sat down next to her. "Chess is being held on a probable cause warrant in Melvin Dial's murder."

"What's that mean?"

"Taylor believes he's guilty, but he wants more time to make his case. He may also be afraid that Chess was about to bolt. My guess is that Taylor is doing his best to link Dial's murder to the murder of Morgana Beck, an antiquities dealer in St. Paul. Have you heard about her?"

"I saw something on the news the other night. She owned a gallery."

"I don't understand what's going on, but Chess is definitely in the thick of it." He pulled his tie away from his collar and unbuttoned the top button of his shirt. "Seems Chess hid Dial's wallet upstairs in your third-floor apartment. The cops found it. If that isn't the final nail in his coffin, I don't know what would be."

"How did he explain it?"

"He didn't."

"Did you tell him you're pulling out, that you're not going to represent him?"

His gaze moved to the top of the oak tree. "As it turns out, it's not that simple. The police can keep him for seventy-two hours on a probable cause warrant. After that, he will either be charged or released. If he's charged, bail will be set at an arraignment. Chess wants out. That's all he's interested in. Doesn't matter how much it costs."

Jane heard the note of wariness in her dad's voice. "But he doesn't have any money."

"He has a check for two hundred and fifty thousand dollars."

"Where'd he get that?"

"He sold something. He said that once he's out, it would take a day or two to clear his bank, and then he could pay me back."

"You? He wants you to put up the bail money?"

"Me or you. Doesn't matter to him."

"Why on earth would we do that?"

"Because——" His jaw tightened. "He's your husband."

"You mean *was* my husband."

"No, honey. He still is. Did you ever really look at the divorce decree he sent you?"

She stared at him, her mouth open. "Are you telling me it was no good?" She erupted off the steps. "That the divorce was a sham?"

He reached for her hand.

"I don't believe you." She backed up. "I don't believe *him*. Why would he want to stay married to me?"

"You'll have to ask him that. Do you have a copy of the decree? I need to see it."

She felt a nauseating heat rise in her throat. "It's in my study." Rushing into the house, she found the folder marked MARRIAGE/ DIVORCE in the filing cabinet and brought it back to him. She crouched in the grass, biting a nail, waiting.

"The marriage was legal," said her father, removing his reading glasses after examining all the papers, "but the divorce documents are worthless. I'm sure he bought them."

"So what does that mean? Does he own half of my restaurants? My house? My investments?"

"I'm not one hundred percent sure about that. It's not my area of law. I'll have to check with a family law attorney."

"Are you kidding me? There's even a possibility of that? How do I get rid of him?"

"Jane, listen. This could get messy. That's why I agreed to help him. We need to keep him happy until I can figure the best way out for you."

She couldn't believe what she was hearing. "I am still *married* to that bastard? Do you know how much he's screwed up my life? I've got people following me around, people staking out my restaurant. Someone attacked me last night. Now I find out he might be able to grab half of everything I've worked for my entire life? I'm supposed to just stand here and take that?"

"For now, yes."

"But why send me fake divorce papers? Was he planning this all along?"

Her father's usual confidence seemed to have vanished. "I don't have the answer to that, but I'll do everything in my power to protect you. I'll call as soon as I learn anything. For the time being, why don't you stick around the house. The restaurants can get along without you for a few days."

"Sure."

"Call Cordelia. Have her bring Hattie and Mel over. You can watch a movie together, order a pizza. I don't want you to worry or be frightened. We'll figure this out."

She wasn't frightened. Not anymore. She was furious.

Irina had called Chess several times on Sunday afternoon and left messages, only to be sitting on the braided rug at the foot of her son's crib in their commandeered bedroom hours later, with no response. She wasn't sure how worried she should be. His cell phone could be out of juice, or he could have misplaced it. There was always the possibility, she supposed, that he'd pocketed the check from Julia Martinsen and taken off for greener pastures. Yet she resisted the idea. He said he loved her. She had to trust that love.

Dusty wiggled on his back under an infant activity gym, his pudgy arms grasping at colorful rattles and soft squeeze toys. Since he was so happily occupied, she tried calling Chess again. After six rings, his voice mail picked up. She leaned her back against the bed frame, closed the phone, and considered what to do next.

Misty had left the house with one of her disgusting male friends around four. Because Irina didn't have a babysitter, she was trapped at home. She hated herself for feeling that way. Dustin was a gift, and it was her responsibility to care for him and make sure he thrived.

The doorbell rang.

Thinking it was okay to leave him on the floor under the gym, Irina got up and dashed into the living room, finding the usual mess. Picking up empty beer cans on her way to the door, she spotted Steve's truck through the front window. He looked oddly subdued when she drew back the door and found him standing on the front steps.

"I thought maybe you'd let me take you out for dinner."

Food sounded good, but without Misty to babysit, it was impossible. "I can't."

"Why not?"

"I can't leave Dusty here by himself. You know that."

He bit the inside of his cheek, thought it over. "Let's take him with us."

"It's not safe."

He stepped inside, closing the door behind him. "He's got to go out sometime. Why not tonight?"

"But the germs."

"Listen to me, honey. I read something yesterday that said kids need to get used to germs. Being exposed to them actually makes their immune systems stronger."

She wasn't sure she believed him. It might be just another one of his ploys to get her to do something she knew was wrong.

"Come on. We need to talk, and by the looks of you, you need to eat."

"What's wrong with the way I look?"

"Nothing," he said, wrapping his arms around her.

The familiar aftershave pulled her in. The strength in his arms eased the tension inside her. She hated herself for being so weak, for needing a man to lean on.

"Can't you, just for a couple hours, bend a few of your rules? I miss you. I want to help you, if you'll let me." He gave her his best lopsided grin.

She did have that new car seat, but she still wasn't sure it was the right thing to do. Turning toward the doorway into the kitchen, she saw that the counter was covered in plates with half-eaten sandwiches, boxes of cereal, open jars of food, empty Campbell's soup cans, coffee mugs, banana peels, and more beer cans. The sink was mounded high with dirty dishes. Misty was using the place as a crash pad and nothing more. This was no place for her and Dusty.

"I'll change my clothes."

"Great," said Steve, rubbing his hands together. "Anywhere you want to go is fine with me—as long as it serves steak."

As she walked past the couch, she noticed that her purse was sticking out from behind one of the pillows.

"Something wrong?" asked Steve.

Misty must have been going through it. Irina picked it up, flipped the top back, and drew out her pocketbook.

"You lose something?" asked Steve.

"Everything seems to be here."

"Misty wouldn't steal from you, if that's what you're thinking."

As if he knew Misty as well as she did. She wasn't sure why he was coming to her sister's defense, because, if history served, he didn't even like her. She stuffed her pocketbook back into her purse, next to the sunglasses she'd found at the gallery. Pulling them out, she held them up. "These yours?"

"Hey, I thought I'd lost them. Where'd you find them?"

She stepped into the hallway, glancing into the bedroom to make sure Dusty was still okay on the floor. "At the gallery."

A guilty look passed over his face.

"You went there?" she asked.

"Your mom called me last Monday, asked me to stop by."

"Mom called *you*? About what?"

He sat down on the edge of a chair and folded his arms across his chest. "Just stuff."

"What stuff?"

"Why do you always push so hard?"

"Because I like to know what the people in my life are saying about me behind my back."

"Why do you assume she wanted to talk about you?"

"Did she?"

He looked down, shrugged. "She was concerned about our marriage."

"Why would she talk to you and not me?"

"She tried talking to you, Irina, tons of times, but every time she did, you blew her off."

This was the last straw. "I don't need people in my life who can't support me."

"Since your mother's dead, I assume that means me."

"I think you'd better leave."

He stood, the muscles along his jawline tightening. "If that's what you want. But first, answer one question. If a person doesn't agree with you completely, with all your choices, all your opinions and every other little goddamn thing you do, does that mean he doesn't support *you*? Or love you?"

"You're twisting my words."

"Listen to yourself. The closer we get to actually having a real conversation about the issues in our marriage—our lives—the higher you build a wall. You cut off all discussion by saying that I don't love you, or that I don't understand you."

"You don't."

"Irina—"

"I know where you're headed. We're talking about Dusty now, right? You don't think I'm taking care of him properly. You think I'm losing my grip on reality."

"Not losing, Irina. *Lost*."

"Okay, so let's talk about the real issue here. The one we've been skirting since the day he was born." She hesitated, knowing that when she said the words out loud, she could never take them back. "You're not his father. You know it and you hate me—and Dustin—for it."

She couldn't read his expression, but when he started to laugh, she got angry.

"You think it's funny that I slept with another man? His name is Chess Garrity. I met him on the trip I took last year to Istanbul."

That stopped him. "You actually . . . you mean—"

"I love him and he loves me."

"This is for real? *He's* for real?"

"He's an antiquities dealer, an American who lives in Istanbul and Amsterdam."

"Antiquities," he repeated, a frown forming. "A friend of your mother's?"

"She knew him, but not that we were in love. As a matter of fact, he's here in town right now. He came to ask me to marry him. I gave him my answer this last night. He loves me, Steve, which is more than I can say for you. He's proud to have such a handsome son."

There it was again, the look she couldn't read. Not that she cared. Not everything she'd told him was the absolute truth, but it was close enough.

Misty burst through the front door looking flushed and buoyant. "I picked up Mom's wheels," she said, pointing out the window at the

Audi Roadster parked in front of the house, behind Steve's truck. She rattled a set of keys. "Drives like a dream. Think I'll keep it."

"Who told you you could have Mom's car?" demanded Irina.

"Nobody," said Misty, giving Steve a wink, "but it was going to get a ticket if it sat there on Grand much longer." She dumped her two sets of keys on the coffee table in the living room and headed into the kitchen.

Irina picked up both sets. She recognized the one that had belonged to her mother because of the custom leather key fob. Misty had only three keys on hers. A house key, a key to her trashy Cougar, and, much to Irina's surprise, a key to the gallery.

Her sister sauntered back into the living room, taking a swig from a can of beer. "What did I miss?" she asked, throwing herself onto the couch. "You two look supremely jolly."

"Walk me out to my truck," said Steve.

Misty glanced at Irina, stuck out her tongue, then got up and followed him out.

Irina watched through the front picture window as her husband, clearly upset, talked animatedly to her sister. Before he climbed into his truck, the two of them embraced. They were generally civil to each other, but this was the first time she'd ever seen them express any physical affection. It startled her. It startled her even more when the embrace went on long past the point of a simple cheer-up hug.

25

 Still *married?*" Cordelia choked the last word through the phone line. "Is this a joke?"

"I wish it were," said Jane, holding her cordless between her shoulder and ear as she searched through the refrigerator, trying to figure out if she had the makings for a quiche Lorraine. Apparently, outrage made her hungry.

"This rarely happens to me, Janey. I'm speechless."

"I'm sure your ability to communicate will return momentarily."

"Stop all that rattling."

"Can't."

"Why not?"

"Because I need to make something to eat."

"At a time like this?"

"Nothing I learned from my dad changes the fact that I'm hungry."

After showering and changing into fresh clothes, Jane had come downstairs into the kitchen and called Cordelia. She'd needed a reality check. Okay, so Cordelia wasn't necessarily the best choice for that, but she was home and therefore available to talk.

"What are you making?"

"A quiche Lorraine. I've got everything but Swiss or gruyère. I do, however, have an excellent Grafton Vermont cheddar, which should do just fine."

"Not if you run into a French chef."

"There aren't any French chefs around the house at the moment, and besides, French cooking is all about theme and variations. I think the Cordon Bleu would even approve, or at the very least grant me a dispensation."

"Should we put out a contract on Chess's life?"

"I knew you'd come up with a workable plan." She looked through a drawer for a cheese grater. "Did I tell you somebody jumped me last night as I was about to get in my car? I almost got my nose broken."

"Last night? I saw you last night when I brought Val to the restaurant."

"It happened later. When I was on my way to my car. The guy was looking for Chess. Since I'm still his little woman—"

"You think they know that?"

"The guy called me his wife."

"I'm coming over. We need to figure out a plan of attack."

"No plans of attack, remember? I'm letting Nolan and the police figure this one out. I've got enough on my hands trying to protect my assets from from a lying ex-friend." The cell in her back pocket vibrated. "Hold on. I'm getting another call. Hello," she said, pressing the cell to her other ear. Both ears were now covered.

"Jane, hi, it's Julia."

"Hey, what's up?"

"Who is it?" demanded Cordelia.

"Just stick a sock in it until I'm done."

204

"What?" said Julia.

"I was talking to someone else."

"Are you alone?"

"Actually, I am."

"And you're talking to someone?"

"To explain would take too much time."

"Explain what?" said Cordelia.

"Listen, I was wondering if you'd like to come over, see my new loft tonight," said Julia. "If you haven't eaten, I could make us dinner. Nothing elaborate. Maybe a Caesar salad. Bread. Wine. It's a beautiful evening. We could eat on the balcony. I guess I'm feeling a little lonely and thought it might be nice to have some company."

Several responses presented themselves. First, Jane could say, "Are you kidding? Cordelia says you're a predator and I should stay away from you." Or she could say, "I'm the last person on earth to help you with your loneliness." Or she could simply grab the nearest crucifix and hold it in front of the phone.

"Tell you what," said Jane, thinking the invitation sounded just dandy. She needed to get out of the house, stop grinding her teeth, and try to develop a little perspective. "I'm making a quiche. What if I prep it here and we bake it at your place? I assume the new loft came with an oven."

"New loft," said Cordelia. "Who has a new loft?"

"Yes, Jane, I have an oven."

"Whoever it is, get rid of them," said Cordelia. "I need to talk to you."

"I'll be there in half an hour."

"Great," said Julia. She repeated the address and then said goodbye.

"You'll be *where* in half an hour?" demanded Cordelia. "I thought I was coming over."

"Julia's invited me to see her new loft."

"And you're going? Janey, you need to see a doctor. Bumps on the head can be dangerous."

"I got bumped on the nose. What does the Mayo Clinic say about that?"

"I'm going to come over there to sit on you."

"I'll be gone before you get here. I'll call you tomorrow."

"Don't you hang up."

Jane hung up.

While Julia finished up in the kitchen, Jane stood on the balcony, breathing in the night air and enjoying the last rays of the peach-colored sunset over Lake Calhoun. It had been the right decision to come. She needed to change gears, to put some psychological distance between herself and Chess's betrayal. Julia wasn't part of the problem, and that made a certain amount of relaxation possible.

Stepping back inside, Jane found Julia sitting at the piano, paging through some sheet music. "I haven't heard you play in years," she said, sitting down on one of the matching love seats.

"I'm out of practice."

"That's what you always used to say."

"It was never truer than it is right now." She thought for a moment. "Here's something."

Jane picked up her wineglass and leaned back against the cushions. She didn't recognize the piece but enjoyed watching Julia. How could there not be a connection after the kind of love they'd once shared? It wasn't love anymore—and yet it was something. It *meant* something.

When the last note sounded and Julia removed her hands from the keys, Jane asked what the song was.

"Mozart. One of his piano sonatas. I have a book of them my mother left me."

"I've never heard you play so beautifully."

"It's the piano."

"Only partly." She'd noticed a certain strain in Julia's eyes during dinner. "Are you feeling okay? You just picked at your food. Or maybe you don't like my cooking."

"I have a headache. I've been having a lot of them lately."

"Have you seen a doctor?"

"Several. And I've had tests done. So far, everything has come back normal."

"Except you've still got the headaches. Must be frustrating."

"Everything about being sick is frustrating. I took something for the pain, but it's not helping much."

"Are you in a lot of pain?"

"Moderate."

"Do you want me to go?"

"I'll have the headache either way. No, stay. I had another reason for asking you to come by tonight." She nodded to a wooden box on the coffee table. "I bought myself a present this morning. I wanted to show it off."

Jane leaned forward and opened the box. Inside was a piece of carved stone, about two inches high and maybe three-quarters of an inch thick. "Looks old."

"It is. It's a Sumerian cylinder seal." She explained everything she knew about it, ending by saying that she'd bought it from Chess. "I met him at your dad's birthday party the other night."

"And he used the opportunity to sell you this?" She wondered how many other people he'd cornered.

"He said he sold antiquities, so I asked him to come by the loft yesterday morning. He didn't twist my arm, if that's what you're thinking. I got it appraised this morning."

"Where?"

"The Morgana Beck Gallery in St. Paul. It's highly reputable. I asked around, called a few people. The woman who did the appraisal encouraged me to take it over to the Institute of Arts to have one of their curators give me a second opinion."

"But you didn't."

"Chess had proof of provenance. Irina Nelson, Morgana Beck's daughter, does this all the time. She's licensed. Very professional."

Chess was accused of murdering Melvin Dial. The police were trying to connect the murder of Dial to Morgana Beck. This was sounding more and more fishy, not to say coincidental. "If you don't mind my asking, how much did you pay for it?"

"Two hundred and fifty thousand dollars."

"Are you kidding me?"

"You act like I got taken."

Jane looked down at the seal cradled in her palm. "I don't know how to say this, other than to just come right out with it. Chess is not somebody I'd trust."

"What do you mean? He's staying with you. You've been . . . friends for years."

"Did he tell you that?"

"That and a lot more."

"Like what?"

Julia hesitated, rising from the piano bench and picking up her wineglass. Folding herself onto the love seat across from Jane, she said, "He said he could tell that I cared about you, so he confided that he was worried about you, that you seemed . . . lost."

"What the hell is that supposed to mean?"

"Don't get angry. He loves you a lot. He told me you two had once been married."

"*What?*"

"Was he lying?"

Jane moved to the edge of her seat. It was all she could do not to get up and start screaming. "No, he wasn't lying. He was manipulating. Gaining your confidence with a confidence of his own."

208

"Are you telling me that the seal is fake?"

"Honestly, Julia, I have no idea. I'm not sure you do either."

"But the appraisal—"

"Morgana Beck was murdered on Wednesday night."

Julia stared back blankly. "I didn't know that. But what's it got to do with the seal? And with Chess?"

"Another man, a collector, was murdered the night before. His name was Melvin Dial. Chess is being held on suspicion—"

"He's in jail?"

"The police think he murdered Dial, and they're trying to link it to the murder of Morgana Beck."

"But . . . that can't be. If he murdered her, why would her daughter be so friendly with him?"

"It's a good question, one I can't answer."

Julia looked around the room, pressing a couple of fingers against her forehead. "He wanted to sell me something else. The Winged Bull of Nimrud. He showed me a picture."

Jane almost laughed out loud. "Sounds like something from a Harrison Ford movie." Then she remembered one of the questions her attacker had asked last night. Something about a bull.

"He gave me a picture of it," said Julia.

"Can I see it?"

"You can have it." She nodded to a small brass box on an end table.

Jane removed a snapshot and leaned toward a row of candles on the coffee table. "He said this thing was real?"

"And enormously valuable."

"How much did he want for it?"

"A million two hundred and fifty thousand." Her eyes hardened. "Nobody swindles me and gets away with it. I'll cancel the check. There's nothing he could do with it today because it's Sunday."

"You wrote him a personal check?" It must be the one her father had told her about—Chess's financial ace in the hole. Now Julia was about to cancel it. Jane felt like a kid at Christmastime who'd just been give the biggest, baddest gift in the world.

"First thing in the morning, I'll call my bank." Julia finished her wine. "Tell me something. Did he ever talk to you about me?"

"You mean about selling you the seal?"

"No, just in general."

"Why would he?"

She ran a finger along the top of her wineglass. "No reason."

Majid glanced at a menu, sitting at a table by the windows. When the waitress finally appeared—she'd been standing by the open kitchen, talking to one of the cooks—he ordered a cheeseburger and fries and asked for a refill on his coffee. She acted as if he were a weirdo for ordering a burger at a Greek restaurant, but it was on the menu, so screw her.

Pushing the empty mug around in his hand, he looked back at the woman who had seated him. She stood next to the cash register talking to a man and a woman who were paying their bill. Majid couldn't use the phone at the gallery, and he couldn't use his cell. That's why he'd driven here so late on a Sunday night. The waitress was probably pissed at him because he'd come fifteen minutes before closing time. If she didn't lighten up, he could easily linger over his meal for hours. He'd brought a book.

Once the customers had left, Majid pushed away from the table and walked over to the counter. "Could I use your house phone? I need to make a call."

The woman handed him a cordless as she rang up the sale.

He removed a sheet of scratch paper from his vest pocket and punched in the number. Stepping over to a bench in the front foyer, he sat down. He'd already decided to use an accent. He might sound like a Texan, but his mother spoke with an Iranian accent softened by years of living in Britain. He had a good ear and could slip into it with no effort at all.

"Hello?" said the woman's voice.

"Is this Julia Martinsen?"

"Who's calling?"

"You bought the Sumerian cylinder seal, yes?"

"Who are you?"

"It was stolen from the Baghdad Museum in Iraq. You must return it. You must not keep it. Do you understand me?"

"Stolen? You mean it's real?"

"Very real, madam. If you thought it was not real, why did you purchase it?"

"I . . . who are you?"

"A friend. Do what is right. You will be cursed if you do not."

He hadn't planned that last bit, it just came out. Smiling to himself, he hung up and handed the phone back and then went to his table to eat his burger. Slowly.

26

The next morning dawned gray and rainy. Shortly after ten, Jane left her house, backing her car out of the driveway in a dreary downpour. She wasn't positive, but at first she thought she was being followed. A van had been parked just up the street. As she passed it, the driver pulled away from the curb. It disappeared in traffic before she turned onto the freeway. When she sped off onto the Lexington Avenue exit, nobody came off after her. She figured she was safe. Even so, it reminded her of an ant crawling up her leg at a picnic. Even when she looked and knew nothing was there, she still felt it.

Parking across the street from the gallery, Jane grabbed her umbrella and slid out. The clouds were starting to break up. Perhaps a change in the weather would give her mood a lift.

Halfway up the front walk, she saw a sign in the front window that said CLOSED. Perfect. She should have called before she drove over, but she hadn't because she'd been itching for movement. She wanted to look at the gallery, maybe meet Irina Nelson, ask if she knew

213

Chess personally, if she thought he had anything to do with her mother's murder.

Jane was studying the turret that jutted off the east side of the house when a man's voice said, "Can I help you?" Turning around, she found a dark-skinned, Arabic-looking man with a trimmed beard, sultry brown eyes, and a serene expression standing a few feet behind her.

"Oh, hi. The gallery's closed." Always good to start a conversation by stating the obvious.

"We'll be open again tomorrow."

She was surprised by the broad Texas accent. "Do you work here?"

"I'm the manager. Majid Farrow."

"I was sorry to hear about——"

"Morgana? Yeah. It was a blow to all of us."

"Do the police know who did it?"

"Not that I've heard." He stared at her for a few seconds. "You look kinda familiar. Have we met?"

Her dad's run for governor had splashed her face across way too many news reports. "Jane Lawless."

"Oh, sure. You're Raymond Lawless's daughter. He lost."

He sounded awfully chipper about it.

"Yes, he did."

"I liked him," he continued, "but when it came right down to it, I couldn't bring myself to vote for him."

"That's okay. I forgive you."

He seemed to like that and grinned.

"Do you give appraisals?"

"Are you a collector?"

Honesty might be the best policy, but it didn't always get you the information you wanted. "I am."

"Sure, we do appraisals. May I ask what you have?"

214

Might as well shoot the moon. She showed him the snapshot of the bull.

"This is quite beautiful."

"It's called the Winged Bull of Nimrud."

"Are we talking the Nimrud gold?"

How the hell did she know? "Of course."

"As far as I know, all of the Nimrud gold is in a vault in Baghdad. Are you sure what you have is authentic?"

"That's what I need to find out—before I buy it."

"So it's not in your possession."

"Not at the moment."

He nodded. "Well, sure. Bring it by." He took out his billfold and handed her a card. "Give me a call and we can set up a time. I'd love to take a look."

"I'll do that. You've been very helpful."

"We aim to please." His Texas accent implied, although he didn't actually add, *little lady.*

"Married, huh?" Nolan eyed her with amusement.

"It's not funny."

"It's kind of funny."

"Not if Chess comes after me and demands half of what I'm worth before he'll grant me a divorce."

"And you found this out after he was arrested?" He blew on his coffee before he took a sip.

"My dad gave me the good news last night."

He whistled. "Bet that's a conversation you'll never forget."

Wiping up a spill off the Formica-topped table with a paper napkin, she didn't answer.

"You're about as tightly wound as I've ever seen you," said Nolan, "and that's saying something."

Nolan had called her as she was leaving the gallery, said he had a few minutes and why didn't they meet at the coffee shop, the only one he ever went to these days—Anodyne on Forty-third and Nicollet. He'd more or less made it his official office away from his home office. He didn't care about the organic coffee, or the grungy chic ambience; it was the cold meat loaf sandwiches that had won his heart.

"I got a lead on why those men are trying to find Chess." She removed the snapshot of the bull from her shirt pocket and handed it to him.

"What's this?"

"The Winged Bull of Nimrud. It's an ancient artifact. Apparently, it's worth over a million dollars. Chess has it. He's trying to sell it to my friend Julia Martinsen. I got jumped on Saturday night by one of the guys watching the restaurant."

"You *what*? Is that why your nose is bruised?"

"Yeah, but listen. The first question the attacker asked me was did I know where Chess was. I lied, told him he was in Chicago. Then he said, 'What about the bull?' I had no idea what he was talking about until I went over to Julia's place last night for dinner. She gave me the snapshot, told me Chess wanted to sell it to her. The more I think about it, the more sure I am that everything that's happened has been related to this bull. Somebody wants it, and they're willing to kill for it."

Nolan handed the photo back. He removed his mirrored sunglasses and began to clean the lenses with a paper napkin. "You think Dial's death and Beck's are related?"

"Yeah, I do. That's why I've got to talk to Chess. I called over to the jail this morning, and they said he can't have any visitors."

"Not until he's charged. And if and when he is charged, unless you're on his visitor's list, you won't get in. 'Course, sometimes those lists are kind of slow getting to the right desk."

Her attention was drawn abruptly to the front windows. A long-haired blond man stood outside looking in. When their eyes met, he turned and took off.

"That's one of them," said Jane.

Nolan glanced over his shoulder.

"The blond guy with the long hair."

Nolan unsnapped his shoulder holster strap with a flick of his thumb and rushed outside. Jane waited a couple of seconds, not sure she wanted to come face-to-face with the guy again, but decided that if Nolan caught up to him, he might need her help. She pushed back her chair and raced out after them. She made it to the next block before she realized she'd taken a wrong turn. She retraced her steps, listening and looking, trying to determine where they'd gone. When she reached the alley behind the coffeehouse, she stopped. Nolan was about fifty yards in, but instead of beating the crap out of the guy, he was crouched down, talking to him.

She sprinted toward them. "Hey."

As Nolan rose, she saw that it wasn't the blond guy he'd been talking to but Lee. He was sitting on the ground, his back against a garbage can, rubbing his jaw and swearing.

"The asswipe clipped me," he said, moving into a crouch and then standing up. "I shoulda had him. I would have, too, except I tripped." He kicked a rock into the garage on the other side of the alley.

"You know this guy?" asked Nolan, still breathing hard from the chase. He was in good shape for a sixty-year-old, but he wasn't as young as he used to be.

"A. J. Nolan," said Jane. "Meet Lee. Don't know if that's a first or last name."

"Lee Northcutt." He stuck out his hand, and Nolan shook it.

"How did you know that man was following me?" asked Jane.

"Because I've been following both of you," said Lee, a red welt appearing just above his jawline. "I had nothing better to do. Actually, it was kind of fun, and I thought it might help you."

217

"I never saw you."

"You wouldn't. I'm a lot better at what I do than those idiots."

"Will someone explain to me what's going on?" asked Nolan, hands rising to his hips.

"This is the guy I told you about," said Jane. "The preacher who noticed the restaurant was being staked out. Let's go back to Anodyne. I'll buy you each a round coffee and we can talk."

"I'd rather have a beer," said Lee.

"Me, too," said Nolan.

The rainy morning had given way to a muggy midday. It was days like this, especially the humid early summer, when Jane felt the entire world was about to mold and rot.

"Fine, beer it is."

They walked over to the Driftwood, where Jane stood at the bar and paid for the brews, then snaked her way back to the table.

They all clicked bottles and took thirsty swallows.

"Lee's an ex-cop," said Jane. "Ex-seminarian. Ex–security consultant."

"At the moment, I'm living on my severance pay. I'm also an ex–army brat. Lived all over the country. I guess I'd like to find a place to settle." He turned the longneck around in his hand.

"Maybe you should become an anti-preacher," said Jane.

"Probably wouldn't pay very well. Besides, at the end of the day, nobody ever changes anybody else's mind."

"I use to be a cop," said Nolan. "Worked homicide."

"I worked mostly vice. In Chicago."

"You know Dwayne Tateum?"

"Sure. I know him well. I was married back then. My wife and me and Dwayne and Ann used to bowl together. We even joined a league one year."

"Small world," said Jane.

"Yup," said Nolan, tipping back his bottle. "You know Al Bruns?"

"Not well. He transferred from vice to narcotics just after I transferred in."

"Where'd you work as a security consultant?" asked Nolan.

"Atlanta. Mears & Hallick. Ever heard of them?"

"Good group."

"But I got sick of it. The pay was okay, but it bored the hell out of me. I guess I need a little more action."

"Ever thought of doing PI work?"

Jane turned and looked at Nolan.

"I knew a few PIs in Chicago. All they did was chase husbands around to see if they were cheating, or sometimes they'd wait in a hotel parking lot all night to get photos of the wife and her lover."

"I don't do that sort of thing," said Nolan. "I only take cases that interest me."

"How do you survive?"

"Very well. I've got one of the best reps in town."

"Huh. Never actually thought a PI could survive being selective."

"Team up with me," said Nolan.

Jane's look turned into a stare. Was he doing this to bait her, to make the point that she wasn't the only game in town?

"Just until we figure out what's going on with Jane," continued Nolan. "I could use your help, and so could she. If you like it, you can stick around, work with me on another case. No strings."

Lee touched the bruise on his jaw. "Hell, I suppose I'm already involved. I'd love to get another crack at that guy." Smiling his gap-toothed smile at Jane and then at Nolan, he said, "Count me in."

27

Jane was prepping the ingredients for the old-fashioneds, getting out the glasses, the maraschino cherry juice, an orange, a lemon, and a lime, finding the rock candy swizzle sticks, and opening up a new bottle of rye, when her landline rang.

"It's *me*," came Cordelia's excited voice. "I'm outside. Let me in, let me in."

"Is the doorbell broken?"

"Don't joke, not at a time like this."

"Use the keypad. I'm in the kitchen cutting up citrus fruit."

"How can you even *think* about vitamin C when—"

"Sigrid is stopping by in a few minutes."

Cordelia barreled into the kitchen, cell phone still attached to her ear. "I was in the 'hood. Thought I'd stop." She grabbed Jane and gave her what she probably thought of as a sustaining hug. To Jane it felt more like being mugged. "You need *moi* at a time like this, not Sigrid." She reached down and gave Mouse a friendly rub.

"Steal something new from the theater's costume department?"

asked Jane, nodding to a silk confection that had come straight out of Maxfield Parrish's drawing of Ali Baba. Red robe over white tunic. Lots of gold braid. All that was missing was the Arabian sword.

"Come," she said, dragging Jane by the scruff of her sweatshirt into the living room and dropping her down on the couch. "Now," she said, pacing back and forth in front of the cold fireplace, "we have to talk."

Mouse hunkered down a few feet away to watch.

"How Chester could have failed me so I will never understand."

"Failed *you?*"

"I'm afraid I come with more bad news." She all but fell onto the couch. "Mel phoned a few minutes ago. Seems the cops finally arrested Chester—officially—and charged him with Dial's murder. Mel said the reports coming across the wire were reporting that you were once married to him. She thinks the story is about to break in a big way."

"Define 'in a big way.'"

"It will make the nightly news, the newspapers, and you might even see a few reporters camped on your doorstep."

Jane put her head in her hands and groaned.

"It's just the kind of juicy personal story people love. *Prominent Lesbian Once Married to Murder Suspect. Details at Ten.* But now, see, it's going to be, *Prominent Lesbian Adoring Wife of Murder Suspect. Lesbian Daughter of Onetime Candidate for Governor, Raymond Lawless, Murder Suspect's Better Half.*"

"You can stop. I get the picture."

"Mel thinks the police leaked the marriage stuff."

"Why?"

"To put pressure on you to cooperate."

"But I have cooperated. More or less."

"They must think you have information you're keeping quiet about."

Everyone, it seemed, had come to the same conclusion.

"This next bit may seem like a parasitic request from a member of the fourth estate, but it's not. It's an offer to help. Mel thinks you should get the truth out there before everybody starts to play fast and loose with the facts. She wants to do an interview with you, to be published in the *Daily TwinCitian* in the next couple of days."

The doorbell rang.

"That must be Sigrid," said Jane, getting up, more eager than ever to get to those old-fashioneds. "Don't say anything about this to her, okay?"

"My luscious lips are zipped, but let's get rid of her fast."

Jane held up a finger for quiet as she hit the OFF button on the security pad and drew back the door. She didn't always engage the security system these days, but since Chess left, she'd had it on constantly.

"Hey, there," said Sigrid, grinning, standing with her hands on the shoulders of her daughter.

"Mia," said Jane, "I didn't know you were coming."

Mia kept her eyes on the ground, twisting her mouth from one side to the other, looking thoroughly disgruntled.

"Julia canceled her meeting with Peter, so he dropped Mia and me off while he takes care of some business in Uptown. We've got about an hour."

"Why'd she cancel the meeting?"

"Not feeling well, I guess."

"Is something wrong with—" Jane nodded to Mia.

"She's monumentally pissed at Peter and me." Sigrid shuffled into the foyer behind her daughter.

Mouse trotted into the room, dropped a bone at Mia's feet, and licked her hand until she petted him. Still Mia didn't smile or look up.

"We found a therapist who can sign," continued Sigrid, checking out Cordelia's getup as she entered from the living room. "I assume the Forty Thieves will be along any minute."

Cordelia gave her a wan smile.

"Anyway, Mia had her second meeting with the therapist this afternoon."

"Not going well, I take it," said Jane, bending down to run her hand gently along Mia's arm. "Hi," she said. "I'm glad you could come. I have an art book for you. I'll give it to you before you go."

Mia nodded, then looked over at Cordelia.

"Wanna play with that chalk in the drive again?" asked Cordelia, signing to Mia as she spoke.

Mia gave a halfhearted shrug.

"Would you rather watch TV?" asked Jane.

Again the girl shrugged. At the moment, shrugs seemed to be her only form of communication.

"Come on," signed Cordelia. "I might even be able to scare us up a black cherry soda if that ogre of a mother of yours doesn't object."

That drew a slight smile.

Sigrid drifted around the kitchen as Jane loaded the cocktail shaker with fruit.

"I didn't expect Cordelia to be here," said Sigrid.

"She stopped by a few minutes ago. If you don't want to talk in front of her—"

"She's family. Besides, she'll pry it out of you, one way or the other. To be honest, there's not much to tell. Peter and I finally worked out our differences. For now, divorce is off the table."

Jane had just finished crushing the fruit in the bottom of the shaker when Cordelia breezed in through the back door.

"Got her all set up with a nice can of pop and the chalk. That Mia is one pissed-off puppy."

"Tell me about it," said Sigrid.

Jane added a generous portion of the rye, a touch of maraschino cherry juice, bitters, and ice and shook it all up together, straining

224

the liquid into three tumblers. She dropped a rock candy swizzle stick in each glass and passed them out.

Mouse, a bone gripped in his teeth, curled up on the rug by the back door. For him, at least, all was well with the world.

"So, you and Peter are back together, riding the happily-ever-after train?" asked Cordelia, sitting down at the kitchen table, pushing out the other chairs with her foot, inviting everyone to join her.

"Pretty much," said Sigrid.

"But at the birthday party," said Jane, "when I asked you if everything was okay, you said 'yes and no.'"

"Oh, I was just angry at him that night. He was being a butt-head."

"What about school?" said Jane. "You wanted to go back and get another master's, and then go on for a doctorate."

"That documentary Peter did of your father's campaign got some real buzz going for him. The finished film will be making the rounds of independent festivals this summer and next fall. He's already had a couple of good offers to work on other documentaries. It may mean that he's out of town more than he'd like, but we'll work it out. I'll go to school part-time. Mia's our number one focus at the moment."

Jane had a sense that there was more to the story, but whether it was because Sigrid didn't feel comfortable talking about the details of her marriage in front of Cordelia, or she simply didn't want to get into it, Jane had no way of knowing. "I've never understood how love can die," she said, sipping her drink. "I know it does. It's happened to me. I still don't understand it. I get even less how you could ever restore love once it's gone."

"Maybe you can't if it's really gone for good," said Sigrid, "but if the spark is still there—"

"I thought you and Peter were finished. That's what you told me. You wanted different things. He wanted kids, a white picket fence, and a conventional life."

"He's got Mia now, which has gone a long way toward filling his need for a child. And he's changed," she said, sucking on her swizzle stick. "After that mess last fall, he's a different man. I can't explain it, except to say that he's willing to take risks now, willing to rock the boat. I can't say we'll be together forever, but for now, our life together is good. More than good."

"It happened for Mel and me," said Cordelia. "We were apart for years before we got back together."

Jane turned her drink around in her hand. "It's still a mystery to me."

"That's exactly what love is," said Cordelia. "Read the philosophers, the romantic poets. Read the biography of my life, once it's written."

"The world is definitely waiting for *that* book," said Sigrid, stifling a yawn.

They talked—and argued—companionably through the first round of drinks and then a second.

"I guess I'd better go get Mia," said Sigrid, tipping the glass back and finishing the last few drops. "Peter should be back any minute. We're having dinner tonight with a documentary director, a woman Peter is hoping to work with. She's in town on business, lives in New York."

Jane and Cordelia remained at the table as Sigrid got up and left through the back door.

"Returning to the subject of the death of love," said Cordelia, dipping her swizzle stick back into the drink. "You weren't thinking about Julia, were you?"

"Yeah, I guess I was. Julia and Kenzie."

"You can do better."

"To be honest, I'm exhausted by the entire subject."

"'The course of true love never did run smooth;'" Willy Shakespeare wrote that."

"A wise man."

Sigrid burst back into the room. "I can't find her."

"Mia?" said Jane, getting up.

"She knows the rules. She's not supposed to go anywhere unless she tells me."

"We'll help you find her," said Jane.

Just as they got outside, Peter drove up. He parked his Mustang in front of the house and hopped out, a big grin on his face. "Thought I might be in time for one of those old-fashioneds." When he saw Sigrid running toward him through the grass, his expression sobered. "What's wrong?"

"Mia. We can't find her."

"She was drawing with chalk in the drive," said Cordelia, nodding to the artwork.

"Here, too," said Jane, seeing a half-finished hopscotch grid drawn in blue and pink chalk right next to the front steps.

"She was so angry at me," said Sigrid, stepping out into the street and looking both ways.

"You think she took off?" said Peter.

"I think," said Jane, "that we're wasting time. We need to spread out."

"You've all got your cell phones?" asked Cordelia. When everyone answered in the affirmative, she headed toward Sheridan and the lake.

"I'll take the alley," said Peter, dashing off.

Sigrid and Jane went in opposite directions down the street.

Jane didn't like the look of that unfinished hopscotch court. Why would a kid start one and not finish it?

As she was passing in front of Sebastian Joe's ice cream parlor a few minutes later, her phone trilled. Digging it out of her back pocket, she said hello.

"Janey, it's Dad."

Her heart sank. She'd been hoping it would be good news about Mia.

"Chess was charged with Dial's murder a few hours ago. He'll be arraigned first thing tomorrow morning. I just got out of the judge's chambers. The bail's going to be set at a million. Not unusual in a case like this. He mentioned that two-hundred-and-fifty-thousand-dollar check again, that he needs to cash it."

"He sold an artifact to Julia. She told me last night that she was calling her bank this morning to cancel it. She's not even sure what he sold her was real."

"Oh, Lord. He won't be happy when he hears that. Anyway, I just wanted to keep you in the loop. Oh, and I talked to a divorce lawyer last night, an old friend. She said that a judge most likely would not allow Chess access to your assets in order to make bail. You're still legally married, but you haven't been in contact with him in decades. In Minnesota, judges rule, in cases like this, on what is reasonable. If we were in, say, Arizona, a judge would more likely stick to the letter of the law and allow him access. That means, unless *you* allow him access, he can't use your money to get out."

"Why on earth would I want to help him get out of jail?"

"I don't know. I do know he's going to try hard to convince you he's innocent. I don't have a crystal ball, Janey, but given his record when it comes to telling the truth, you'd be crazy to trust him. I'll represent him, for now, but in my opinion, you're safer with him in jail rather than out."

"I couldn't agree more."

"The bad news is, when it comes time for a divorce, Chess is entitled to half of your assets. He might not ask for it, but it's his if he wants it."

"Are you kidding me?"

"Maybe we can make a deal with him. I'm one of the best criminal defense lawyers in the state, and he knows it. I'll tell him that I'll represent him *if* he agrees to keep his hands off your estate. We'll get it in writing."

If only it could be that easy.

"You're being careful, right?" asked her dad.

She wasn't sure if she should tell him about Mia. She made a quick decision to call him later, hopefully with good news. "You don't need to worry."

"Yes, I do, honey. When it comes to my kids, it's my job."

An hour later, Jane trudged up the sidewalk to her front door. Cordelia was already back, sitting on the steps, her turban askew, her robes drooping from the heat and humidity.

"Nothing?" asked Cordelia, fanning her face with a copy of the *Southwest Journal.*

Jane sat down next to her. "Nothing. It's so frustrating that she can't hear if we call her name."

"Tell me about it."

"I just talked to Sigrid. She and Peter are going to stay at it a while longer. I told them we'd stick around the house in case Mia comes back. Apparently, Mia's run away from them before. Twice. She came home on her own the first time. The second time, the cops found her in a park, hauled her back."

"If she wants to get lost, it's not hard."

"What did Mia say to you while you were setting her up with the chalk?"

"Not a lot," said Cordelia. "Just that she was really angry at her mom. She wished things could go back to the way they were last fall, with Peter living on one side of a double bungalow and Sigrid on the other. She said it wasn't Peter's idea for her to see a therapist, it was her mom's. She doesn't understand why she has to talk about things that are painful. She wants to live with Peter. She wishes her mom would move out."

229

Jane looked up at the cloudless summer sky, wiping sweat off her forehead with the back of her arm. "I suppose she could've gone for a walk and gotten lost. She's not familiar with this neighborhood."

"I suppose."

"Or—"

"What other options are there? She got lost or she took off."

Jane was so frightened by one other possibility, she couldn't even bring herself to say it out loud.

28

Irina glanced to her right, anxious to make sure Dusty was okay in his car seat. She hated that her mother's car didn't have a backseat, but she had to make do. She sped through the dark streets toward the River Bay Marina south of Hastings, where her mother's houseboat was docked in a rented slip. Her little boy's brown eyes were open, and he seemed to be alternately looking out the window at the lights whizzing past and playing with his toes. He'd sneezed once, just as she was getting him strapped into his seat, which concerned her. She wasn't sure if the windows should be open or closed. She couldn't bear to think he was breathing in bacteria, microorganisms, or viruses that could hurt him. She'd finally decided on keeping the windows closed, with the air-conditioning running. Mothers had a sixth sense about their own kids, and that's what Irina had to trust.

This was the second time she'd taken Dusty out in the last few days. She thought about Steve's comment, that babies needed to be exposed to germs to help them develop their immune systems. Conflicting information, especially when it came to children's health, seemed to be the norm. It was probably just something Steve had made up because he wanted to go to a restaurant and wolf down a steak while he tried to convince her to come back home.

Not only was it impossible for her to return to Apple Valley, but she couldn't stay at the old family house another minute. Earlier in the evening, Irina had seen the same truck drive past the house three times in the space of ten minutes. She called to Misty, told her come look, but as luck would have it, once Misty had joined her at the window, the truck never came by again. She eventually gave up trying to convince her sister that they weren't safe, that they should both leave, and instead she'd gone into the bedroom and packed up her suitcase and Dusty's diaper bag, then crept out the back door. She'd lifted her mom's key fob from Misty's purse on the way out. Misty's rattletrap Cougar, with the ashtray filled to overflowing and the ripped, dirty seats, was the least hygienic place in the northern hemisphere. Her sister would be angry when she learned what Irina had done, but in a few days she'd be able to buy five Audi Roadsters if she wanted them.

Arriving at the marina shortly before ten, Irina drove through the security gate and then began her search for a parking space. Her mother rented a liveaboard slip, which meant that the boat was moored on one of the outer fingers. After finding a spot reasonably close to the walkway, she unstrapped Dusty's car seat and lifted the entire seat onto the pavement next to her. Then she grabbed her suitcase, hung the diaper bag over her shoulder, and lugged everything—and everyone—to the far side of the marina.

Under a starry sky on the aft deck, she unlocked the door to the first-floor salon. A night-light that her mom always kept on in the galley burned at the back of the large, open room. She loved the feel of being on the water, although this wasn't exactly a normal boat. The two-story floating mansion was sixty-two feet long, custommade to her mother's specifications, using only the finest-quality materials—teak, ebony, mahogany, leather, glass block, and polished marble. She wasn't sure how much it was worth, but she would learn tomorrow when she and her sister met at the lawyer's office to go over the trust documents. She couldn't stand the idea of having the boat trashed by Misty and her sleazy friends. She intended to buy her sister out. Misty would inherit stocks and the house in Merriam Park. Irina would get the gallery, more stocks, some bonds, and her mother's condo in Woodbury. Misty had been the black sheep in the family forever, but still, Irina thought the bequests were generous.

Irina spent a few seconds checking the refrigerator to see if there was any food on board. Her mom normally spent the weekends here. It struck her as achingly sad that her mom would never come here again, a place she'd loved so much. Tears formed, but she fought them. She would have the rest of her life to mourn her mother's passing. For now, she had to stay focused on keeping herself—and Dusty—safe. Finding that the refrigerator shelves were stocked with cheeses, fruit, champagne, and even a slice of pâté and a paper carton of crab and corn chowder from Surdyk's, she turned back to her son.

"Let's get you upstairs to bed," she said, carrying him and everything she'd brought with her up the staircase. She moved quietly down a hall lit by more tiny night-lights, bumping the wall with the suitcase, past the guest cabin and one of the four bathrooms. Standing at last in the master suite, she wondered for a moment if she should run back downstairs and find the cleaning supplies, scrub the room down before they spent the night. It seemed too much, even to her. One night in a room she hadn't inspected from top to bottom, but one that she knew was cleaned regularly by a professional service, would probably be okay. She could open the sliding glass doors that led out to the foredeck if she wanted fresh air.

Irina set Dusty's car seat in a chair and pulled it over next to the bed, where she sat down with a tired thump. It was times like this that she truly loathed the people in her life. Where was their support for a young mother with a sick baby? If it took a village to raise a child, her village was full of nothing but slackers and critics.

Irina gave Dusty a quick bath in the master bathroom. She dressed him in a clean Onesie and then gave him his bottle. He fell asleep on her shoulder as she walked around the darkened room, patting his back and humming softly. She held him in her arms for a long time, just looking down at him, smelling him, kissing his cheek, marveling at how beautiful and sweet he was, and how grateful she was that she'd finally been able to cary a child to term.

After getting him settled back in the car seat and tucking a blanket around him, she stretched out on the bed, feeling another wave of sadness wash over her—this time, for Chess. He would never know the joy of having a son, and Dusty would never know his father. It seemed pretty clear to Irina that Chess had taken off. She'd been afraid he'd do something like that all along. He hadn't returned any of her calls. Unless he was lying dead in an alley somewhere, a victim of whoever was searching for the bull, there was no other reasonable explanation for his silence. He was gone. In many ways, she didn't blame him. They'd gotten in way over their heads, with no exit strategy. She didn't have a gun anymore, but she did have an ace in the hole if the thugs came after her again. She intended to stand her ground, refusing to flee as Chess had done, but she wouldn't allow herself to be a sitting duck, as she had the other night.

Had she ever really loved Chess, she wondered, or had he simply represented a way out of an unworkable life with Steve? She might be greedy, and she might have been attracted to the idea of a secret romance, but she was also a practical person—maybe too practical for her own good. She was a little surprised that she could think this clearly at such a stressful time. Yes, as she mulled it over, she did want to marry Chess, but not at any price. The fact that he'd run off without so much as a phone call meant she was expendable. The biggest error she'd made was not telling him about Dusty. If she could do it all over again, she wouldn't make the same mistake.

Back in the galley, Irina removed the champagne from the refrigerator, noting that it was French and expensive. She found some crackers in the cupboard and returned to the master cabin, where she disrobed, opened up the sliding doors to the foredeck, removed the hot tub cover, and climbed in. The heat felt good against her chilled skin. Above her, a yellow half-moon floated peacefully in the night sky. She drank directly from the champagne bottle, feeling the alcohol ease the knots in her tired muscles.

It had been a long day. She'd spent most of the morning arranging the funeral. She'd driven to the funeral home, picked out a casket, arranged for flowers, and contacted the church and talked to the minister who would officiate at the service. He was a man she'd never met before, but he seemed to understand her desire to keep things simple. There would be two eulogies, one delivered by her uncle, her mother's brother, who would be flying in with his family from Pittsburgh, and the other by her mother's best friend, a woman who lived in town.

In the afternoon, Irina had called all the relatives and friends her mother would have wanted to come. For some on the list, she'd left messages. Those were the easy calls. Many of the others had wanted to talk. It seemed to Irina that they were, tacitly but unmistakably, asking her to make *them* feel better instead of offering her comfort. The entire day had been exhausting and confusing.

Misty, of course, felt she deserved time off for good behavior because she'd babysat Dusty for several hours while Irina was off taking care of the funeral business. And frankly, it was fine with Irina if Misty left the house. When she was around, so were her friends. Irina planned to confront her sister and Steve about their cozy embrace last night, but not until after the funeral. Her emotions were already on overload, and at the moment, it was more than she wanted to know.

Lying in the tub, with the jets turned off, drifting to sounds of the quiet lapping of the waves against the hull, Irina began to wonder about mold. Boats were in contact with water, which was a perfect environment for mold to grow. It didn't smell moldy inside the houseboat. If anything, it smelled like lemon oil and eucalyptus. Still, it might not have been the best idea to bring Dusty here. With every decision she made, she was compromising his health. She pushed up out of the water and sat on the edge of the tub, naked, alone, half drunk. She was a miserable excuse for a mother. She didn't deserve such a wonderful son. She started to cry, unable to stop herself this time.

An odd feeling—perhaps a sensation of movement or a shifting in the boat's balance, something almost but not quite perceptible—caused her to look back into the cabin. She climbed out of the water as quietly as she could manage and grabbed her bathrobe from the bed, sure as she could be that she was no longer alone on the boat. Standing in the darkness, with moonlight streaming in through the sliding glass doors, she listened, hoping with all her might that she was wrong.

Creeping to the edge of the door, she looked down the hall. A light snapped on in the salon, throwing a shadow against the stairway.

She backed up and looked around for something to use as a weapon, but unless she wanted to smother the intruder with a pillow, or smack him with a lamp, she was out of luck. That's when she remembered her knitting needles. She'd brought along the tiny blue sweater she was making for Dusty. Easing over to her suitcase, she dug through her clothes until she found them. She pulled several free and tested them by poking them into her palm. It was a puny effort, but if she could get close enough without being seen, she could do some damage.

Standing behind the door, she waited, taking shallow breaths, praying that Dusty wouldn't wake and start to cry. The wood stairs creaked under the weight of heavy footsteps. A second later he was in the hall moving toward her. She couldn't see him, but she had the sense that he was big. And then he stopped. Just stopped.

She pulled her head back as a light burst on in the bathroom. A slice of brightness slid across the cabin rug. She watched, feeling eerily calm, as the shadow moved into the doorway. Her hand tightened around the knitting needles. She was sure of only one thing. She would kill to protect her son.

The shadow hovered.

She could hear his breathing, feel his nearness.

Without warning, the door slammed back at her, driving the needles against her stomach. She cried out in pain, lost her balance, and fell back against the wall.

The overhead light flipped on. She found herself staring up at Majid. "What . . . what are you doing here?"

His black eyes swept over her, taking in the cabin, the open suitcase, her clothes tossed over the bed. He zeroed in on the car seat. His expression was inscrutable.

"Here," he said, extending his hand. "Let me help you."

Continuing to hold the knitting needles in her fist, she righted herself and stood up. "How did you get in? Did you break the lock?" She would call the police, have him arrested.

"No," he said, scrutinizing her face. "I have a key."

"You stole it?"

"No, of course not. Your mother gave it to me."

"Why would she do that?"

"Someone got into my apartment this afternoon, tossed it good and proper. Probably the same people who murdered Morgana and ransacked the gallery. The police told me I couldn't stay there, so I drove out here thinking I'd spend the night."

"The police?"

"I called them, reported what happened. It's a crime scene now."

"But why would my mother give you a key to her houseboat?"

He walked over to Dusty and stood looking down at him.

"Answer me."

"Did you happen to look in the closet?"

"The closet?"

"I stay here a lot. Your mama and me, we were lovers. More than that. We loved each other. Check out the closet, you'll find my bathrobe, my shirts and slacks. My shaving kit is in the bathroom."

She gripped the knitting needles tighter. "Get away from him."

He turned, a look of pain crossing his face. "I'm grieving, too, Irina. You're not the only person who lost someone important."

"You should be ashamed of yourself. Seducing a woman so many years older than you."

"It wasn't like that. It happened so slowly that we almost didn't realize it until one night when we were working late and . . . we had to face our feelings."

"That's disgusting. She was old."

"Not to me."

A thought seized her. "Do you expect to be included in the trust?"

"Why do you hate me?"

"Get out. Get out of here or I'll call the police."

Holding up his hands as if she were pointing a gun at him, he moved toward the door. "Just calm down, okay?"

"I'm very calm."

"Great. Fine. I'm leaving," he said.

"Give me the key."

"What?"

"The key to the downstairs door. I want it. I don't want you coming back in here in the middle of the night."

"To do what?"

"I've never trusted you." She held out her left hand, her right hand holding the needles like a dagger.

"I'd never hurt you. You must know that." He dipped his hand into his pocket and pulled out a key ring. Unscrewing the end, he took off several keys until he came to the right one.

Irina recognized it and took it from him. "Now, get off the boat and don't come back."

With one last glance at the baby, he turned and walked back down the hall.

Irina stepped out on the foredeck and watched him move silently back up the walkway to the parking area. When he was out of sight, she ran back down to check that he'd locked the door. Throwing the double lock, something she should have done right away, she went into the kitchen and began removing the Lysol, the Ajax, the 409, the rags and scrub brushes. She'd never get to sleep now. She might as well clean.

29

At the Hennepin County jail the next morning, Jane sat down across from Chess at the far end of an institutional anteroom, a new, unwelcome hardness in the center of her stomach. She didn't want to be here. She never wanted to see Chess again, and yet she had to come.

Separated by a Plexiglas wall, speaking to each other via phones attached to the side walls, they worked their way through the formalities. Jane touched the Plexiglas, saw where others had left fingerprints behind. The surface was hard, practical, oppressive. It was, of course, meant to protect the visitor from the visited. In this case, however, it was the other way around.

Chess looked awful, his face puffy, his hair disheveled. He tried gamely to smile, to shrug off his current condition, even to make light of it, but they both knew it was an act. The odd thing was, he did seem happy to see her.

"I tried to phone you right away, he said, but they told me I couldn't make any calls."

"Now that you've been charged and arraigned you can." She tried with little success to drain the coldness from her voice.

"It's so good to see you. What happened to your nose? It's all bruised."

The comment made her appreciate how utterly removed he was from what his sudden reappearance had done to her life. "You have no clue what it's been like for me the last couple of days."

"For you?"

"I was attacked in the Lyme House parking lot on Saturday night. Two guys have been staking out the place. I didn't find out why until I got jumped. The man wanted me to tell him where my husband was."

Both eyebrows shot up. "I never thought—"

"What? That the people who are after you would come after me? What are you mixed up in?"

"Jane, look—" He ran a hand over his unshaven face. "I'm not even sure where to start."

The anger inside her exploded. "Let me help. Why did you send me fake divorce papers?"

"I didn't know they were fake, I swear. Not until years later, when I was thinking about marrying someone. I gave the divorce decree to my lawyer, and he told me they were no good."

"And you didn't think it might be nice to let me know?"

"Why? I never intended to come back."

"Do you ever think about anyone but you? All that talk about solidarity—gays and lesbians sticking together. I felt sorry for you, thought you'd been wronged by your parents. Sure I wanted the money you offered, but that's not why I agreed to marry you. For all I know, you're not even gay."

His eyes skirted away.

What he'd just said finally penetrated. "You were going to get *married*? To a woman? It was *all* a lie? What did I ever do to you, Chess?" It took every ounce of her self-control not to stand up and scream at him. "The cops think you not only killed Dial but Morgana Beck. It's all about that gold artifact, right? You turn my entire life upside down by showing up and you have the nerve to sit there and smile at me? Who the hell *are* you?"

"You know who I am. Jane, please——"

"We made today's *Star Tribune,* in case you're interested. It wasn't the headline, but the article was on the front page. Want to know the lead?"

"Don't."

"*Daughter of Raymond Lawless Once Married to Accused Killer.* Don't you just love that? Has a nice titillating ring, don't you think? I wonder what they'll do when they find out we're still married? Why did you have to come back here, Chess? Why couldn't you just leave me alone?"

"If you'll just give me a chance, I can explain."

"You must think I'm pathetic. Stupid, wide-eyed, gullible Jane."

"I don't."

"Well, *I* think I'm pathetic. Why did I allow myself to be taken in by someone like you? What's wrong with me that I could be so credulous?" She felt gutted, like her insides had been clawed out and tossed on the floor. "Fool me once, shame on you. Fool me twice . . . that's where we're at. I invited you into my home again, even asked you to come to my father's birthday party. What did you do? You spent the evening trying to swindle my friends with that crap you sell."

"I did no such thing."

"Julia? The cylinder seal?"

"She was the only person I talked to about it—and it's worth every penny."

"And we know that *because*? Because you said so? Because you showed her some fake provenance papers? We all know what your word is worth."

"Stop."

"The first time around, you bribed me with money. This time, you gave me a ring." She pulled the gold snake off her index finger and held it up. "Get it in a Cracker Jack box, Chess?" She turned and hurled it against the concrete wall behind her.

"You're angry. I don't blame you. But the ring is real. So is the cylinder seal."

"I don't believe you," she said, barely controlling her fury. "Not that it matters. Julia stopped payment on the check yesterday morning."

His lips thinned, tightened. "She shouldn't have done that. I need to get out of here, and fast."

"Why? So you can hightail it out of Dodge?"

He put his hand up to the Plexiglas and spoke softly, but with more feeling. "I swear to you on everything I love, I didn't kill Dial or Morgana Beck. I'm innocent. I may bend the truth more than I should. I'm not proud of that. But I'm not a murderer."

"Then who did kill them? What's going on? Why are those men following you?"

He rested his head against his hand. "They want the bull."

Something she already knew. She just wanted to see if he would feed her another lie. "Who are they?"

"At first, I thought maybe Dial's next-door neighbor might have had something to do with it. Something about him struck me as phony. His name's Smith. He said he'd lost his job, that he and his wife were having a tough time financially. The problem is, he saw me coming out of Dial's door last Wednesday around noon. I'd just found Dial dead in the living room and tried to leave without anybody seeing me."

"Wait, wait, wait. You told me that you went back to Dial's house on Wednesday because you realized you'd left your passport there. Nobody was around, but the door was unlocked."

"I, ah, bent the truth a little there. I had to. I thought if I told you what really happened, you wouldn't believe me, and you wouldn't ask your father to represent me."

244

This guy was unbelievable. "Go on."

"Like I said, we played poker on Tuesday night. I got drunk and ended up outside, in the backyard. I must have been trying to get into the hot tub, but keeled over right next to it and fell asleep. I woke up on the concrete walk next to the tub on Wednesday about noon, went into the house, and found that it had been ransacked. Dial was on the floor in the living room. He'd been knifed. I would have been killed, too, I'm sure of it, if whoever got in had found me. It was just a stroke of luck that I'd wandered outside. I thought that maybe I could get away from the house without anybody knowing I'd been there. I left by the front door. About the same time, the neighbor, Smith, came out on his front steps to get his newspaper."

"Are you saying you thought he'd killed Dial?"

"I don't know, but something about him seemed off. Not that it matters. After thinking about it for the last few days, I came to the conclusion that someone else is after me. Three people to be exact. There's a story that's been making the rounds of antiquities dealers for almost a year. Three people, an Englishwoman living in Italy, an Egyptian professor of ancient history, and an ex-major in the Iraqi army, have formed a cabal to hunt down the antiquities stolen from the Baghdad Museum, and the thieves who did the stealing. Dealers and buyers have been killed mysteriously all over the world—in alleys, pushed off buildings, drowned in swimming pools. These people are ruthless, single-minded, and apparently have money."

"Go back for a second. *You* stole the bull?"

"No, not me. But yes, it was taken illegally. I knew that when I bought it. I hoped I could keep it. It felt—you're going to think I'm crazy—but it was like I'd owned it before in a previous life. Like I had a right to it."

"You are a world-class liar, even to yourself."

"Maybe I am, but I've always been drawn to the past, to the Middle East and Egypt. Particularly to Babylon. That's where I first landed on

245

this earth, took my first breath. You don't believe me, I can see that. It's fine. There's no reason you should. But haven't you ever been drawn to something not entirely rational?"

"This isn't about me."

"No, it's not. It's about me, what I did to you that I never intended. I'm sorry, Jane."

That was too easy. "You came to the Twin Cities to sell the bull."

"To Dial, yeah."

"Did he know it was stolen?"

Chess gave a noncommittal shrug. "We weren't doing anything others haven't been doing for millennia. But he was killed before we could make the exchange, the money for the statue. I assume that whoever is searching for it thought Morgana must know something about it, too. She didn't."

"So you tried to sell it to Julia."

"I'd sell it to anybody for the right price."

"Okay, let's talk about that. The 'right' price, as you put it."

This was the moment of truth. She removed a piece of yellow legal paper from her back pocket. "Yesterday, my brother's little girl went missing. Her name is Mia. She's eleven. We thought she'd run away. She'd done it before. But this morning I found this." She unfolded it, held it up to the Plexiglas so he could read it.

"I don't have my glasses. What's it say?"

With a trembling hand, she spread it out on the small counter in front of her. The note was written in black ink, all caps. " 'Mrs. Garrity,' " she read, clearing her throat, trying to tamp back the tears burning her eyes. " 'We have your little girl. We will not hurt her if you give us what we want. An even trade. The girl for the bull. If you contact the police, you will never see the girl again. We are not unreasonable, but we will tolerate no interference. You have forty-eight hours. We will contact you about the exchange. We are not ama-

246

teurs. If we feel our safety is compromised, you will not hear from us again.' "

Jane looked up.

Chess's face had turned ashen.

"You have to give them what they want."

"I can't."

She felt her anger heat up again, like a boiling wave crashing over her. "Even *you* can't be that callous."

"I don't know where it is. I gave it to Irina to keep it safe."

"Irina Nelson? Morgana Beck's daughter? She was in on this?"

"She put it in a safety deposit box, but for some reason, she removed it and hid it in the basement of the gallery. We went to get it on Saturday night and it was gone."

Jane's skin felt suddenly too tight.

"The only person who had access to the basement, other than Irina and her mother, was a man named Majid Farrow. It has to be him. He works there. I was planning to talk to him on Sunday afternoon, offer to cut him into the deal—or beat the crap out of him until he told me where he'd hidden it—but I was arrested."

She struggled to compose herself. "Majid? The manager?"

"You know him?"

"We've met."

"But see, your niece . . . that's even more reason why you have to help me get out of here."

She knew it would come down to this. "You'll leave if I do."

"I won't leave, Jane. I promise you. I'll stay and do everything I can to help find the bull."

"And then you'll leave with it."

"I won't!"

"I don't believe you."

"Jane, please. I'm the only one who can find it."

"I've got two days." She hung up the phone, pushed away from the table, and got up.

When Chess began pounding on the Plexiglas, a man came out of a side door and grabbed his arms, yanking him out of his chair. He was still yelling, still waving at her to come back, when she turned and left the room.

30

Chess bent over the telephone, keeping his voice low. The guard had made it clear that he couldn't talk long.

"Irina, it's me." He could hear a gasp.

"I thought you'd left. Why didn't you return any of my calls?"

"I was arrested. For Dial's murder."

"I haven't seen a news broadcast in days, or read a newspaper. Oh, Chess, that's awful, but it's so good to hear your voice."

"Have you made any progress finding the . . . you know?"

"Sorry, no. Oh, baby, where are you?"

"The Hennepin County jail."

"Are you okay?"

"The bail was set at a million dollars. I need to put up one hundred thousand to get out. You've got to help me. Did your inheritance come through yet? You could put up the gallery for collateral."

She didn't say anything for several seconds. "I'm in the waiting room at my mother's lawyer's office. We're going over the trust documents this morning. I don't know how long it will take for my mom's assets to be transferred to me, but as soon as I have the money, I'll get you out."

"I'm dying to see you."

"Oh," she said, sighing into the phone, "I'm so glad you called. Wait."

He heard some rustling, a door closing. "What's going on?"

"I left the office because I didn't want Misty to overhear. I found out something important. Remember we thought Majid was the only other person with a key to the gallery? Misty has one. Mom gave it to her because she wanted her to start working there part-time. She's had it for at least a week."

This was a major break. "And she needs money badly. Sure, that makes sense. Maybe she went down to the basement to look around. She found the statue and took it."

"Or gave it to one of her slimy friends. If that's the case, we may never see it again."

Chess refused to give up that easily.

"You have no idea how crazy these last few days have been for me. I left Steve, moved in with Misty, but I couldn't stay there. I'll tell you about it when we have more time. I'm living on my mom's houseboat at the moment. I'm terrified those people who killed Dial and my mom will find me. Plus I have Dusty to protect. I've been so careful about his environment ever since he was born. Now I've had to move him twice in two days."

"Is he doing okay?"

"He sneezed last night. I think he may have sneezed again this morning when I was getting out of the shower. I'm worried about the mold on the boat."

A sneeze. Right. Potentially deadly in anybody's book. "Is Steve taking care of him today?" He didn't really care; he was just making conversation.

"Absolutely not."

"If Misty's with you—"

"I left him back at the houseboat."

"With a friend?"

"I don't know anybody out there. No, he'll be fine. I'm only going to be gone for a couple hours."

"You left him *alone*? Irina, he's only a few months old."

"I spent half the night cleaning the master cabin. It's the safest place for him right now. I couldn't exactly leave him in the car. It's going up to ninety today. And I refuse to bring him into this huge office building."

Had he heard her right? Sure, he'd joked about her mental health when it came to her son, but now he was beginning to think she actually had gone over the edge.

"Misty's calling me," said Irina. "Time to meet with Zeller."

"Come see me as soon as you can."

"Maybe I'll swing by after the meeting."

"But what about Dusty?"

"It means a lot to me that you're so concerned about him. If I'm gone an extra hour, it's not a problem. He's all strapped into his car seat. He'll be fine."

"Really, though—"

"I'll see you soon."

Inside Leonard Zeller's office, Irina sat next to Misty, hands in her lap, acting patient even though she felt as if she had an engine revving inside her chest. Zeller was a fussy old man, which was why they were here. He insisted on meeting with them in person, probably intended to do a formal reading. It was the kind of folderol she didn't need in her life, especially with everything else on her plate.

Misty tugged on her too-tight Diesel jeans. Since last night, she'd cut her hair even shorter, dyed it black, and painted her fingernails and toenails a matching black, no doubt in preparation for the big day. If she was trying to impress Zeller with her sense of style, she couldn't have made worse choices. Zeller was old-school. A gentleman. White-haired, with round Harry Potter glasses, three-piece tweed suits, French cuffs peeking just the right amount from the sleeves of his jacket. Next to him, Misty looked crude, the Rolls-Royce of tacky.

Zeller studied the papers in front of him. When his intercom buzzed, he picked up the phone. "Thank you, Janet. Yes, please send him in."

Irina turned to find Majid coming through the door. "What's he doing here?"

"Since he's mentioned in the trust, I asked him to come by," said Zeller. He motioned Majid to a chair.

Looking uncharacteristically subdued, Majid sat down and crossed his legs without so much as a nod to either Irina or Misty.

Leaning toward them, Zeller passed out copies of the trust agreement. "Morgana made several changes a few weeks ago."

This was the first Irina had heard about changes. "Such as?"

"The disposition of some of her assets."

Misty stopped chewing her gum. "Huh?"

"Just cut to the chase," said Irina. If Majid was going to ignore her, she could play the same game.

"All right," said Zeller, leaning back against his buttery brown leather chair. "You can all take your copies home and read them at your leisure. If you have questions, you can, of course, call for clarification. Cutting to the chase, as you put it, here are the changes: The gallery—the building, the name, the stock, all debt and all bank accounts associated with it—has been given to Majid Farrow."

Irina's eyes opened wide. "That gallery is *mine*."

"You are to receive your mother's condo in Woodbury, the houseboat, and financial assets in the amount of approximately nine hundred thousand dollars."

"What about me?" said Misty indignantly.

Zeller checked his copy of the trust. "You are to receive your mother's car—an Audi Roadster—the house in Merriam Park, and approximately four hundred thousand dollars in various securities."

"What's all this 'approximately' stuff?" demanded Misty.

While Zeller explained that stocks and bonds fluctuated in value, Irina seethed. She couldn't believe her mother had taken away her inheritance and given it to her boy toy. The gallery had *always* been the major part of her inheritance. She glared at Majid, but he refused to meet her eyes.

"I think I deserve some sort of explanation," said Irina, giving Zeller a fierce look. "Did my mother state a reason why she made the decision to leave the gallery to Majid instead of me?"

"We've been together for years," said Majid, keeping his voice low. "It was a show of her love for me, and her trust in my ability and dedication."

"Bullshit," said Irina. "You played her."

Through clenched teeth, Majid said, "I know this is hard for you, but for once in your life, just shut the fuck up."

Fussing with his French cuffs, Zeller rolled his chair closer to his desk. "There is another provision I need to explain to you, Irina. I won't mince words. Your mother was deeply concerned about the state of your mental health. Rest assured, your inheritance is secure. I have been named the executor of that inheritance. According to the terms of the trust, nothing will transfer to you until you've been diagnosed by a licensed psychologist, and are in some sort of treatment—either in-patient within a mental health care facility, or in outpatient care. I have been given full discretion on this. I will release funds to you so that you can get the help you need. However, until I receive a report that you have made sufficient strides toward recovery, I cannot release the balance of the estate to you. Do you understand?"

253

Irina sat in her chair, her face flushed a deep red. Her body felt suddenly swollen, decaying, like a forgotten tomato that had been left out in the garden to rot. "I don't believe this."

"I know it's a blow," said Zeller, his voice kindly, "but there was no way to sugarcoat the terms of the trust. You must face facts."

"It's what I've been saying for months," said Misty. "You think we all hate you, that we're trying to make your life miserable, but it's not true. You've gone off the tracks. Every day you get a little bit worse."

"This is all about Dustin," whispered Irina.

"Of course it's about Dustin," said her sister.

"I have to go," said Irina, rising abruptly. "I can't stay."

"Irina, please," said Zeller, holding out his hand to her. "I thought perhaps you could stay after everyone else had left. We could talk this over. I have some suggestions for you."

"I don't need any suggestions." What she needed was to tell Chess that he had a son. Once he knew, once he understood the kind of care Dusty needed, he'd back her up. They would sell the bull, bank the money, and go off somewhere to live happily ever after.

31

Standing just inside the swinging kitchen doors, Jane looked out one of the round windows into the main dining room. She spotted Lee sitting at a table near the windows, eating breakfast and reading the morning paper. She waited for one of the waiters to come through the door, then walked out, crossed through the room, and pulled out the chair opposite him. It was centering to feel the familiar hum of the restaurant breathing around her.

"Morning," she said, sitting down. "Another wonderful day in paradise."

Setting the paper down next to a book titled *Early Christian Scriptures,* Lee replied, "Ain't that the Bible truth."

If she told Nolan about the ransom note, he'd tell her to ignore the part about not calling the police. She figured Lee would be of the same opinion, so instead of telling him about it and getting a lecture, she asked, "You or Nolan learn anything new?"

"As a matter of fact, yes." He fiddled with his cell phone for a few seconds and then handed it to her. "You recognize that guy?"

She stared at the image. "I can't really see his face." It was a picture of a man on a motorcycle riding past her house.

"Here," said Lee, reaching over to flip to the next picture. "Keep pressing the right arrow. This guy drove past your place at least three times yesterday afternoon."

Jane studied the images. "He looks Middle Eastern." Then it struck her. "I met this guy over at the Morgana Beck Gallery in St. Paul. He's the manager. Here, I've got his card." She pulled it out of the pocket of her jeans and handed it to him, recalling that Chess had just told her that Majid might have taken the bull from the basement of the gallery. "What do you think he was doing?"

"Casing your place."

If the statue was in his possession, why would he care? "Was he one of the men staking out my restaurant?"

"Never seen him before."

"Did you show this picture to Nolan?"

"He agrees with me. This bozo on the motorcycle is connected in some way. We'll follow up on it."

She would, too, privately. "You like working with Nolan?"

"Yeah, I do. He showed me some of his old cases last night. He's a smart guy."

"Think you'll stick around, work with him a while longer?"

"I just might. He's looking for a partner."

"I'd heard that." She glanced around the room. "Well, I have a meeting I need to get to."

"You go," he said, picking up his coffee cup and taking a swallow.

As she stood, she said, "You doing any preaching today?"

"That's on hold now that I've got something more interesting to do with my time."

"Glad I could provide you with a little diversion."

"Go on, get out of here. I'll call if I learn anything more."

On her way back into the kitchen, Jane talked to one of the waiters and told him not to charge Lee for breakfast. She grabbed a bowl of meat scraps for Mouse and then went back down to her office.

After paging though the St. Paul white pages and not finding a listing for Majid Farrow, Jane called the gallery. She figured she'd have to leave a message but was surprised when a male voice answered, "Morgana Beck Gallery of Antiquities."

"Is this Majid Farrow?" she asked.

"Speaking."

She would have preferred to talk to him in person, but because she was hoping for something to tell Peter and Sigrid when they arrived, she pressed on. "This is Jane Lawless. We met yesterday morning in front of the gallery."

"Of course. You showed me that picture of the Nimrud bull."

As far as she could see, there were three possibilities. He didn't have the bull. Or he had it, but wasn't part of the murderous group sent here to find it. Or he was part of the group, and might or might not have it. The only thing that really mattered at the moment was whether or not the bull was in his possession.

"You wanted me to appraise that statue before you bought it."

"That's right. I could bring it by this afternoon."

"Wonderful," he said eagerly. "I would be delighted to take a look. Let me grab my appointment book."

He hadn't hesitated for even a millisecond. That told her everything she needed to know. Someone had the bull, but it wasn't him.

"I could do three o'clock."

"I have to be somewhere at three," said Jane.

"This evening might work. Say around seven."

"Let me call you back."

"May I ask you something? How much do you know about the Nimrud gold?"

"Not a lot."

"I hope you don't mind if I speak plainly. It's generally conceded that the Nimrud gold belongs to the Iraqi government. Or perhaps the Iraqi people. Questions about who owns history and how culture is preserved are large and difficult, but it's my opinion that if your statue is part of the Nimrud gold, you may be buying it illegally. It's something to consider. I myself wouldn't want to be any part of that."

"You've been very helpful." She thanked him and hung up, realizing she'd hit another dead end. Majid might be a good actor, but he didn't sound like a kidnapper or a killer.

Cordelia arrived early for the meeting, looking subdued in her black capri-length leggings, red satin tunic, and yellow flip-flops. "Show me the note."

Jane handed it to her and watched as she sank down on the couch, stroking Mouse's head as she read.

"How can people like this exist?" she asked, leaning back and draping herself over the cushions. "I mean, they abduct a living, breathing child just to get some stupid statue back?"

"That stupid statue is worth a whole hell of a lot to the people involved."

"Yeah, well." She muttered a few X-rated words under her breath. "What did that snake in the grass Chester have to say?" She stared straight ahead and listened as Jane filled her in.

With so much hope riding on her talk with Chess, Jane had felt utterly demoralized as she walked out of the jail. He'd given her virtually nothing to go on, although he had verified the seriousness of the situation. The only way out was to find the bull, a task that could take days, weeks—a lifetime. She tried to banish all thoughts of what Mia was going through from her mind, but somehow, the fear found the back of her throat and lodged there, a lump that wouldn't go away.

The food arrived as they were talking the situation over. Juice, a coffee carafe, a covered chafing dish filled with scrambled eggs, sausage, and bacon, a plate of cut fruit, and a tray of pastries. Jane pushed the cart back against the wall. She couldn't do much, but at least she could feed her family.

"Where's Hattie this morning?" she asked after thanking the waiter.

"She's supposed to be at Y Camp," said Cordelia, "Except for the duration, until Mia is home safe and sound, Hattie's staying inside. Mel took some time off to be with her."

"Not going to hire that ex-nurse?"

Cordelia shivered. "My loft will not be used as a way station for ex–sheep ranchers."

Peter and Sigrid arrived a few minutes later. They both looked exhausted. Sigrid's eyes were red and puffy, her expression tight. She demanded to see the note, just as Cordelia had. Peter stood behind her, reading over her shoulder.

"What's this *bull* stuff about?" asked Peter, sitting down on the couch next to Cordelia. He moved like an arthritic old man, as if his whole body hurt.

Jane had been dreading the question. Her relationship with Chess was like a nightmare octopus with ever-growing tentacles. Each time she thought she'd seen them all, a new one would appear. She started in, talking about Chess, about her marriage to him. When she faltered, Cordelia picked up the story, explaining everything that had happened. Jane was grateful. Once again, her problems had leaked over onto her brother's life. She started to apologize, but Peter cut her off.

"It's not your fault, any more than what happened last fall was your fault. You saved my life, Janey. I wouldn't be here today if it weren't for you."

She supposed it was one way of looking at it. There were others.

"So this bull was stolen?" asked Sigrid, wiping tears away from her face.

"From the Baghdad Museum," said Cordelia. "Chess showed up here because he had a buyer for it, but then the buyer was murdered."

"We have to call the cops," said Peter.

"No we don't." Sigrid stood rigidly next to the fireplace.

He glanced up. "I thought we agreed."

"I'm her mother. I should get the final say in what we do or don't do."

"Meaning what? Since I'm not her biological dad, I don't have *any* say in the matter?"

"Let's not start in on ourselves," said Cordelia with a sigh. "We're all we've got." She rose and dished herself up some food. When she realized everyone was staring at her, she said, "What? I don't think well on an empty stomach."

"If we're voting, I'm with Peter," said Jane.

"And I'm with Sigrid," said Cordelia.

"We're not voting," said Sigrid. "It's my call. No police."

"Then what do we do?" Peter's face had grown flushed. He perched on the edge of the couch. "How the hell are we supposed to find this bull all by ourselves?"

"Any way we can," said Sigrid.

"What about Nolan?" asked Peter, looking over at Jane.

"He'd tell us to bring the police in."

"Does that mean he won't help?"

She'd been thinking about that ever since she found the note. "I can pretty much tell you what he'd say. Start contacting antiquities dealers in the area. Ask if anyone has called or stopped by wanting to sell them a gold statue. See if they have any connections with private collectors who buy antiquities. When we've exhausted the local market, we start calling galleries around the country."

"That could take forever," said Peter.

"Unless we catch a break, it's all we've got."

Cordelia held her fork in the air, thinking out loud "There are four of us. And we've got"—she glanced at her watch—"forty-five hours."

"What about Chess?" asked Sigrid. "Can he help us?"

Jane shook her head. "He says he doesn't know where the bull is."

"Do you believe him?"

"He's lied to me so many times, I have no way of knowing."

"We should call Dad," said Peter.

Jane tapped a pencil against her desktop. "There's nothing he can do. Why worry him?"

"He and Elizabeth would make two more people to make phone calls," said Cordelia.

"She's right," said Peter. "I'll phone him."

A heavy silence descended as they each weighed the impossibility of the task.

"If we don't get Mia back, I'll hunt those people down and kill them with my bare hands," said Peter. "I mean it."

Just what the world needed, thought Jane. Another vendetta. Except she felt the same way. If anything happened to Mia, she'd be right there with him.

32

Irina looked down at the chair, then up at the Plexiglas partition. There was a time in her life when filth hadn't bothered her. She might not even have seen the grimy, greasy fingerprints, the dried spit, the dark red lipstick imprint where some silly woman had kissed the Plexiglas. Yet now, inside this narrow, airless room, she struggled to breathe. She would make the meeting quick. She'd made a decision on the way over and couldn't wait to break the news to Chess.

Sitting down on the edge of the chair, she gazed anxiously at the phone hanging from the wall, imagining the crawling bacteria, the slithering microbes, knowing that in just a few moments, she would need to touch the cold black plastic with her bare hand. She would be strong—for Dusty's sake. For Chess's sake. And for her own. She would get through this and then go back to the houseboat and stand in the shower for as long as it took her to feel clean again.

The door at the back of the room opened, and Chess walked out. He was smiling, his hand reaching to touch the Plexiglas separating them as he sat down. Her heart twisted inside when she saw how tired he looked, but she couldn't bring herself to press her hand to his. She lifted her arm, tried to force her hand forward, but she couldn't do it.

He seemed to understand and picked up the phone.

She hesitated before she did the same. "I've missed you so much," she whispered.

"I've missed you, too," he said, still smiling. "You look wonderful."

She looked strung out and knew it, but she appreciated his hopefulness, the yearning in his eyes. It meant more to her than anything he'd ever said or done before—because it was real.

"What did the lawyer say?" he asked. "When do you get the money? When can you get me out of here?"

"It's not going to happen. My mother tied up all the funds. The trust states that I have to see a shrink before I get any of it."

"So go see one. Today. This afternoon. Call a psychiatrist and make an appointment."

"I don't need to. We'll sell the bull, get the money that way."

His eyes darted around the room. He gave his head a tight shake. "You mean that beautiful little bullfrog figurine you bought in China last year? Sure, I can help you sell that, once I get out of here." He flashed his eyes at her.

She got the message. This wasn't a safe place to talk.

"But you lost the bullfrog," he said casually.

"I did, but then I found it again. Last night."

His eyes registered shock. "You *found* it?"

"I'll explain it to you later. I thought you'd be happy."

"I'm thrilled. But . . . you're sure about this now. You're not just pulling my leg, telling me what you think I want to hear."

"No, I have it. It's safe and sound."

He sat back, tapped his fingers on the counter, studied her for a few seconds. "You know, I may have a buyer for you."

264

"Of course we have a buyer. Julia Martinsen."

"She's, ah, no longer interested. This is someone else. Someone who'd pay top dollar. You remember I told you about that friend of mine, Jane Lawless? She'd love to own it."

"No way. I don't like her."

"You don't even know her. Besides, right now, we can't be choosy. I'll call her. I'm pretty sure I can persuade her to post the bond. Maybe she can still get it done today. If not, I'll be out tomorrow for sure. You said you were staying at your mom's houseboat, right? Where is it?"

She didn't like this. She didn't want that woman involved. "The River Bay Marina."

"Okay, here's what we do."

"No," she said, sitting up straight. "The bullfrog belongs to me. I get to say how this goes down."

"I *have* to get out of here."

"I understand that, but I don't want to sell it to that woman. Go ahead and phone her. If she agrees to put up your bail money, great. You can ditch her once you're free."

"How am I supposed to do that?"

"You're clever. Figure it out. If you have to bring her out to the marina, fine. We'll handle things there. I'll rent a car this afternoon. I'll swab it down with disinfectant and get it all ready for a nice drive with you and me and Dusty. You know, out in the country. Maybe we can even have a picnic."

"A picnic sounds good."

She would miss her mom's funeral if they left the state, but that couldn't be helped. "Take a cab to the marina. Or if you have to come with her, I'll meet you on the foredeck." She explained where the boat was moored. "I've got a surprise for you."

"A surprise?"

"No hints. I'll need you to bag all your clothes before you come

265

aboard, and then I want you to shower, get all the grime from the jail off you. I'll buy you some clean clothes at Target this afternoon. We'll dump your old clothes before we leave for our drive."

"You're going to the store now?"

"As soon as I leave."

"What about Dusty?" He glanced at his watch. "When did you leave the marina?"

"Around eleven."

"That's almost four hours ago. You need to get back there."

"He'll be okay. It won't take me that much longer."

"But the poor little guy. What if he starts to cry? What if he's scared?"

"He'll be fine." She wished people would stop telling her what was best for her son. "We'll make this work, Chess. You're with me, right?"

"All the way."

She felt exhilarated, ready for action. "Call me when you know what time you're getting out." She finally understood the desire to put her hand on the partition. She wanted to touch him, even if it wasn't for real—but her revulsion caused her better judgment to kick in. They could touch all they wanted later, under the immaculately clean sheets in her mom's cabin. She would hold that thought—until he could hold her in his arms.

Jane searched through the local yellow pages before her family left her office. She wanted to divide up their investigative work but quickly learned that the only gallery of ancient art in all of Minnesota was the Morgana Beck Gallery of Antiquities.

"What do we do now?" asked Peter, dropping down on a chair.

Jane logged on to the Internet and began a wider search. She clicked around until she found an article from the *St. Louis Post-Dispatch*. "Says here that there are lots of ancient art galleries associated with museums of fine arts, like California's Getty and New York's Metropolitan, but fewer private galleries, where people can actually buy the artifacts."

"Maybe that makes it easier for us," said Cordelia.

Jane read on. "Get this. Most reputable museums actually own stolen artifacts. The concept of 'provenance' appears to be tricky—and murky—when you're dealing with something that ancient. Museums are generally wary of tighter laws because they feel those laws would drive art antiquities underground—into the hands of private collectors. Cultural sensitivity notwithstanding, the black market is booming."

"Great," said Peter. "Private collectors aren't going to list themselves on Google."

"Maybe we can get to them through some of the more reputable galleries," said Jane.

"How?" said Sigrid.

"Come at it generally. First ask about Babylonian art. Then ask about any gold artifacts they may have from that time period. If they bring up the Nimrud gold, run with it. If they don't, maybe we should act dumb—like we've heard about it but don't know a lot, whether it's for sale or not."

"Makes sense," said Peter.

"I think we should also ask if they know any private collectors who have a collection from that period."

Jane made a printout of a list of private galleries around the world. They each took a chunk. Once again, she could see in everyone's eyes how overwhelmed they were by the impossibility of the task, and yet they all knew they had to do something.

With assignments in hand, and a feeling that the next few hours would be critical, everyone left the office except for Jane and Mouse. They would all use landlines to make the calls, leaving their cell phones free to phone each other with updates.

Supplying herself with a pot of coffee, Jane sat behind her desk and began to call galleries in northern Europe. She spoke a little French, enough to ask some basic questions.

Two hours later, she tossed her pencil down and ran her hands through her hair. She'd talked to dozens of people and gotten exactly nothing. This felt worse than trying to find a needle in a haystack. At least with the needle, you knew it was *in* the haystack. Jane wasn't at all sure where the statue was. It could easily be in somebody's trunk.

"Mouse, come on. We've got someplace we need to be." She felt a little guilty as she clipped the leash to his collar. She should be spending every waking minute calling galleries, but she had an idea and wanted to follow up on it.

She drove by her house on the way to her destination, seeing two men sitting on the front steps and a WTWN-TV truck parked by the curb. Had to be reporters. She wondered how long they'd stick around.

She pulled up a few minutes later across the street from Melvin Dial's house, a stately redbrick Colonial with tan shutters, white trim, and a dark green door. The house on the south side was less palatial—a one-and-a-half-story Craftsman-style bungalow with a FOR SALE sign in the front yard. The neighbor Chess had talked about, a Mr. Smith, lived there. Jane wasn't surprised to see that the house was for sale. Chess had mentioned that the man and his wife were having financial problems due to a lost job. Chess had also thought there was something off about the guy, so Jane figured it made sense to check it out. It would probably lead nowhere, but she didn't want to leave any loose ends.

Opening the door of her Mini, she flipped the seat forward, and Mouse jumped out. She secured the leash to his collar, then walked him across the quiet, sun-dappled street to a box attached to the underside of the FOR SALE sign. The real estate company had stocked it with brochures about the house, so she might as well take a look. As she reached inside, a gray-haired woman came out of the house next door to move the yard sprinkler from one side of the grass to the other. When she saw Mouse, she stopped and smiled.

"Nice dog," she said, raising a hand to shield her eyes from the sun.

"Thanks," said Jane.

"I used to have a Lab. He was black, not brown. His name was Thaddeus."

"This is Mouse."

The woman laughed at the name, walked a few paces closer, and held her hand out for him to sniff. "He friendly?"

"He loves people."

Mouse sat down and held up his paw for her to shake.

"He's showing off," said Jane.

"He's a charmer," said the woman, taking hold of his paw and pumping it a couple of times. "You looking to buy a house?"

"Actually, yeah. Has this one been on the market long?"

"The sign went up yesterday."

"You know the owners?"

"Just one owner. A single guy. He's only been living there a month or so. I knew the old owners really well—an older couple. They moved to Baltimore to be closer to their kids."

"Do you know why he's selling?"

She shrugged, folded her arms over her stomach. "He's not around much. Seems friendly enough when he's outside working on the yard." She moved a little closer. "The weird thing is, he's living in there without any furniture."

"You're sure about that?"

"There was never any moving van, not even a U-Haul. I'm not the only one who noticed. Sometimes I see him leave at night and he doesn't come back for days. There's a chandelier in the dining room. He keeps that on when he's gone. That's how I know. When he's around, it's off. He's been around a lot the last few days."

"What's he do for a living?"

Before she could answer, a white Ford pickup pulled into the driveway behind the house. A bald, portly man in cargo shorts and a New York Yankees T-shirt got out carrying what looked like a sack of groceries. He hustled up the back sidewalk and disappeared inside.

"That's him," said the neighbor.

Either Chess was lying to Jane, or this guy had lied to Chess. Whatever the case, something wasn't right.

Speaking a little more softly, the woman said, "He says he's a music teacher."

"High school? College?"

"He may have told my husband, but he never said anything to me."

Jane glanced down at the brochure in her hand. "I guess I'll have to take a look."

The woman gave Mouse's head a couple of quick strokes. "Nice to meet you, big guy." To Jane, she added, "Good luck with your house search."

Jane sat in her car for the next few minutes, watching the bungalow and wondering what it all meant. Who was this guy? Why buy a house and never move any furniture in, and then turn around a month later and put it back on the market? Was it just a coincidence that this man had moved in next to Melvin Dial? Why had Chess found this guy's behavior odd? She wished now that she'd pressed him about it, but at the time it hadn't seemed important. She went back and forth, deciding that it was an almost complete leap in the dark to even *entertain* the idea that this man was connected to the people who were searching for the bull. Still, if Smith was one of them, it was possible he was also connected to Mia's abduction. Had she stumbled over the place where Mia was being held captive? Was she building a scenario that had no basis in reality? Whatever the case, there was no way she could walk away and not check it out.

Flipping her cell phone open, she tapped in Cordelia's number.

Three rings later, Cordelia's voice answered breathlessly, "Did you find the bull?"

"No."

"Me neither. This is a frickin' waste of time. But I know, I know. Mel and I will keep calling."

"I need your help with something else."

"Of course you do. Like what?"

"Tonight. I'll call and let you know what time."

"You discovered something?"

"I don't want to get anybody's hopes up if what I have turns out to be a dead end. We have to check this out."

"*Now* you're talking. You're finally back in the saddle, Janey, right where you belong. Me and you. Jane and Cordelia ride again!"

33

Chess sat on his mattress, his back against the cold concrete block. He'd made a mistake, pissed off a guard. Who knew the guy would be so sensitive about his weight. Chess was hardly one to cast stones, but if he could joke about his girth, why couldn't the guard? Some people had no sense of humor.

Chess needed to make another phone call, but the guard had to call someone to take him, and at the moment, he was standing inside the guard box in the main part of the cell block, talking about "them fuck-tastic Twins" to one of the other guards. Chess couldn't stand it anymore and so came back into his cell to get away from being ignored.

The harsh fluorescent lights irritated his eyes. He was used to the smell of unwashed bodies, but not the nervous sweat that came along with the sometimes furtive but more often hard looks he got from other prisoners. He had the perfect "get out of jail" card, but that tubby pissant wasn't going to let him play it.

After another four-star jailhouse dinner, accompanied by a generous glass of complex, subtle, yet full-bodied Minneapolis tap water, Chess strolled around the main room. Most of the men were watching TV. The asshole guard had left and didn't seem to be coming back.

"I need to use the phone," he said to a different guard who had just come on duty. Chess had met the man the day before. He seemed nice enough.

"Yeah?"

"It's about my bail."

"You want out of here? Why, I thought you liked our ambience." He mispronounced the last word.

It was a slap at Chess's cultured bearing, but it didn't matter. Chess would suck anything up, become one of the guys, spit on the floor, scratch his crotch, or be sophistication itself—whatever it took to get what he wanted.

The guard sat down behind the desk and tapped in a couple of numbers. He spoke quickly, said what he needed, and then joked for a couple of minutes with the person on the other end of the line.

After what seemed like hours, Chess was moved to another room, where he sat on a folding chair and called Jane's cell. He closed his eyes as the phone began to ring. "Pick up," he whispered. "Please, pick up."

"Hello?"

"Jane, it's Chess." When she didn't respond, he said, "Are you there?"

"What do you want?"

"I've got great news. I know where the bull is. I mean, I know who has it."

"Who?"

"Irina Nelson."

"I thought you said she lost it."

"I think she may have been lying to me. She's in love with me. The sale of the bull was going to finance our life together, but she didn't trust me to stick around once it was sold."

"That I believe."

274

"Just listen. She's gone into hiding. She's sure that the people who murdered her mother and Melvin Dial are after her now. I told her you'd get me out, that you'd do it in exchange for the bull."

"She agreed?"

"She thinks the plan is to double-cross you. She's rented a car. She wants to ditch you and take off as soon as I get out."

"Where is she now?"

"She'll never talk to you without me. I swear to you, as soon as I get my hands on the bull, it's yours."

"You're a real piece of work, you know that? You actually expect me to believe you? You pile one lie on another, build a house with them, and then turn around and point at it as if it's evidence of something real."

"I'm not lying. Not this time."

"Ever hear about the boy who cried wolf?"

"One hundred thousand dollars. If you write a check, you don't have to talk to a bail bond service and put up collateral for the rest of the money. Go to your bank tomorrow morning. Put the money in your checking account or get a cashier's check. Then come down and get me out of here. It won't take long. You can come with me to where Irina is hiding. Bring a gun for all I care. I'll get you the statue if it's the last thing I do. Everything that's happened is my fault. I take full responsibility."

"That's big of you."

The anger in her voice irritated him. He wasn't sure what he was expecting, but a little gratitude might be nice. "Do you have a hundred thousand liquid?"

"Maybe."

"Will you do it?"

"You really think you can play me like this?"

"You told me you had forty-eight hours. The clock is ticking, Jane. I may be your last hope."

34

Just after ten that night, Cordelia slipped into the front seat of Jane's Mini. She was dressed in black jeans and a black turtleneck and had on an oversized pair of dark glasses.

"I see you still have your breaking-and-entering gear," said Jane, drinking from a can of Mountain Dew.

"You never go wrong with basic black. Works for every occasion."

"It would have been so much easier if I could've arranged for a real estate agent to show us the house tonight, but I couldn't make it happen. Apparently, the owner wanted the sign put up to start generating interest, but he won't allow any showings until the end of the week."

"Weird."

"Tell me about it."

"Hey, I talked to Peter before I left the mother ship," said Cordelia, pulling out a Snickers bar and tearing off the wrapping with her teeth. "He'd just phoned your dad. Nobody has been able to shake anything loose about the bull. Mel and I covered most of the calls you didn't make."

"If I'm right and Mia is in that house, we won't need to make any more calls. We'll have her back and the kidnappers can go to hell."

Cordelia offered Jane the first bite of the candy bar. "It's good for you. It has peanuts."

"Eat it fast," said Jane. She tipped her can back and finished the soda. "Smith came out around eight and drove off. The chandelier is on in the dining room, so I'm hoping that means he won't be back."

Chewing maniacally, Cordelia asked about Nolan.

"I called him earlier, gave him the license plate number for Smith's truck. Maybe he can chase something down." She waited until Cordelia had swallowed the last bite of her Snickers and then said, "Are you ready?"

"I'm about to hyperventilate. That must mean something."

"Lose the glasses."

"Really?"

"Do you see any sunlight out there?"

"It's all about my *look,* Janey. The idiom I'm trying to project."

"Off."

"You have no sense of style."

Jane removed an athletic bag and a car blanket from her trunk. After Smith had left the house, she'd driven to a hardware store to buy everything she figured she'd need.

"I think I can get us in," she said, glad that it was a hot night. Most people had their windows closed and their air-conditioning running, thus muting any loud outside noises.

Cordelia stuck close to Jane as they pushed through a privacy gate into Smith's backyard. They didn't need to worry about anybody seeing them on the side of the house that faced Dial's place.

"Hey, Janey?"

"Keep your voice down."

"I just remembered something."

"What?"

278

"I don't like breaking and entering."

Jane crouched next to one of the basement windows. Thick white peony bushes by the fence sweetened the night air around them. The peonies actually smelled a lot like roses. It had never occurred to her before that the two smelled similar. How she could allow a thought like that to flit through her mind at a time like this truly amazed her. She dug in the bag for a hammer and a retractable-blade metal scraper.

"You going to break the window?" whispered Cordelia.

"No, I'm going to build a garage." Folding the towel, she added, "We're lucky. This is a single pane. No bars or security system. Shouldn't be too hard to get inside."

"Janey, I'm just spitballing here, to quote one of my favorite Jack Nicholson movies, but have you looked at the narrowness of that window and then taken a good look at me?"

"Your point?"

"When I was ten years old, I couldn't fit through it. I certainly can't now."

"I thought I'd let you shinny up the side of the house and come down the chimney."

"Drop the sarcasm."

"I'll climb in, and then I'll let you in the back door."

"I like it. Always good to have a Plan B."

Jane tapped at the window through the blanket to mute the sound of breaking glass. Handing Cordelia a small flashlight, she said, "I need to make sure I chip off all the broken edges before I climb in." After a few minutes' work with the hammer and a pair of pliers, finished off by the metal scraper, the remainder of the jagged glass was gone. To protect her skin from any shards she'd missed, she pulled a leather jacket and a pair of heavy leather work gloves out of the bag and put everything on. She'd already tucked her long hair up under a baseball cap. With Cordelia's help, she lowered herself through the opening; Her feet dangled for a few seconds and finally hit the floor. "Now pass me down the flashlight."

"What's it look like in there?"

"Empty," said Jane, aiming the beam around the open, unfinished space. It was clean but dank, one long room with a concrete floor and water-stained walls. A freezer stood at one end. On the other end was a small laundry area. She remained still and listened, but no sound stood out, nobody moving around upstairs, no TV, no music.

She was about to head up when she looked once again at the freezer. The image forming in her mind was too vile to even consider, and yet she had to. She walked over, stood next to it with her hand on the lid, telling herself that she'd seen way too many horror movies in her life. She flipped the top back.

"Empty," she breathed. Thank God.

Wiping sweat off her forehead, she crept up the stairs into a narrow hall that led to the back door. Cordelia was standing outside.

"What took you so long?"

Jane held a finger to her lips.

The house was a typical bungalow. Most likely two bedrooms downstairs and an attic or possibly a finished room upstairs. On the kitchen counter was a fifth of vodka, a half-eaten bag of tortilla chips, and a Hershey's bar.

"He's well fed," whispered Cordelia. "Every essential food group is represented, except for one."

They checked inside all the cupboards and one tall broom closet, then passed into a long room that was probably meant to be both a living and dining room, completely empty of furniture. Entering a hallway, they stood in front of a bathroom. On either side were the bedrooms. One door was open, one closed. Shining the flashlight in through the open door, Jane found nothing but another empty room. The closet door was open, no clothes inside.

Cordelia opened the other door. "Mia?" she whispered.

Jane came over and stood behind her. On the floor, tucked into the far corner, were a sleeping bag, a digital clock radio, a stack of newspapers, a six-pack of bottled water, and two cans of Jolt.

"There's the last food group," said Cordelia. "Caffeine."

Again the closet door was open and empty.

"He stays here occasionally," said Jane, "but you could hardly say he lives here."

She led the way up the stairs to the second floor. Rounding the top of the steps, she walked into a large finished space with a deeply slanted ceiling, one that rose to a peak in the center of the room. The walls were wallpapered with tiny yellow and purple violets on a cream-colored background.

"Doesn't look promising," said Cordelia, creeping in behind her.

Jane felt flattened. Ever since she'd learned about Smith earlier in the day, she'd been so amped up she could hardly sit still. She'd been sure they were going to find the little girl.

"Hey, here's another closet," said Cordelia. "A big one."

Jane held her breath and pointed the flashlight at the sliding door as Cordelia drew it back.

"Empty as a piggy bank with a hole in it," she said, stepping inside and looking around.

For the next few minutes, they drifted through the room, tapping the walls.

"There could be a secret panel," said Cordelia.

They inspected every imperfection in the wall but once again found nothing.

"Where do you suppose that little door leads?" asked Cordelia, nodding to one next to a couple of windows. "Lilliput?"

"Has to open onto the flat roof above the sunroom." Jane recalled seeing it from the front yard.

"I'm glad we didn't say anything to Sigrid and Peter," muttered Cordelia.

Jane felt a sick swirl inside her stomach.

"Then again, you can't say we didn't try."

Hearing an engine and seeing a burst of brightness outside three small windows facing the backyard, both Jane and Cordelia rushed over to get a look.

"He's back," said Jane.

"Yikes! We gotta get out of here."

Smith was already out of his truck and making his way up the back walk.

"We'll never make it to the front door in time," said Jane.

"We need another Plan B."

"I don't have one."

The back door opened.

Jane rushed to the small door, flipped back the lock, ducked, and pushed out onto the roof. Cordelia became wedged when she tried to move through the small opening. She held out a hand for Jane to help yank her through.

When they were finally outside, Jane stepped carefully over to the edge of the sunroom roof. "We've got to jump."

"In the dark? Are you crazy?"

"It's only one story. If we can manage to hoist ourselves over the side and hang on for a few seconds, the drop should only be five feet or so. Piece of cake."

Jane began to lower herself over the side. When Cordelia hesitated, she whispered, "It's either this or we try to explain to Mr. Smith what we're doing in his house."

"I'll take my chances with Mr. Smith."

"Really? We've illegally entered the home of a man who is mostly likely entirely innocent. We can't tell the police why we did what we did because Sigrid said no cops. You really want to stick around and try to talk your way out of that?" Jane dangled from the roof and then dropped into a bed of juniper bushes. Disentangling herself, she brushed off her pants and then repositioned her cap. "Come on."

"I am *not* a Navy SEAL."

"I never said you were."

Gingerly, she dropped one leg over the side.

"That's right. Good job."

She hoisted the other leg over and sat for a few seconds on the edge.

"The jump wasn't bad. There are some bushes right underneath you. Do it slow and you'll be fine."

"I can't."

"Don't be a baby."

"I'm *not* a baby. I am Humpty Dumpty about to have a great fall."

"Cordelia!"

She turned around and, inching downward, her feet trying to find purchase on the wood siding, attempted to swing away from the wall.

"No, no. Just drop straight down."

Pushing off, she fell to the grass like a sack of bricks.

"Oh Lord," she groaned, doubling over, grabbing her ankle.

Jane bent down to take a look. "Think you sprained it?"

"I'll never walk again."

"You have to." With both hands, she tugged her up. "Lean on me. I'll get you back to the car."

"What if Smith is watching from one of the windows?"

"Then we're toast. Just hang on and take it slow."

"It's ballooning, Janey. Even in the dark, it looks like I have a grapefruit attached to my ankle."

"We'll put some ice on it."

"Ice? You think ice will help when all the king's horses and all the king's men—"

"Quiet down. We're almost home free."

35

Jane's eyes panned across the waiting room at the front of the Hennepin County Public Safety Facility, otherwise known as the downtown Minneapolis jail. She was waiting for Chess to come out. She'd done all the paperwork, handed over the check, but for some reason it was taking longer for him to be released than she'd expected. She was about to ask the cop behind the reception desk what was going on when she saw Chess come through a door. The smile of relief on his face was a sharp contrast to the frown on her own. She watched him rush forward, as if he intended to hug her.

Backing away, she said, "Where are we going?"

He seemed miffed. "I'll tell you in the car."

"No, now."

He looked around him. Speaking more softly, he said, "The River Bay Marina south of Hastings. You know where it is?"

"On the Mississippi? Why a marina?"

"Irina's mother has a houseboat. That's where it's moored."

She stared hard into his eyes. "If you're lying to me—"

"If you spend all your time second guessing me, we're never going to get anywhere."

They trotted down the outside steps and headed for Jane's car.

"Did you call Irina? She's expecting us? She's got the statue?"

"Everything's set."

"You said she expects you to double-cross me. What's that mean?"

"She wants to leave you tied up on the boat. Once we're well out of town, we would call someone and tell them where we left you."

Jane hadn't told a soul about getting Chess out of jail. After what happened last night, she didn't want to raise anyone's hopes about finding Mia—not even Cordelia's. She stopped before she unlocked the car door. Now that he was out, the power balance had shifted in his favor. She felt a wave of helplessness break over her. She was being asked to trust a man who lied as easily as he breathed. "If you screw this up, if you don't keep your word—"

"I said I'd get the bull for you, and I will—but you've got to promise me something in return. You have to let Irina and me go. I told you she rented a car. What you don't know is that she has a baby. A little boy named Dustin."

"What's that got to do with anything?"

"She's been acting strangely. It's got to be all the stress she's been under. Her mom's death. The breakup of her marriage. I'm worried about the kid. I don't think she's caring for him the way she should be. I know you don't think I have a conscience, but I do. I feel like I owe her for seeing me through this mess—the same way I owe you. If Irina and I and the baby all disappear, it will mean that you'll forfeit the hundred thousand you just paid the county treasurer, but I figure it's a small price to pay for getting your niece back, right? And I'll be gone from your life forever."

"Like you were last time?"

"You're worried about the divorce. I don't want anything of yours. Honestly."

286

"Just the hundred thousand."

"Yeah, just that. Come on, Jane. We're wasting time."

She was on her own this time. No Nolan with his gun and his years of experience. No Cordelia cracking jokes to relieve the pressure. Just Jane, with the instincts Nolan found so impressive. Crazy as it sounded, her instincts told her she could trust Chess this time. Her brain told her she didn't have a choice.

Chess was a convincing talker, a good salesman. Still, it took every ounce of the persuasion he could muster to get Jane to stay on the pier while he went in to talk to Irina. As he stepped onto the open aft portion of the houseboat, he could see Jane about twenty yards away, sitting on a bench overlooking the river. The clouds were a few shades lighter than the water, with the blue-green trees at the horizon line breaking up the unremitting gray. Jane had on a pair of sunglasses, which hid the strain in her eyes. It hardly mattered. He knew it was there.

Angry as he was at her for the way she'd treated him, he couldn't let her down. Not this time. As far as he was concerned, he was done with his precious Winged Bull of Nimrud. He might have owned it, even loved it, now and in an earlier life, but in this one, hanging on to it would be nothing short of a death sentence. He wanted out— out of jail, out of the Twin Cities, and out of the country. What he'd told Jane was true. He was worried about Dustin. It was more than that, though. Much to his continuing amazement, he was concerned for Irina, too. Maybe he felt sorry for her. That was more palatable than thinking that he cared for her.

He knocked on the door. Irina appeared a few seconds later, all smiles and eagerness, but then her face turned wary.

"Take off your clothes," she ordered, looking as if she weren't quite sure she wanted to let him come aboard. "We'll toss them in the garbage. I bought you new socks, underwear, slacks, and a shirt.

We can buy more when we're on the road. You have to shower right away. I've scrubbed the entire boat."

"Irina, no." She retreated to the center of the room as he pushed inside. "I'm not going to shower."

"But Dustin—"

"He'll be fine. I won't hurt him, you must know that."

Her eyes softened.

"Where's the bull?"

"It's here."

He looked around the salon. It was one of the nicer houseboats he'd been on. He could smell coffee, but the smell was mixed with pine cleaner. It turned his stomach. "Show me," he said.

"First things first."

"Irina—"

"At least take off your shoes."

He gave a frustrated sigh as he kicked them off.

"Now the sport coat."

"I need to see the bull."

"Please. Just that. And go back to the kitchen and wash your hands and face."

He charged past her and did as she asked. Before he turned around, he opened the refrigerator and grabbed himself a beer. Twisting off the cap, he took a couple of thirsty swallows.

"Follow me upstairs," said Irina.

"Why?"

"There's someone I want you to meet." She gave him an impish smile.

The only other person on the boat was Dustin. Why make such a big deal out of meeting him? Especially now.

Standing in front of a closed door on the upper story, Irina turned around and took his hand in hers. She seemed both solemn, and bursting with excitement.

"You know that Dusty is a special little boy."

288

"Of course he is."

"But do you know why?"

If he played along with this for a few minutes, then he could demand that they get down to business. "I don't."

"Do the math," she said, pressing her lips together to keep them from trembling.

"Math?"

"I told you that he was born four weeks premature. That was late April. Count back eight months and what do you have?"

"Please don't make me play games."

She looked crestfallen.

He closed his eyes, did the mental calculation. "August."

"He was conceived during the week I spent with you in Istanbul."

He wasn't sure if he should laugh or take her seriously. "You're saying I'm his father?"

"You have a beautiful little son, Chess. Now that you know who he is, I want you to meet him. I've been looking forward to this day since I found out I was pregnant."

"What about your husband?"

"What about him?"

"I thought Dusty was his child."

"He doesn't look a thing like him."

"That's your proof? The way he *looks*?"

"Here, put this mask on." She handed him one and then put one on herself. "Come on," she said, opening the door to the master cabin and tugging him inside.

The smell of bleach was even stronger up here.

Irina walked over to a chair, where a child's car seat sat facing sliding glass doors that led out to the foredeck. "Come meet him," she said, holding out her hand. "See who you think he looks like."

He slipped the mask on as he walked over to the chair. The sight that met his eyes took a few moments to fully register.

"Isn't he beautiful?"

"*This* is Dusty?"

"Our little baby. He has your brown eyes. Every time I look at him, I see you."

"Irina—" He swallowed, looked up.

"Our precious little boy."

"It's . . . a teddy bear."

"I don't know why everyone keeps saying that. It's incredibly mean and I won't allow it."

It wasn't just any teddy bear. This one had on a diaper and was caked with layers of white baby powder. But what really made the hairs at the back of Chess's neck stand up straight was that the fur had been scrubbed off in patches. The bear looked diseased.

"He's sleeping now, but when he wakes up, you can see what a wonderful smile he has."

Whatever part of his brain was supposed to rise to the occasion and figure out something to say had been stunned into silence.

"Stop looking at me like that."

He pulled off his mask, let it dangle from his hand. "Honey . . . sweetheart, we need to talk."

"I can see what you're thinking. You're just like everyone else. I thought you'd be different, but obviously I was wrong. You don't understand what it's like to have a child with a compromised immune system. I have to keep his environment immaculate. When I try to scrub him off after he's been playing, sometimes he cries and fights me. I hate it. But I *have* to keep him clean. A mother knows what's best."

"Sure she does. I completely agree."

"There are people in my life who think I've gone off the deep end with all this concern over germs."

"You're a wonderful mother. Dedicated. Self-sacrificing. Anyone can see that."

She felt inside Dustin's diaper. "He's wet. I should change him."

"Let him sleep," said Chess. "He looks so peaceful. Why don't we take a look at the bull, figure out what we're going to do with Jane."

She narrowed her eyes. "Did she come with you?"

"She's outside sitting on one of the benches. We owe her something. She did put up the money so I could get out of jail." He pulled her into his arms. "Just show me where you've hidden the bull." When he tried to kiss her, she pulled away. "You need to brush your teeth. You stink."

He smiled and ground his teeth at the same time. "Tell me where there's a toothbrush and some toothpaste."

"No," she said backing farther away. "You can't use mine." She gave a shiver of revulsion.

"Irina, what's wrong? It's me. I'm not going to hurt you or Dusty. Surely you know that."

She closed her eyes, pressed her arms to her stomach. "I want you to go."

"But the statue."

"That's all you ever think about."

"Irina, where is it?"

"Do you realize that you lower your voice when you try to act like you're in charge? It doesn't work on me anymore."

This time he almost screamed. "Where is the bull?" He grabbed her by her shoulders. "Tell me."

"I don't have it."

"But you said—"

"I lied. People lie all the time."

"I don't believe you."

"Okay, I do have it, but it's not here."

"Then we'll go to wherever it is."

"I don't think so." She picked up the teddy bear and cradled it in her arms. Walking around the room, she began humming "Twinkle,

Twinkle, Little Star." "Actually, it is here, on the houseboat. But you'll never find it."

He was inside a carnival fun house. This was Irina's mind.

"Maybe I'll give it to you."

"Will you?" he said. "When?"

"I'll have to think about that." As she sat down on the bed, she inadvertently knocked a thin sliver of the caked baby powder off the bear's paw. "Give me a few minutes. You've upset me."

"I didn't mean to."

She caressed the bear's ravaged head. "Go outside. When I'm ready to show it to you, I'll call for you."

"Then it is here."

"Of course it's here."

He didn't have a choice. He couldn't exactly beat the truth out of her.

What he was going to tell Jane was another matter. His credibility with her was already shot. She was never, in a million years, going to believe this.

36

Jane paced back and forth in front of the houseboat, waiting for Chess to come back out. All she'd done all morning was wait—first at the bank, then at the jail, and now on the pier. Time was ticking away. She'd already received three phone messages from Cordelia on her cell, two from Peter, and one from her father. They had to be wondering where she was and why she hadn't called back.

Hearing a door open, she turned and saw Chess hop back onto the pier and come toward her.

"Where's the bull?"

He stopped a few feet away and sank his hands into his pockets. "I don't know where to start."

"She doesn't have it?"

He looked across the river toward the far shore. "Honestly? I don't have a clue."

"Either she has it or she doesn't."

"She's sick. Mentally ill. She's got a teddy bear in there that she thinks is our baby. It's grotesque. Jesus, I need a cigarette." He felt inside the pocket of his sport coat but came up empty.

This was starting to sound like a bad joke. "So this how you two are planning to play me? Your girlfriend has suddenly gone crazy? Sorry, I don't buy it."

Chess bent over, hands on his knees, as if he'd just run a marathon. "If I were you, I wouldn't believe it either."

"I'm going in," said Jane.

"No." As he stepped in front of her, his eyes darted over her shoulder. "What the hell's a cop doing here?"

She turned to see a uniformed officer jogging toward them.

"Shit. I knew it," muttered Chess. "That's Smith. Dial's neighbor. This is bad news."

She supposed he could be Smith. He had the right girth, but he was wearing a hat, which covered his head.

"We gotta get out of here," said Chess, tugging at her arm.

They didn't have any good options. They could jump into the river or they could climb aboard one of the houseboats and try to play hide-and-seek.

Chess was halfway to the end of the pier when the officer pulled his gun and ordered him to stop.

"I mean it, Garrity," called the officer. "Back here. *Now.*"

Chess came to a halt. Without turning around, he called, "What do you want?"

"We both know the answer to that."

"I don't have it."

"Where's Mia?" demanded Jane. "I'll give you anything I have. Just let her go."

"Shut up," ordered Smith. "Garrity, you give me what I want and I let you and your wife here live."

Chess turned to face him. "I told you. I don't have it."

294

"You're pissing me off."

"I can't produce it out of thin air."

"That's it." He motioned for Chess to stand next to Jane, then ordered them to move back down the pier.

Halfway up the hill to the parking lot, Chess said, "Are you really a cop?"

"It's as good a disguise as any."

They stopped when they reached the same white Ford pickup Jane had seen in Smith's driveway the night before.

Smith tossed the keys to Chess. "You drive. Wifey sits next to you."

It was an extended cab. Smith sat in the back and directed Chess.

Staring out the front window, Jane watched the names of the streets as they passed. They were heading south on back roads away from the marina. Chess kept the needle at a steady forty miles an hour, five miles under the speed limit.

"Tell me where my niece is," said Jane. "I'll do anything you want, just let her go."

"Shut up."

"Or what? You'll shoot me?"

He cracked her on the head with the butt of the gun. "There's a lot I can do to you short of killing you. When I say shut the fuck up, I mean it."

She gripped the door handle and waited for the pain to subside.

A while later, Smith touched the barrel of the gun to the back of Chess's neck. "You see that red and white sign on the left about a hundred feet ahead?"

"Yeah?" said Chess.

"Turn there."

They headed into the woods, bumping down a dirt road until they came to a dead-end about fifty yards from a lake. Jane had a headache the size of Texas, and she was lost. Even if she tried, she doubted she could give anyone directions to their position.

"Get out," said Smith, opening the back door and jumping out ahead of them. He motioned for them to stand by the front fender. "Now," he said, backing up a few paces, his heavy boots breaking the dry twigs. "I'm giving you one more chance. You tell me where the bull is. I'll send someone to get it. Once it's in our hands, I'll leave."

"We're supposed to believe that?" said Chess. "After what you did to Dial and Morgana Beck?"

"Please let Mia go," said Jane. "She's got nothing to do with any of this."

"I've been paid to do a job. Your husband's the one who started it all by stealing an artifact that didn't belong to him. If you want to blame someone, blame him."

She saw only coldness in the man's eyes. No compassion. Not even a sliver of pity. "I'm going to tell him the truth," said Jane, turning to Chess. "The statue, it's at one of my restaurants. The Lyme House. In my office in the back of my black filing cabinet."

Scared as he was, Chess's face betrayed only the faintest tremor. But Jane caught it. She glanced back at Smith and saw that he had, too.

"No it's not," said Smith. "Nice try."

"Irina Nelson's sister has it," said Chess, as if he were finally giving in. "She took it from the storage room in the basement of the gallery. Irina and I were trying to get it back when I was arrested."

"Nope. No cigar."

"How could you possibly—"

"I *know*," he said flatly.

"Look," said Chess, sweat dripping off his forehead, "if I had it, wouldn't I tell you?"

"People are funny. I stopped trying to figure humanity out a long time ago." His cell rang.

Out in the woods, the ring seemed out of place, a reminder that the world they lived in was far away.

"What?" Smith asked, stepping back another couple of paces. Rubbing the stubble under his chin, he said, "Nah, we're not going to get it. I hear you, but we get paid either way. I want everyone packed and ready to leave by six. Pass that on. And pass the word to get rid of the girl. You know where to dump the body."

Something hard and cold clenched in the center of Jane's chest. She lunged at him. "No," she screamed.

He trained the gun on her, his eyes inviting her to keep coming.

Seeing the grin playing on his lips, she finally understood. Her death meant nothing to him. Shooting her would be like swatting a fly.

Folding the phone closed, Smith said, "Makes no difference to me what you do. I was sent to find the bull. If I don't get it back, you don't walk out of here. It's that simple."

Chess stared at the ground. With a voice empty of emotion, he said, "Then I guess we don't walk out."

"How can you be like that?" demanded Jane. "She's a little girl. She never hurt anybody."

Smith shrugged. "Nothing personal." Motioning with the gun, he said, "Both of you, move toward the lake. When you get to the shore, kneel down."

So this was it, thought Jane. This was what her last day on earth looked like. Her skin felt clammy, and she wasn't sure that her legs would support her. As she stepped cautiously away from the truck, she felt Chess take hold of her arm. His touch buoyed her, if only briefly. She looked up and saw a hawk riding the thermals. Two squirrels chased each other around the trunk of an oak. She was terrified, and yet it all seemed suddenly so beautiful.

They knelt down together by the water, their arms around each other's waists.

Jane looked at Chess, saw that he was crying.

"Can you ever forgive me?" he whispered.

She heard a burst. In that instant, her mind disconnected. Chess fell forward, his face pressed into the sand, a small hole ripped in the center of his sport coat. A red oozing stain in the sand spread out beneath his body. She leaned toward him, her hand finding his. Holding her breath, she looked up, trying to find the hawk one last time.

Two blasts broke the stillness. They sounded farther away, with a higher pitch. She waited for impact, refusing to shut her eyes.

"Drop the gun," shouted a familiar voice.

She spun around.

Smith was down on one knee, blood spouting from a wound in his shoulder. His eyes were fixed on the woods to his right. He fired three quick rounds as he scrambled behind a broken tree trunk. Crouching there, he fired another shot, then curled up and began to moan.

Jane half stumbled, half ran toward the woods. "Nolan?" she called, jumping over rocks and brambles. She felt light, graceful, her mind disengaged from her body. She floated from tree to tree, her eyes scrutinizing, sifting, scanning until she found him. He was on the ground, his legs spread out in front of him, propped up on one elbow. She assumed that he was staying low, but as she came closer, she realized that he, too, had been hit. She skidded into the dirt next to him. "Are you okay?"

It was a stomach wound. Bleeding like crazy. He held his hand over it, but the blood seeped through his fingers and soaked into his shirt.

"Take my Glock," he said, forcing it into her hand. "I've got my cell. I'll call for the police and the EMTs. You go make sure Smith is out of commission. If he's still moving, hold the gun on him until the cops get here."

"I shouldn't leave you."

"Move," he ordered. "And be careful."

She pushed to her feet and ran back through the woods. Instead of coming out where she'd entered, she doubled around behind where Smith had gone down. Crouching behind a tree, she saw that he was still there. That was when it hit. A feeling she'd never experienced before. She thought of Peter, when he'd murdered that man last fall. Was this what it had been like for him? She thought of Mia. She looked toward the lake, saw Chess's body sprawled on the shore. Melvin Dial was dead. Morgana Beck. At that moment her hatred surged so hot that it bordered on physical pain. Something deep, a feeling beyond words, broke like a thunderstorm inside her.

Holding the gun in both hands, she walked up to the man who had become, in the space of a few seconds, the center of her fury. He was bleeding from the shoulder wound, but also from a hole in his chest. His skin had gone deathly white, and his breathing was labored. His eyes cracked open as she moved in close to kick the gun away from his hand.

"Don't," he said weakly. "Please don't."

She was overwhelmed by disgust. This guy thought he had the right to beg for mercy when he'd shown none to others.

"Tell me where Mia is."

He coughed a couple of times. "It's hard to kill, ain't it."

"Not for you. Of course, like you said, there's a lot I can do to you short of killing you. The thing is, I've never fired a gun before. I would imagine I'm not a very good shot."

His eyes registered caution.

"Tell me where you're keeping Mia."

"Doesn't matter. She's dead by now."

She aimed for his foot, pulled the trigger. The recoil thrust her hand up into the air.

Smith screamed.

When she looked down, she saw that she'd hit his thigh. He was grinding his hands into the dirt, swearing and groaning.

"You probably won't die from that, but I'll bet it hurts. Too bad. Nothing personal. Tell me where you're holding my niece. If you do, I'll call and get the paramedics out here for you."

He looked up at her, made a guttural sound in his throat—and then his mouth opened and blood drained down his chin. He watched her with a kind of animal terror in his eyes. A few seconds more and the expression faded. He was still looking at her, but his eyes had grown dull and vacant. In that instant, her emotions thudded back to earth. He'd been her last link to Mia, and now he was gone.

Slowly, with the immense weight of loss pressing down on her, she picked up his weapon and walked back into the woods. Nolan was unconscious when she reached him.

"No," she cried, crouching down next to him. "Can you hear me?" His cell was open. "Hello?" she said, pressing it to her ear.

"This is 911 dispatch. Who am I talking to?"

"I'm a friend of the man who called you. He's unconscious, and he's lost a lot of blood."

"We have a unit on the way."

"How long?"

"A few minutes."

"Tell them to hurry."

She tossed the cell onto the dirt, moved up next to him, and cradled his head in her lap. "Hold on," she whispered, bending over him, kissing his forehead, her cheek pressed to his. She smoothed back his wiry gray hair. "Please, God," she whispered, her voice shaking, "help him hold on."

300

37

The next few hours were a blur. When the paramedics arrived, sirens wailing, they immediately called for a medevac helicopter to transfer Nolan to Regions Hospital in St. Paul. Smith and Chess were pronounced dead. They started Nolan on an IV because he'd lost so much blood and moved him to a stationary board before transferring him to the van. They drove him back to an open field, where the helicopter landed a few minutes later. Jane asked if she could go with him, but the police had already arrived and wanted her to stay at the crime scene to answer questions.

Sitting in a police cruiser, talking to an officer from the Dakota County Sheriff's Office, she'd explained everything she knew. Her first concern was Mia. The officer radioed back to his dispatcher and gave him the information and told her an Amber Alert would be issued. Jane figured that it was probably too late, but there was no reason now not to do it.

The more she talked, the more she realized how much she didn't know. For example, she had no idea how Nolan had managed to find her. If someone had been following the truck, she was positive a man like Smith, a professional assassin, would have noticed it. She also didn't have Smith's real name or any credible information about who had hired him, other than Chess's wild notion about a foreign cabal formed to hunt down antiquities stolen from the Baghdad Museum— and the people who took them. Whatever the case, others were involved locally, specifically the men who had been staking out her restaurant, but Smith had given an order to get ready to leave—and the order to get rid of Mia. If Smith was the head of the snake, with him gone, the rest would scatter.

Sergeant Kevante Taylor from the Minneapolis homicide unit arrived half an hour after the Dakota County Medical Examiner truck had driven in. By then, Jane was sitting alone with her back against a tree, watching the crime scene unit take pictures, gather evidence, draw maps, take blood samples and generally investigate the scene. Taylor knew more of the story than anyone else. She spent another hour with him, filling in all the gaps in his information, walking around the taped-off perimeter. He still wasn't convinced that Chess hadn't had a part in Dial's and Beck's murders, but by then, Jane no longer cared.

Standing by the ME van a while later, Jane watched as Chess's lifeless body was zipped into a body bag for transfer back to Regina Medical Center in Hastings. Once he was gone, there was no reason for her to stick around. Taylor offered her a ride back to the marina, where she'd left her car. In response to her question about Irina Nelson, he said that several officers had been dispatched to the houseboat. That was as much as he knew.

On her drive back to Minneapolis, Jane tried to determine if there was anything else she could do to find Mia. Was there a stone she hadn't turned over? Was there a question she hadn't asked?

It was going on four in the afternoon when she passed through downtown Minneapolis heading for St. Louis Park and her brother's house. Smith had given the order to "get rid of the girl" three hours ago. There was no reason to believe that Mia was still alive, and yet Jane couldn't let go. She had to think of a way to break the news to her family without removing all hope. The Amber Alert was, to quote an oft-used cliché, like closing the barn door after the horse was already gone, and yet it was something they could hang on to, at least for a little while. In the end, Mia might have been a loose end that, with one quick comment, Smith had tied up, but Jane would never believe it until she was forced to.

She had won the race against the clock enough times before that she'd felt, deep down where she truly lived, that she'd be able to beat it again and bring the little girl home. If Mia really was gone, it was too enormous to even contemplate, let alone believe. Yet she would, of necessity, need to become the messenger of the worst news her brother and sister-in-law would ever receive. She turned on the radio, found some rock music, and turned the sound up to ear-shattering, hoping to blast all thought from her mind.

Just before five, she pulled up to the house her brother and his wife had recently rented in St. Louis Park. She turned off the motor and sat for a few minutes, her hands at the top of the steering wheel, her forehead resting against her hands. She wanted to be anywhere but here. Her emotional circuit boards had been fried by the crises of the last few days. She could move around, walk and talk like a normal person, but underneath it all she felt dazed, frozen. She prayed that the numbness would last a little while longer.

Before she got out of the car, she placed a call to Regions Hospital to see if she could find out any news on Nolan. She was told that his condition was listed as critical and that he was in surgery.

Sigrid answered the front door and let her in.

"Where were you?" she asked, calling up the stairs for Peter to come down.

"Could I have a glass of water?" asked Jane.

Peter came into the living room as she was about to sit down. "We've been calling you all day. What the hell is going on?"

She waited for Sigrid to return to the room and then said, "I'm afraid I've got some bad news." She'd practiced the line but could hardly get it out.

Sigrid dropped the glass. Water shot up all over Jane's jeans.

"What?" said Peter. His face flushed.

"I don't want to hear it," said Sigrid, pressing her hands to her ears, twisting away from them.

Peter grabbed her, pulled her next to him. "Tell us."

Woodenly, Jane sat down. She told them everything that had happened. She didn't cry. Her voice was composed. She explained about the Amber Alert—that the cops were looking for Mia. She tried to be a cheerleader for the idea that there was still something to hang on to. She was pretty sure that Sigrid started screaming at one point, but she kept on talking, the words themselves feeling like a buffer. If she could explain, if she could make sense out of it for them, everything would be okay . . . but the longer she talked—the harder she struggled to make sense of the senseless—the more confused she became. Eventually, she just stopped. In the middle of a sentence. The words dried up, and the tears came pouring out.

"I'm sorry," she said. "I tried my best."

By then, her audience of two was well past hearing.

38

Standing between the outer door and the inner door of the psych unit, feeling as if he were in an airlock on a space station, Steve Nelson waited for the nurse to come in and talk to him. She would need to know why he was here before he would be allowed in. It was a locked facility. Rules were rules.

He explained that his wife was Irina Nelson and that she had just been admitted. He needed to see her. While he had little clout, or money, Irina's mother did—or had—and her lawyer had paved the way for him by calling one of the leading psychiatrists in Minnesota, Dr. Albert Darling, to head Irina's psychotherapy team.

At the mention of Dr. Darling's name, the nurse's voice turned creamy. Did he want to see Irina in her room? Yes, it was a private room. Yes, she'd been served a late lunch, although she'd refused to eat. Of course, they would be happy to get him a cup of coffee. Make him a peanut butter sandwich. Rub his feet. Press his slacks and shine his shoes while he waited.

"Is the doctor still here?" he asked.

"I believe he is," said the nurse, walking him down the hall toward his wife's room. "I saw him in the staff lounge. I'd be happy to get him for you."

Before she could scamper off, a fat man in an expensive gray suit came out of a closed door.

"Dr. Darling," said the nurse, tugging on a small pearl earring. "This is Steve Nelson, Irina Nelson's husband."

Darling stuck out his hand. It was as limp as the proverbial dishrag. Steve took an instant dislike to him.

"Let's talk in the conference room." Turning to the nurse, he said, "Will you get me that bag?" Without waiting for a response, he pivoted and strode away.

Steve offered the nurse his thanks and walked erectly to a room across from the patient lounge. He didn't like hospitals and he didn't like doctors. Once they were seated at a long rectangular table, he said, "How is she? Is she awake? Is she rational?"

"She was fairly agitated when she was admitted to the ER. I ordered a sedative. For the moment, I'd say she's resting comfortably."

Leonard Zeller had called Steve and explained that the police had found Irina on her mother's houseboat a few hours earlier. He detailed the state she was in, said that she'd been hugging a teddy bear, refused to give it up, and was making very little sense. The police had taken her to a mental health facility. Steve could visit her there if he chose.

Darling nodded to Steve's desert camo pants tucked into his hot-weather, steel-toed combat boots. "Are you in the military?"

"Ex-military."

"I see."

Steve wasn't sure what he saw and had no interest in pursuing his preconceptions.

"Tell me about your wife's pseudocyesis," said Darling.

"Her what?"

"Her false pregnancy." He smoothed his mustache hairs with the tips of his fingers.

"Look," said Steve. "We talked about it, her family and me. At first, we all thought she was having a real baby. She's been through a lot since we've been married. I did three tours in Iraq. She's been pregnant twice before. One ended in a miscarriage and one in a stillbirth. I was gone when she lost them, so she had to deal with it pretty much on her own. I know it took a toll. But she's always been so levelheaded, so unflappable. I just didn't see this coming."

Darling continued to smooth his mustache. "Go on."

"One day I came home and she'd bought this teddy bear, put it in the crib. She'd carry it around, diaper it. She acted like it was a real baby and got pissed when I didn't play along. I thought she'd gone nuts. She'd lose her mind and start yelling at me when I referred to it as Smokey. You know? Smokey the Bear? *Only you can prevent forest fires?* I thought a little humor might break the ice, get her to see what she was doing. I get in trouble with my humor sometimes. Maybe I went a little too far."

Darling didn't respond; he just sat there, hunched in his chair.

"Anyway, I kept telling her that she had to see a shrink, but that got me exactly nowhere. She wasn't the crazy one, I was. And I was selfish. A terrible dad. Uncaring. Mean. So I changed my approach. Started calling it marriage counseling. She still wouldn't budge. This past Sunday, she told me that she's romantically involved with some antiquities dealer from Istanbul, an American who lives there. She says she loves him. That the baby is his. What the hell was I supposed to think?"

"Do you want to participate in your wife's psychotherapy?"

He sat up straighter. "I love Irina. I know that she doesn't always believe that. I've had problems with her mother in the past, problems that have leaked over into our marriage. I was planning to leave again, this time for Kabul. I've been offered a job with a private military

307

contractor. You may not understand this, but it occurred to me that if I went away, she'd be forced to get better, to deal realistically with the world around her. But I can't leave. Not the way things are. I have to stick by her if she'll let me."

There was a knock on the door.

"Come in," called Darling. He stood up and took a diaper bag from the nurse. He never said thank you, he just sat back down and watched her leave. He was either deeply preoccupied by weighty psychological issues, or he was a jackass. Steve favored the latter.

"Is that Irina's?" he asked, recognizing the orange and fuchsia balloons.

"The officers who brought her to the ER said she refused to let go of it." Darling set it on the table in front of him. "The bag was filled with diapers, toys, baby wipes, the usual. They didn't see any harm in letting her take it when they left the houseboat, but when she was admitted to the mental health unit, she had to give it up. The unit doesn't allow patients to bring personal items into their rooms. Someone on the staff makes a list of the items, and then everything is locked away. When I got here, I was informed that the bag contained something unusual." He removed a fleecy scarf that appeared to be balled around something heavy. Removing the scarf, he set a statue on the table.

"Is it gold?" asked Steve.

"That would be my guess."

It was a winged ox or maybe a bull, the size of a small kitten. The eyes were two iridescent blue gemstones. They looked like they might be sapphires. The horns were a whitish brown. Could be stone, or ivory.

"It's old," said Steve. "Most likely something Irina took from her mother's gallery."

"I'd like to give it to the police, let them figure out what to do with it."

"Fine with me," said Steve with a shrug. "Look, I'm happy to talk you, answer any questions you have, but right now I want to see my wife."

"That's fine," said Darling, glancing at his Rolex. "We can talk more tomorrow. Her recovery will take time, but with love and support, and the correct therapy protocol, I believe she has a good chance of making it all the way back."

Steve stood in the doorway, marveling at what a room on a psych ward *didn't* contain. There was no bathroom. No clothes closet—no closet at all. The bedside table had no drawers in it and was attached by bolts to the wall. One long curtain was drawn over a large window. Staring for a few seconds at a square of metal mounted on the wall, trying to comprehend what it might be, he finally decided that it had to be a covered and locked thermostat. The patients couldn't even turn up the heat if they were cold.

Irina was lying in a single bed, on top of the white bedcovers, looking like a homeless waif, which, he supposed, in many ways she was. Her eyes were closed, her arms at her sides. For a woman who was always in motion, always tensely focused, she seemed unusually peaceful. She wore teal-colored scrubs and looked as if she'd lost even more weight. The bones in her cheeks protruded. She was without makeup, her hair unwashed. He wasn't sure he would have recognized her if he'd seen her on the street.

"Irina?" he whispered. The room was so dimly lit, so quiet, he figured his normal voice would be too jarring.

Her eyes opened. "Chess?"

"No, it's Steve." He walked over. "Can I sit on the bed with you?" There was one other piece of furniture in the room, a chair, but it was too low, too far away. He wanted to be closer.

"I guess," she said. As he sat down, she gripped his wrist. "Have you seen Dusty? Is he okay? Where are they keeping him? Why won't they let me have him?"

He pried her fingers off and held her hand. "He's fine. I've got him."

"What do you mean you've got him? You're here. How could you be here and be taking care of him at the same time? Am I crazy? That's a logical question, isn't it? Why am I here? They act like there's something wrong with me. Mental. Up here." She tapped her head. "Why won't they let me go? One of the other patients said the doors are locked. How can the doors be locked? I'm an American citizen. I have rights."

"Of course you do."

"Then why can't I have my son? I need him. Nobody else knows what's best for him."

"Misty's with Dusty. He's fine. Everyone's fine."

"She's not smoking around him, is she? Or drinking?"

"Absolutely not."

"Are you sleeping with her? Tell me the truth."

He started to laugh but stopped himself. "Where did you get that idea?"

"You can admit it. I'm tougher than you think."

His smile turned tender. "She's the last person on earth I'd want a relationship with. Give me a little credit."

She lay back, exhausted by her outburst. "I'm tired."

"I know you are. You need to rest. I heard you didn't eat any lunch."

"I'm not hungry. How can I be hungry when my son is God-knows-where."

"I told you. He's safe. You're safe."

"Did you call my mother? Tell her what happened?"

He hesitated. "Not yet."

She turned her face away. "Why does everything keep spinning?"

"Is that what it feels like?"

"I don't know what's happening to me."

"I'm here for you."

"Are you? Are you really?"

"If you want me."

She turned back to him, gazed up into his eyes. "I don't know what I want."

"That's fine. It's a starting place."

"Aren't you going back to Iraq?"

"I'm staying here with you. Until you're feeling better."

"Then what?"

"Then I'll bring you home."

Still gazing deep into his eyes, she said, "Where's home, Steve?"

"With me."

"And Dusty?"

He pressed his lips together, swallowed a couple of times. "And Dusty."

"All I ever wanted was for us to be a family."

"I know that now."

"I still love you."

In Steve's lexicon of important human character traits, courage and steadfastness in the face of trouble were at the top of the list. A man without courage was a man lost. "I love you, too," he said, kissing her hand, holding it against his heart.

39

Jane felt like the angel of death passing through the land of Egypt. She drove from place to place, bringing the news about Mia to her family. She tried to stay positive. She'd talked to one of the police officers working with Amber Alerts and been told that they already had several leads to follow up on. She spent an hour in Cordelia's living room. Melanie sat on the floor, holding her little dog, petting his head. Cordelia, reclining on the couch with her injured ankle up on a pillow, alternately cried and scolded herself for crying. Only Hattie, unaware of the significance of what was happening, continued on with what she was doing. She'd lined up the three felines that shared the loft with them and was instructing them on how to be better cats. At any other time it would have been funny. This afternoon, it was just background noise.

Jane went to her father's office and got her dad and Elizabeth out of a meeting. She didn't stay long. Her dad offered to drive her home, but she said she was okay. She said she'd monitor what the police learned from the alert and let them know.

She spent the rest of the evening at the hospital, sitting next to Nolan's bed in the ICU. He finally opened his eyes around nine that evening. After the nurses and doctors had been in to talk to him, to check his vital signs and make notes about all the monitors he was hooked up to, Jane was finally alone with him for a few minutes.

Standing next to the bed, she said, "Welcome back."

He looked around to get his bearings, then held up his right arm, glanced at the IV taped to his hand, and followed the tubes to where a bag was hanging on a stand next to the bed.

"You saved my life," said Jane.

"Water?"

"Ice chips," said Jane. She spooned a couple into his mouth. "They put a tube down your throat. Is it sore?"

"Yeah."

"How do you feel?"

"Like I was hit by the entire Vikings defensive line." His voice was softer than normal, weaker. "But it looks like I'll live."

Jane fought back tears because she knew something he didn't. The bullet that Smith had fired had lodged next to his spine. The doctors weren't able to remove it. There was a possibility that he might be paralyzed from the waist down.

"How long you been here?"

"A while."

The new nurse came in to check his IV bag. Nolan winked at Jane, then introduced her as his daughter.

"Well," said the nurse, glancing from face to face, taking in their different skin colors. "That's really nice she could be here."

"She's that kind of daughter."

"I'm Jane."

"Lois. I'll be your father's nurse this evening. Do you live in town?"

"Minneapolis."

She checked his blood pressure. "How's the pain?" she asked. "On a scale of one to ten, ten being the worst."

"Five," he whispered.

"You're due for more pain meds. I'll go get them."

After she'd left, Jane bent over and kissed his cheek. "Thanks, Dad."

"Don't mention it."

"Do you feel up to a little conversation?"

"Thought that's what we were having."

"Do you remember what happened?"

Slowly, woozily, he said, "I got shot in the stomach, not the head."

"How did you find me?"

"Tiny GPS unit. I put it on Redzig's truck last night."

"Who's Redzig?"

"Eddy Redzig. I'm a PI, you know." Another slow wink. "You knew him as Smith. Followed him to the marina this morning. Then the woods. More ice."

She spooned more chips into his mouth.

He looked up at the TV, then over at the window. "I gotta close my eyes."

"I'll sit here a while longer."

"No, go home. Come back tomorrow." His eyes fluttered shut. A few seconds later, he was asleep.

On the way back to her house, Jane's cell rang. Thinking it might be the police with an update, she answered without checking the caller ID.

"I just saw an Amber Alert on TV about a little girl named Mia Lawless," came Julia's excited voice. "Is it for real? Peter and Sigrid's daughter?"

"I'm afraid so," said Jane.

"Is there anything I can do? Anything at all—"

"I wish there was."

"Do you have any idea who took her?"

Jane offered a few details but kept them general.

"I'm so sorry. If there's anything I can do to help, you'll let me know, right? If Sigrid needs a sedative to help her sleep? Of if you do, or Peter."

"Thanks."

"At a time like this, nothing else is important—but I thought I'd tell you that I took the cylinder seal I bought from Chess over to a curator at the Institute of Arts. I gave them the provenance papers. I should know in a few days if it was stolen or not. I'll let you know. If it wasn't taken illegally, I suppose I'll have to write him another check. I canceled the one I gave him on Sunday."

Jane simply couldn't deal with it. "I suppose so."

"Well, take care. And keep in touch."

By eleven that night, Jane was sitting again on her back porch with a brandy, her dog's head resting in her lap. Her mind was caught in familiar filaments of thought. Sometimes her life felt more like a circle than a straight line, with issues and themes doubling back on themselves, never truly reaching a conclusion or a sense of completion. Just hours ago a man had died within inches of her, one of her best friends was shot, and she'd been moments away from her own death. She'd experienced the world in a way she never had before, and yet here she was, falling back into the same old grooves, with the same questions swirling around inside her. Did a human have to look back in order to move forward? She remembered a favorite line from *Alice in Wonderland*. "It's a poor sort of memory that only works backward." Yet that's where she was stuck. She would be caught and held forever in the past until she knew for sure what had happened to Mia.

Over the course of the afternoon and evening, she'd talked to the police half a dozen times. None of their leads had panned out. She could tell that the man she'd last spoken to was trying, in an official yet gentle way, to prepare her for the worst. She decided to wait until morning before she talked to Peter and Sigrid again. She had nothing new to add and didn't want them to hear the pain in her voice.

By midnight, the numbness had, gratefully, returned. She remembered a line of scripture her mother sometimes quoted. "Sufficient unto the day is the evil thereof." Jane had always taken it to mean "Time for bed." That was the way her mom used it. When enough bad things had happened, it was best to call it a day and hope for a better tomorrow.

Headlights hitting the garage door alerted her to a car pulling into the driveway. She opened the screen for Mouse and then walked out after him.

Lee was just getting out of the driver's seat of an older-model Chevy van. "Hey," he said. "I just heard about Nolan."

Mouse lunged for the fence.

"It's okay, boy." She grabbed his collar, ordered him to sit.

"Dogs and me don't mix. Never have. Maybe they smell a cop. Look, I, ah . . . I decided that the Twin Cities isn't for me after all."

"You're leaving?"

"Thought I'd come over, say my good-byes."

"Where are you headed?" she asked, stepping up to the gate.

"Not sure. I was thinking about Seattle. Go west, young man, isn't that what they say?"

"Planning to do more preaching?"

"Oh, I suppose. It's cheap entertainment." Covering the gatepost with his hand, he continued, "You okay?"

She took a deep breath. "Not so good. Those people who were staking out my restaurant, they not only shot Nolan, but they kidnapped and may have murdered my niece." The act of saying the words out loud gave them a reality she still resisted.

Lee's eyes panned across the yard.

317

"I've never felt so helpless."

"Yeah . . . about that."

The hesitation in his voice caused her to look him squarely in the eye. "What? Do you know something?"

"I'm sorry for the part I played in this whole mess."

"Your part? What are you saying?"

"I was part of the group hired to retrieve the bull. My job was to get to know you. Feel out the situation, see if you knew where it was."

"Where *is* she?"

"Give me a minute, okay?"

She stood very still, almost afraid to breathe.

"There's stuff I need to explain. I never worked with Redzig before. I mean, that guy was bat-shit crazy. A psychopath. The other groups I've been a part of weren't like this one. I was recruited two years ago by a friend I first met in seminary. He told me he was working for an ex-major in the old Iraqi army. The more he talked, the more interested I became. I agreed that returning looted antiquities to the museum in Baghdad was a just cause. What I told you is true. I'm not much of a Christian, but the Bible and the history it represents is important to me. And hell, I needed a job, something that required more than pushing papers around a desk. So I signed on. But I never signed on for what happened here."

"I don't want your excuses, *I want to know where my niece is.*"

"I never expected to like you so much."

"Where is she?"

He extracted an envelope from the back pocket of his jeans. "Here."

She ripped it open. Inside was a page torn from a legal pad. She couldn't make out the words, just that they were written in all caps. "What's this?"

"It's a list of all the people who are part of the operation—the ones I've come in contact with in the last few years. Down at the bottom, you'll find info on the three who run the show. They call themselves the Baghdad Union. Names, phone numbers, addresses, e-mails. Everything the FBI will need to track them. Don't ask me how I got it. Just take it and give it to the police. The cops will be the least of my worries if that's ever traced back to me."

"I don't care about this. I want *Mia*. Is she alive? Dead?" She grabbed the front of his shirt, but he backed away. Walking around to the rear of the van, he motioned for her to join him—and then he opened the doors.

The little girl was lying on her stomach atop a sleeping bag, one that had been spread over a bare, dirty mattress. Her eyes were closed. "Is she—"

"She's alive."

Jane lunged inside, lifted her into her arms, and pulled her out.

"She's been sedated," said Lee, following Jane through the back gate into the house. "I made sure she was treated well. I told her right off that I wasn't going to hurt her, that she'd be home in a couple of days. She was scared at first, sure, but she got over it. We watched movies together. I bought her all her favorite fast foods. We played games. When Redzig gave the order to get rid of her, I slipped her out the back door and took off."

Jane laid the little girl down on the couch in the living room. She sat down next to her, brushed the hair away from her forehead.

"She'll wake up soon."

She checked her breathing, looked for cuts or bruises, felt for a fever.

"She's fine," said Lee.

"She's not fine!" She stood, coming face to face with him. "She was kidnapped. We thought she was dead. Do you have any idea what this has done to my family? What it's done to her? To me?"

"I brought her back. All I ask is that you let me go. If you can't do that, at least give me a few hours. A day if possible. Please," he said. "Twenty-four hours."

"Get out of here."

"I'm sorry."

"Get out."

She walked with him to the front door. After he'd gone, she threw the bolt and turned the security system back on. Returning to the living room, she eased down next to Mia, gazing at her niece's impossibly young face. Her fury at Lee was white hot, and yet she knew he could easily have taken off and never looked back. Instead, he'd saved Mia, brought her back. Right then and there she made a decision to give him his twenty-four hours. She owed him that much.

"You're home," she whispered, pulling Mia into her arms, feeling her strong, steady heartbeat. Holding her tight, she stroked her hair and rocked her until the reality of her return fully sank in. "You're going to be okay. Everything's going to be okay now that you're back." She prayed with all her might that those words were true.

Holding her for a moment more, Jane finally relaxed and released Mia, laying her back down against the pillow. Then, with a heart fairly bursting, she opened her cell phone to call her family.